"Why would ... You don't even know me."

Mack kept his gaze fixed on hers. "I know more than you might think. I know that the father of your baby isn't going to be around to take care of you or the child."

Addy's jaw dropped, then closed with an angry click of teeth. "You don't know any such thing."

"Yes, I do," he replied calmly. "If his past actions are any indication, you'll never hear from Ty again."

Her eyes widened. "You – you know Ty?"

"He's my half-brother."

"You mean, you knew about me and the baby before – "

"Yes, that's why I dropped by your house. I was there to offer you money."

Steam all but came out of her ears. "Well, you can tell Ty to keep his damn money. I don't want it."

"The money's not Ty's. It's mine."

"Well, I don't want your money, either, Mack McGruder." She pointed a stiff finger at the door. "Get out. And don't bother coming back."

Reunion of Revenge
by Kathie DeNosky

᠔ᠵ᠊᠊ᠧ

> **From the desk of Emerald Larson, owner and CEO of Emerald, Inc.**
>
> To: My personal assistant, Luther Freemont
>
> Re: My newly discovered grandson, Nick Daniels
>
> My grandson, Nick, will be leaving at the end of the week to take over running the Sugar Creek Cattle Company in Wyoming. Please be advised that he won't be particularly happy when he discovers that his ranch foreman is the woman he was to have married thirteen years ago. To ensure the success of my plan and avoid the fallout of his displeasure, I am instructing you to intercept all calls from him until further notice.
>
> As always, I am relying on your complete discretion in this matter.
>
> Emerald Larson

Available in April 2007
from Mills & Boon Desire

The Convenient Marriage
PEGGY MORELAND

Reunion of Revenge
KATHIE DeNOSKY

MILLS & BOON®

Desire™

First published in Great Britain 2007
Harlequin Mills & Boon Limited,
Eton House, 18-24 Paradise Road, Richmond, Surrey TW9 1SR

The publisher acknowledges the copyright holders of the
individual works as follows:

The Convenient Marriage © Peggy Bozeman Morse 2006
(Original title: The Texan's Convenient Marriage)
Reunion of Revenge © Kathie DeNosky 2006

ISBN: 978 0 263 85013 0

51-0407

Printed and bound in Spain
by Litografia Rosés S.A., Barcelona

THE CONVENIENT MARRIAGE

by
Peggy Moreland

PEGGY MORELAND

published her first romance in 1989, and continues to delight readers with stories set in her home state of Texas. Winner of the National Readers' Choice Award, a nominee for *Romantic Times BOOKclub* Reviewer's Choice Award and a two-time finalist for the prestigious RITA® Award, Peggy's books frequently appear on the *USA Today* and Waldenbooks bestseller lists. When not writing, you can usually find Peggy outside, tending the cattle, goats and other creatures on the ranch she shares with her husband. You may write to Peggy at PO Box 1099, Florence, TX 76527-1099, USA, or e-mail her at peggy@peggymoreland.com.

To my daughter, Hilary.
Thanks for your willingness to read my work, your
encouragement when I need it most and for the
smile you put in my heart.

Prologue

War is fear cloaked in courage.
—William Westmoreland

Smoke hung in the air cloaking the darkness, its acrid scent burning the noses of the soldiers hiding in the tall grass. Some had taken advantage of the lull in activity and had stretched out, eyes closed, their guns held at the ready across their chests, their packs pillowed beneath their heads. Others were hunkered down, watching…and waiting.

Antonio Rocci, or Romeo as he was called by his friends, wanted to sleep but couldn't. Fear kept his eyes open and his ears cocked for any sound of movement in the inky darkness. In the distance, red embers and thin curls of smoke marked where a small village had once stood. Reconnaissance had reported that Vietcong soldiers had infiltrated the village and were using the area to store artillery. Earlier that day, while the sun was still up, an air attack had taken place. Constructed mainly of grasses and bamboo gathered from the surrounding countryside, the hooches that had once formed the small village had gone up like dry kindling. All that remained were burning embers and the cloying smell of smoke.

When morning came, it was the job of Romeo and the other soldiers in his unit to go into the village and search for the cache of artillery and ammunition reportedly hidden there. A side duty was checking for survivors and counting the dead. Bile rose in Romeo's throat at the thought of what he might face, and he quickly swallowed it down. It's war, he reminded himself. It's either us or them, and he'd a hell of a lot rather it be them.

"Romeo?"

He jumped at the voice, then forced the tension from his body when he realized it was Pops, their team leader, who had spoken.

He set his jaw to steady his voice, hide the fear. "Over here."

He heard a slight rustle of grass, and angled his head, watching as Pop's shadowed form moved closer.

"You okay?" Pops whispered.

Romeo released his grip on his gun long enough to drag his arm across the nervous perspiration that beaded his forehead, then settled his finger over the trigger again. "Yeah, but I'd feel a whole lot better if I knew we were the only ones out here."

"Yeah," Pops agreed soberly. "I hear you."

Silence settled between them, as both continued to watch the darkness.

Romeo would never admit it, but he felt safer, less vulnerable with Pops at his side. Older than most of the others in the unit, Pops—the nickname given to Larry Blair by the rest of the team—had already completed one tour of duty in Vietnam and was working on his second. Romeo couldn't imagine why anyone would willingly sign on for another tour. From the day he'd arrived in country, he'd felt as if he'd been dropped down into the bowels of hell and couldn't wait for the day he could board the plane that would carry him home.

"Pops?"

"Yeah?"

"Do you ever regret signing on for a second tour?"

"No sense regretting what you can't change."

Romeo angled his head to peer at the man whose opinion he respected as much as he would his father's. "Do you ever get scared, Pops?"

"Yeah," Pops admitted quietly. "It's the soldier who fears nothing that gets himself killed. If you use fear to your advantage, it'll keep you alert, on guard, prepared. Give in to it and it'll make you helpless, weak."

Romeo considered that for a moment, but found little comfort in Pop's advice. He'd always considered himself brave, even cocky. Now he wondered if he had a bright-yellow stripe running down his back.

"Is being afraid the same as being a coward?" he asked hesitantly.

"No. A coward runs and hides."

"Some of the guys think Preacher's a coward."

"Well, they're wrong. Preacher just can't bear the thought of taking a human life. It's his beliefs he struggles with, not cowardice."

Romeo considered that a moment, then shook his head sadly. "Hell, it doesn't matter if you're a hero or a coward. We all die just the same."

Pop pulled a package of gum from his pocket. "Don't think about dying," he warned, and offered a piece to Romeo. He unwrapped one for himself and folded the strip of gum in two, before popping it into his mouth. "Think about living, about what you're going to do when you get home."

Romeo gulped, thinking about what he'd left behind, what would be waiting for him when he returned. "Have I ever told you why I joined the service?"

"Can't say as you have."

"I got a girl pregnant."

He felt Pop's gaze and, for once, was grateful for the darkness so that Pop couldn't see his face, his shame. "She was putting pressure on me to marry her. I figured the army was as good a way to get out of it, as any."

If Pop had an opinion, he kept it to himself, which Romeo appreciated. He wasn't looking for absolution…or a lecture. What he wanted was a sounding board, someone who would listen.

"It was wrong," he admitted with regret. "Running

away, I mean. Even if I didn't want to marry her, I should've at least agreed to share responsibility for the kid. It's mine, a part of me. I shouldn't have left her to deal with it alone." He glanced over at Pops. "Do you think it's too late?"

Pop frowned in confusion. "For what?"

"To provide for the kid. I was thinking maybe I could send her some money."

"I'm sure she'd appreciate it," Pop replied.

"Yeah," Romeo said, warming to the idea. "And when I get home and get a real job, I could send her a set amount every month. Kinda like the child support my dad had to pay my mom after they divorced."

"Sounds fair," Pops agreed. "A man should take care of what's his."

Romeo frowned, as a new thought rose. "But what happens if I don't make it home?" He glanced over at Pops. "Who'll take care of my kid then?"

Pops clasped Romeo's shoulder, gave it a squeeze. "Don't talk like that. You're going to make it home. We all are."

Though Romeo appreciated the reassurance, he knew Pops was blowing smoke. There were no guarantees. Not for any of them. And if he did get killed, what would happen to the baby he'd fathered? He didn't have anything of value to leave behind. No savings, no property. Hell, he didn't even own a car. He'd sold his old heap to his cousin, before he'd left for 'Nam.

"Pops?"

"Yeah?"

"Remember the deed that rancher tore up and gave to us the day before we shipped out?"

"Yeah. What about it?"

"The old man said he was going to give us his ranch when we got home. My portion of the deed is in my footlocker back at camp. If something happens to me, would you see that my kid gets it?"

"Nothing's going to happen to you," Pop maintained stubbornly.

"But if something does, promise me you'll send it to Mary Claire Richards. Tell her it's for the baby."

There was a long pause of silence, before Pop said quietly, "Consider it done."

One

Addy pressed the heel of her hand against the ache building between her eyes. Another five minutes on the phone with her mother and it would surpass the one that had throbbed low in her back all day.

Drawing in a deep breath, she searched for patience.

"I know you don't like to talk about my father," she began, choosing her words carefully. "But this is important. A lady called. Stephanie Parker. She said her father served with mine in Vietnam."

"So what if he did?" her mother snapped. "Thousands of American soldiers went to Vietnam."

Ignoring her mother's bitterness, Addy forged on, determined to get through this conversation without screaming. "Stephanie told me that her father sent her mother a letter from Vietnam with a torn piece of paper inside. She thinks Tony might have had a similar piece and sent it to you."

"The only thing Antonio Rocci ever gave me was *you* and that was an accident."

Addy didn't flinch at the jab at her illegitimacy. She'd had the circumstances surrounding her birth thrown in her face so often over the years that hearing it no longer had the power to sting.

"This paper may be valuable," she persisted. "Do you remember Tony sending you anything like that?"

"That was over thirty years ago! How am I supposed to remember something that happened that long ago? I don't even remember what was in yesterday's mail."

"A torn piece of paper, Mom. That's odd enough that you should remember."

"If you called to talk about *him,* I'm hanging up. I'm missing my shows."

Before Addy could say anything more, the dial tone buzzed in her ear.

"The baby and I are doing fine, but thanks for asking."

Scowling, she slammed down the phone, furious with herself for letting her mother's lack of concern get to her. Mary Claire Richards-Smith-Carlton-Sullivan was a neurotic, self-centered woman who raced from one bad marriage to the next, fueled by a bitterness she'd clung to for more than thirty years and oblivious to anyone else's needs, including her daughter's.

With a sigh Addy swept a stray lock of hair from her face and told herself it didn't matter. She'd survived thirty-three years of her mother's disregard. Why should she expect her to show any concern now?

She stooped to untie her shoelaces but froze when she caught a glimpse of her reflection on the patio door. Straightening slowly, she stared, barely recognizing the woman who stared back. Her stomach looked as if she'd swallowed a soccer ball, her feet and ankles so swollen they looked like an elephant's, and her long, black hair—which she usually considered her best feature—was wadded up in a frizzy knot on top of her head. Add to that lovely image nurses' scrubs in a putrid shade of green and a well-worn pair of Reeboks and she was almost glad Ty wasn't around to see her now.

Grimacing, she reached to untie her shoelaces again. "As if I'd let him past the front door," she muttered under her breath. Ty Bodean was a lying snake and she was better off without him, even if it did mean she'd be raising her baby alone.

She caught her lower lip between her teeth as she eased the shoe off her swollen foot, thinking what all that meant, what lay ahead of her. Money was going to be a problem. Eighteen months ago, she'd bought the house, which had depleted her savings and shackled her to a mortgage payment that already stretched her monthly budget to the limit. At the time she'd made the purchase, it had seemed a wise investment. She'd always wanted to have her own home, and the previous owner had offered it to her at a ridiculously low price. Of course, when she'd agreed to buy the property, she hadn't been pregnant and had no plans of becoming pregnant in the near future. An unforgettable—albeit brief—affair with Ty Bodean had changed all that.

The second problem—which was tied directly to the first—was child care. She hated the thought of her baby being raised by strangers, but as the major and *only* breadwinner in the family, there was no way she could quit her job and stay at home with her baby.

The third problem was raising a child in a single-parent home. Again she had no other option, but she was determined to do a better job of it than her own mother had done in raising her.

The reminder of her mother sent her thoughts segueing to the father she'd never known and the phone call she'd received concerning him. She frowned thoughtfully as she considered the torn piece of paper Stephanie Parker had mentioned.

Could it really be valuable? she asked herself, then sputtered a laugh. Even if it was, which she seriously doubted, she couldn't cash in on something she couldn't find. She supposed she could paw her way through the trunk her mother had left in her garage for safekeeping. If it was anywhere, it would be there.

But not tonight, she thought, heaving a weary sigh. She'd put in a long, back-breaking eight-hour shift in Emergency, and she wasn't doing anything more strenuous that evening than propping up her feet and watching TV.

Bracing a hand against the counter for support, she lifted her foot to tug off her remaining shoe. As she did, a pain knifed through her midsection, stealing her breath. Eyes wide, she hugged an arm around her middle and sank slowly to her knees. With a hand propped on the floor to keep herself upright, she forced herself to take slow, even breaths, and tried to think of a logical explanation for the pain. It couldn't be labor, she told herself. Her due date was still almost two months away. It had to be Braxton Hicks, she decided. False labor. She'd experienced similar pains before. None as severe as this, but she knew it would soon pass, just as the others had.

But as she knelt, waiting for the pain to lessen, it grew stronger, more intense, as if a vise had been clamped around her middle and cinched up tight. Sweat broke out on her brow, beading her upper lip. She couldn't move, could barely breathe. She glanced up at the counter and the phone just out of reach, and gulped back the nausea, the fear, knowing she had to call for help. But who? She hated to call 911, if this turned out to be false labor. She worked in Emergency. She knew how much manpower and time was wasted on expectant mothers who were convinced they were in labor.

She'd call her neighbor, she decided. Mrs. Baker would stay with her until she could determine that this was the real thing and not a false alarm.

As she lifted a hand to the counter to pull herself up, another pain, nearly blinding in its intensity, dragged her back down to her knees. Moaning, she curled into a ball, trying to smother the pain. She felt a gush of moisture between her legs and watched in horror as a dark stain spread from the crotch of her scrub pants, soaking her to the knees.

She squeezed her eyes shut against the sight, knowing all too well what this meant.

"Oh, God, please," she prayed tearfully. "Don't let me lose my baby."

Mack climbed from his car and checked the number on the house against the return address on the envelope he held, then tucked it into his shirt pocket and studied the house. Its modest appearance and old-fashioned charm surprised him. Similar trips in the past had taken him to ultramodern condominiums in singles' neighborhoods and upscale apartment high-rises, but nothing even close to this. This house seemed almost...well, homey. From the border of impatiens that lined the sidewalk, to the baskets of ferns that swung lazily from hooks on the porch eaves, it looked like a place where a family might live.

Reminded that it was his own family who was responsible for him being here, he swore under his breath and started up the walk, anxious to get the unsavory task over with. Reaching the door, he rapped his knuckles against wood painted a warm, cheerful red, then rocked back on his boot heels and waited.

After a full minute passed without a response, he lifted a hand and knocked again. Frowning, he strained to listen for any sound coming from inside that would indicate that someone was home. He heard a female voice call out, but wasn't sure what was said. An invitation to come in, he wondered, or simply a signal to let him know she was on her way to the door?

Figuring it was the latter, he waited, listening for the sound of footsteps from inside. When he heard nothing but silence, he tried the door and found it locked. Frowning, he glanced to his left and noticed a set of windows. Though covered by blinds, he crossed to peer through them, hoping they would offer him a peek inside. A narrow gap between the slats provided him with a slim view of the living room. Finding no sign of life, he shifted his gaze to a hallway beyond that led toward the rear of the house. A flutter of movement on the floor caught his attention and he pressed his nose against the glass for a better look.

"What the hell," he murmured, as he stared at what appeared to be an outstretched hand, its fingers clawing against the hardwood floor. Was the woman drunk and had fallen? he wondered. Had she OD'd? Either possibility wouldn't surprise him, considering the crowd Ty ran with. But it was the other possibilities that came to mind—attempted burglary, possible rape victim—that had him leaping off the porch and running around to the rear of the house. His heart thumping wildly, he cleared the back porch steps in one leap and shoved open the door.

Braced for a possible attack, he stepped cautiously inside. "Ma'am?" he called. "Are you okay?"

"Help me…please."

The voice, weak and thready, came from the opposite side of the room.

He quickly rounded the island that separated the

room and found the woman lying on the floor, her back to him. From her sprawled position, it appeared she had heard his knock and had tried to drag herself to the front door.

He dropped to a knee behind her and laid a hand on her arm. "Are you hurt?"

"I—"

Moaning, she curled tighter into herself.

"My…water…broke," she managed to gasp out between breaths.

A chill skated down Mack's spine. He had known the woman was pregnant but hadn't realized she was that far along. "How far apart are the contractions?"

She dragged in a breath, slowly released it, then rolled to her back and looked up at him.

"Continuous." She wet her lips. "Please…help me." Tears welled up in her eyes and spilled over dark lashes. "I don't want to lose my baby."

He set his jaw against the fear in her eyes, the desperation in her voice. He didn't need this nightmare, he told himself. He could walk out the door right now, tear up the check he'd brought along to end whatever responsibility the woman felt his family owed her, and no one would ever be the wiser.

Her hand closed over his, her fingers digging deeply into his skin. "Please," she begged. "You've got to help me."

He hesitated a moment, then swore under his breath and pushed to his feet. With his mouth slanted in a scowl, he snatched the phone from its base and punched in 911.

* * *

Mack paced the waiting area of the Emergency Room, his stomach in knots, his palms slick with sweat. His uneasiness wasn't due to his concern for the woman who had been wheeled away by EMS thirty minutes earlier. It was the hospital. He hated them. The antiseptic smell. The sterile decor. The constant pages over the PA system for doctors and nurses and the dreaded words "code blue." He didn't know what had possessed him to come here. He'd done what the woman had asked of him. He'd called 911, then stayed with her until the ambulance arrived. He'd done his duty. If she lost her baby, it was no skin off his nose. It wasn't his kid.

He dropped his head back with a groan, unable to believe that he would even think such a thing. He didn't wish the woman ill. And he sure as hell didn't want her to lose her baby. He knew what it was like to lose a child. The grief, the guilt, the hole it left in your heart, in your life.

"Mr. McGruder?"

He whirled at the sound of his name and found a nurse standing in the doorway. "Yes?"

"Ms. Rocci is asking for you." She opened the door wider. "If you'll follow me, I'll show you the way."

He hesitated, knowing it was a mistake to see the woman again, to get involved any deeper than he already was. He should leave. Go back home where he belonged. Forget about Adrianna Rocci and her unborn child.

Instead he found himself following the nurse down a long hall.

She glanced over her shoulder. "You're a bit of a hero around here, you know."

He frowned, uncomfortable at being tagged as such. "I'm no hero."

"You are to us. You came to the aid of one of our own." At his confused looked, she explained. "Addy works here. If you hadn't happened along when you did, there's a chance she would've lost her baby. Maybe even her life."

Before he could think of a response, she stopped before one of the curtained-off cubicles, pushed back the drape and held it aside.

When he hesitated, she gave him a reassuring smile. "Don't worry," she whispered. "She's resting more comfortably now."

Taking a deep breath, he stepped inside. The room was so small the curtain brushed the backs of his legs when the nurse dropped it into place. The woman—Addy, he remembered the nurse calling her—lay on a gurney parked no more than a foot from where he stood, a sheet draping her from chin to toes. A white identification bracelet circled her left wrist and an IV needle was taped to the back of her hand. He followed the tube to a bottle hooked to a stainless steel pole wheeled close to the bed, then shifted his gaze to her face.

With her eyes closed and her hands folded over her swollen stomach, she looked serene, peaceful. Thinking she was asleep, he eased closer to the bed and was relieved to find that there was more color in her face than there had been when the attendants had loaded her into the ambulance.

She wasn't beautiful, he thought as he studied her, but she wasn't homely, either. Her complexion was dark, as was her hair, a testament to her Italian surname, he supposed. Her cheekbones were high ridges, her neck long and graceful.

As he stared, trying to remember the color of her eyes, her lashes fluttered up. Brown, he noted. Her eyes were brown.

She smiled softly and reached for his hand. "I can't believe you're really here. I was sure that I had imagined you."

Her voice was husky, barely more than a whisper, but he heard the wonder in it. "The nurse said you wanted to see me."

She gave his hand a grateful squeeze. "To thank you." She closed her eyes, gulped. When she opened them again, a single tear slipped from the corner and slid down her temple to disappear into her hair. "I don't know what would've happened to me and my baby if you hadn't come along when you did."

He averted his gaze, unsure what to say. When he glanced back, she was studying him curiously, as if only just now wondering at his identity and why he was at her house.

"Do I know you?"

He hesitated a moment, then figured she'd never make the connection. "John McGruder, though most folks call me Mack."

"Mack," she repeated, as if testing the sound of the name, then smiled. "That's a good, strong name. It suits you."

Before he could think of a response, her eyes slammed shut and she arched up high off the bed, her fingers digging into the mattress.

Panicking, he glanced around for a call button. "Should I get the nurse?"

She released a long breath, then opened her eyes and forced a reassuring smile. "No. I'm okay. The doctor was able to stop the labor, but he said I should expect a few more pains."

He blew out a long breath of his own, relieved that it hadn't lasted any longer than it had. "Does that mean you get to go home?"

"No. In fact, an orderly is on his way right now to take me up to Labor and Delivery."

"But I thought you said the doctor was able to stop your labor?"

"He was…for the time being. But I have to stay in the hospital. They need to be able to monitor the baby's vital signs, plus keep me off my feet."

"How long will you have to stay?"

She lifted a shoulder. "Until the baby's born. My actual due date isn't until July 15, but Dr. Wharton says he doubts I'll make it that long."

He did the math in his head and shuddered, knowing he'd go nuts if he had to stay in a hospital bed for six weeks. "Is there anyone I can call for you? Family you want notified?"

She shook her head. "The only family I have is my mother, and she lives in Hawaii."

He pulled a pen from his pocket. "Give me her number, and I'll give her a call. She'll probably want to catch the next plane out."

"You're sweet to offer, but it isn't necessary. She wasn't planning on coming for the baby's birth. Me going into labor early won't change her mind."

He pressed the pen against the paper. "Why don't you let her decide that?"

She hesitated a moment, then sighed. "I guess it wouldn't hurt to let her know what's going on. Her name is Mary Claire Sullivan and her number is—"

Mack jotted down the number she rattled off, then slipped the paper and pen back into his pocket. He glanced uncertainly around. "Well, I guess I better get out of here before they run me off. Is there anything I can get for you before I leave?"

She lifted a brow. "About six more weeks of pregnancy?" Smiling, she flapped a hand. "Just kidding. I'll be fine."

He shifted uneasily from foot to foot, anxious to go, but reluctant to leave her alone. "You take care of yourself, okay?"

She reached for his hand and gave it another grateful squeeze. "Thanks, Mack. For everything. I owe you one."

As Mack stepped through the Emergency Room doors, he pulled his cell phone from the holster clipped at his waist and punched in the number Addy had given him, wanting to make the call to her mother before he hit the road.

When a woman answered, he asked, "Is this Mary Claire Sullivan?"

"Who wants to know?"

Mack scowled at the woman's suspicious tone. "Mack McGruder. I'm calling for your daughter. Addy," he added, thinking she might have more than one. "She went into labor earlier this evening and was rushed to the hospital. The doctor was able to stop the labor, but she's going to have to remain in the hospital until the baby is born."

"Are you the one who got her pregnant?"

Startled by the unexpected question, he gaped, then scowled again. "No. I'm just passing on information. Figured you'd want to make arrangements to come and stay with her."

"If she thinks I'm going to fly all the way to Dallas to hold her hand, she's got another think coming! Nobody sat by my side while I was giving birth to her. No siree. I sweated out twelve hours of labor all by myself. Twelve *long* hours," she added. "And even if I wanted to come, which I don't, I've got a husband to see after. I can't go flying off and leave him to fend for himself. You tell Addy that she's the one who got herself into this mess, and she'll have to see it to its end. I've got troubles enough of my own to deal with, without taking on hers."

Stunned, Mack stood slack-jawed. How could a mother be so callous about her own child? So uncaring?

"If it's the cost you're worried about, I'll arrange for your flight."

"A man who'd offer to do that either has a guilty conscience or money to burn."

Mack ground his teeth. "I'm just trying to be helpful. I'd think you'd want to be with your daughter at a time like this."

"She got pregnant without my help. She can deliver without it, too."

"But she's your daughter!" he shouted, unable to contain his frustration any longer. "She needs you."

"I did my duty by Addy. I raised her, didn't I? And without any help from the sorry SOB who fathered her."

Mack wanted to curse at the woman, strangle something, preferably her. How could anyone, much less a mother, be so cold-blooded?

"I'm sorry I bothered you," he muttered, and disconnected the call before he gave in to the urge to tell the woman exactly what he thought of her. Scowling, he stuffed his cell phone back into its holster at his waist, then dragged his hands over his hair. Lacing his fingers behind his head, he glanced over his shoulder at the Emergency Room door and envisioned Addy lying on the gurney, probably worried out of her mind about her baby, and without a soul to lean on for support.

Dropping his arms, he headed for the parking lot, telling himself it wasn't his problem. He'd done his duty. He'd called the ambulance for her, made sure that she'd arrived safely at the hospital. He'd even called her mother for her.

He did an abrupt about-face and marched back to the Emergency entrance. Once inside, he quickly spotted the nurse who had taken him back to see Addy and motioned her toward him.

"Leaving us?" she asked, smiling.

"Yes, ma'am. I've got a good four-hour drive home." He fished a business card from his wallet and handed it to her. "I'd appreciate it if you'd give me a call if there's a change in Addy's condition. My cell number is there at the bottom. Call day or night. Doesn't matter. I'll answer."

She hid a smile. "And you claimed you're not a hero," she scolded.

"More like a janitor," he grumbled, and turned for the door.

"Janitor?" she repeated in confusion.

He paused in the open doorway and glanced back. "Yeah. Seems I've made a career of cleaning up other people's messes."

Two

Addy thrust her head back against the pillow and clenched her teeth, sure that the pain was going to rip her apart. In spite of her efforts to suppress it, a low animal-like groan slid past her lips, and she began to pant, determined to stay ahead of the pain and not give in to it.

Busy adjusting an intravenous drip, Marjorie glanced her way. "Bad?"

Gulping, Addy nodded. "Did you call Dr. Wharton?"

Satisfied that the fluids were transferring at the proper rate, Marjorie took Addy's hand and held it between her own. "He's on his way."

Addy gulped again. "He better hurry."

Her expression sympathetic, Marjorie stroked Addy's

damp hair back from her face. "I know you don't want to hear this, but you're a long way from delivering."

Groaning, Addy closed her eyes. "I can't be. The pain is already unbearable." She opened her eyes and looked at Marjorie, tears blurring her friend's image. "You'd tell me if something was wrong with the baby, wouldn't you?"

"Of course I would," Marjorie assured her.

Addy searched her friend's face, trying to determine if she was telling the truth or just saying that to keep Addy from becoming more upset. Unsure, she looked away. "You should go back down to Emergency. You're on duty."

Marjorie glanced toward the door and worried her lip. "I really should. There was a bus wreck on the interstate. The call came in just before I came up to check on you."

Addy pulled her hand from Marjorie's. "Then go. They need you more than I do."

"But I hate leaving you alone," Marjorie fretted.

"I'll be okay. Really."

"I'll call Mack," Marjorie said, already digging in her pocket for her cell phone. "He gave me his number and said for me to let him know if there was a change in your condition."

"No, please," Addy begged. "He's done enough for me already. Promise you won't call him."

Marjorie eyed Addy stubbornly for a moment, then sagged her shoulders in defeat. "Oh, all right," she said, and shoved the phone into her pocket. "I'll come back and check on you again as soon as I can."

"Thanks, Marjorie."

Addy waited until the door closed behind her friend, then covered her face with her hands and gave in to the tears that had threatened since her labor had started again. She couldn't lose her baby, prayed God would keep it safe. She wanted this baby so badly, needed it. In spite of all the sacrifices she would have to make to support and care for it, she wanted this baby to live.

And while she was praying, she added a thanks for Mack's unexpected appearance at her house and the steps he'd taken to protect her baby's life.

Even as the prayer formed, she lowered her hands from her face and frowned, wondering about Mack and realizing that, although she'd asked him his name, she'd failed to ask him why he'd been at her house.

There were any number of plausible explanations, she reminded herself. He could be a bill collector or a solicitor. Her frown deepened. But that didn't make sense, as she didn't have any outstanding bills and solicitors were prohibited in her neighborhood. She supposed he might have become lost and simply stopped to ask directions, which wasn't unusual, as her neighborhood was made up of a tangle of streets that baffled even the most gifted map reader.

Whatever his reason, she thought, dismissing her concerns as unnecessary considering his kindness to her, she wished he was still with her. She knew it was stupid, foolish even, to yearn for someone she didn't even know. But while he'd been with her, both at her house and in Emergency, she'd felt safe, more in control, better capable of handling the pain, of facing whatever happened. Not so alone.

She opened her hands to look at them, remembering how sure his grip had felt on hers, how firmly he'd held her hand. How strong he'd seemed, so in control. He didn't even know her, yet he'd followed the ambulance to the hospital, stayed with her, even offered to call her mother.

Why couldn't she have fallen for a guy like Mack? she asked herself miserably. She bet he wouldn't have stolen from her or lied to her as Ty had done. And he probably wouldn't have run the way Ty had when she'd told him she was pregnant.

Gulping back the regret that crowded her throat, she closed her eyes and willed her body to relax and her mind to clear, knowing she had to keep her thoughts focused so that she could deal with the next pain when it came.

There'd be plenty of time for regrets later.

A thick band of clouds blocked what light the moon might have offered, leaving the interstate a black ribbon that stretched for miles and miles in the darkness. But Mack didn't mind the darkness or the lack of traffic he encountered. In fact, he welcomed it. It gave him time to think.

And Adrianna Rocci—or Addy, as her friend had called her—had given him a lot to think about.

An unplanned pregnancy. An irresponsible boyfriend. A mother who ranked right up there with Joan Crawford on the nurturing scale. And now her baby's life was in jeopardy. How much more could the woman take, before she snapped?

It wasn't right, he told himself. No one should have to go through something like this alone. She should have a husband or, at the very least, family with her to offer emotional and physical support. Hell, the woman was going to be all but tied to a bed for the next six weeks! Who would take care of her house? Get her mail? Pay her bills? Who would sit with her to help pass the time? Hold her hand when she was scared? Stand at her side during the birth?

He narrowed his eyes at the dark highway ahead, wishing he could get his hands on Ty. Castration came to mind as sufficient punishment, but even that seemed too kind. Getting a woman pregnant, then abandoning her... It just wasn't right. Yet that was Ty's style. Hit and run, love 'em and leave 'em, that was his standard modus operandi. In Mack's estimation, Ty was immature, irresponsible and a royal pain in the ass. Unfortunately, women seemed to find him irresistible. And why wouldn't they? he asked himself. Ty was a good-looking man, smooth talking, fun loving. It was in the integrity department that he came up short. Just like his old man.

Mack scowled at the reminder of his stepfather. Jacob Bodean was nothing but a two-bit con artist out trolling for a free ride, when he'd met Mack's mother. Recently widowed and still grieving over the loss of her husband, his mother had been an easy mark for a scumball like Jacob. Playing on her weakened emotional state, within two months Jacob had sweet-talked her into marrying him. Another fourteen months and Ty had been born.

It had taken Mack's mother six years—and the loss of a large chunk of the fortune Mack's father had left her—before she'd figured out that Jacob was only interested in her money and was going through it as fast as he could write checks. It had cost her another chunk of money to get rid of him and to win custody of Ty. Mack often wondered if she wouldn't have been better off washing her hands of them both.

But Ty is blood, he told himself, as his mother had often reminded him and, like it or not, he was now Mack's responsibility. On her deathbed, his mother had made him promise that he would look after his half brother. The trust fund she'd set up for Ty prior to her death, naming Mack as executor, had added a legal obligation to the moral one he'd already assumed.

Both had been stretched mighty thin over the years.

Mack had bailed Ty out of more trouble than he cared to think about and was sick and damn tired of mopping up a grown man's messes. For God's sake, he thought, his anger with his half brother building. Ty was thirty-four years old! It was past time for him to settle down and take care of his own damn mistakes.

Mack drew in a long breath and slowly released it, telling himself that working up a steam over Ty wasn't going to help Addy's situation. And Addy definitely needed help.

He patted his shirt pocket, remembering the check he'd planned to offer her, in hopes of buying Ty's way out of yet another paternity suit, if that's what she'd had in mind. But after finding her lying on the floor already in labor, he hadn't been able to bring himself to broach the subject. How could he, when she was worried sick she might lose her baby?

But he had to do something, he told himself. He couldn't just leave her hanging out there alone. She'd seemed like a nice person, nothing at all like the other women Ty associated with, who had greedily snatched up the money he had offered them. Yet, what options did Mack have other than to offer her money? He sure as hell couldn't force Ty to do the honorable thing and marry the woman and give the baby his name. Even if he could, he certainly wouldn't be doing Addy any favors, saddling her with a man like Ty.

His cell phone rang, and he quickly plucked it from the console, where he'd laid it, and flipped it open. "Mack," he said.

"This is Marjorie Johnson. The nurse from the Emergency Room?"

He tensed at the hesitancy in the woman's voice, knowing the call had to be about Addy. "Has something happened to Addy?"

"Her labor started again. The doctor says he can't stop it this time. I wanted to stay with her, but I'm on duty and don't get off for another five hours."

He glanced at the illuminated clock on the dash and quickly calculated the time. "I can be there in less than two."

"Oh, thank you," she said in relief, then added in a

rush, "But please don't tell her that I called. When I suggested it, she insisted that I not bother you. Said you'd done enough for her already."

He saw an exit sign up ahead, and took it.

"Don't worry. Your secret is safe with me."

Mack headed straight for Labor and Delivery and the room number the attendant at the information desk had given him.

The room he entered was larger than the tiny cubicle he'd left her in during her stay in the ER. There was also more equipment on hand, all of which was humming and blinking, busily monitoring her vital signs as well as those of her baby.

She lay facing the dark window, her back to him. From his vantage point, if he hadn't known better, he would never have suspected she was pregnant. Her shoulders and hips appeared slim beneath the bedcovers, her waist a shallow dip between the two.

He thought for a moment that she was asleep, then heard a low groan and watched as her fingers curled around the edge of the mattress. He waited until they slowly relaxed, then said quietly, "Addy?"

She glanced over her shoulder, and her eyes widened in surprise. Shifting awkwardly to her back, she stretched out a hand. "Mack."

Her voice was no more than a whisper, but the relief in it resonated through him and settled somewhere near his heart. He crossed to the bed and gripped her hand within his.

"I thought you were going home," she said.

"I was," he admitted, then shrugged. "Decided I didn't want to miss the birthday party."

She narrowed her eyes in suspicion. "Did Marjorie call you?"

Mindful of his promise, he avoided her question by asking one of his own. "How are you doing?"

"Okay, I guess." Tears filled her eyes and she shook her head. "I'm scared, Mack. More scared than I've ever been in my life."

He chafed her hand between his. "Everything's going to be all right." He tipped his head toward the row of equipment and teased her with a smile. "Hell, there's enough technology in this room to send a man to the moon and back. Getting a baby here safely ought to be a snap."

She glanced toward the machines and winced. "It does seem a bit much, doesn't it?"

"What I want to know is, do all patients get this kind of preferential treatment or is it reserved for hospital employees?"

She laughed softly. "Since I've never been a patient, I wouldn't know."

She opened her mouth to say something more, then slammed her eyes shut and emitted a low groan.

He tightened his fingers around hers. "Another pain?"

Her teeth gritted, she nodded.

He racked his brain, trying to remember the techniques he'd learned in the Lamaze classes he'd attended with his wife. "Look at me," he ordered.

She opened her eyes and fixed them on his.

"Breathe slowly," he instructed. "Work with the pain, not against it."

He kept his gaze on hers while she hauled in a deep breath, released it, drew in another. Unconsciously he matched his breathing to hers, while he waited for the pain to pass. After what seemed like hours, her grip on his hand slowly relaxed and she released a long shuddery breath.

"Better?" he asked.

She wet her lips, nodded. "They're coming faster now. Harder."

He gave her hand a reassuring squeeze. "You're doing just fine. A couple more like that one, and I'll bet that baby will be here in no time."

"I'm going to hold you to—"

Her eyes went wide, her body rigid.

Without thinking, he laid a hand on her stomach and felt the tautness beneath his palm and knew she was already having another contraction. "Relax," he soothed, and began stroking his palm over her stomach.

Eyes wild, she fought him, struggling to escape his hold on her, as well as the pain.

He clamped down hard on her hand, refusing to let go. "Look at me, Addy," he ordered sternly. "Focus. We can do this."

She shook her head wildly. "Maybe you can, but I can't. It hurts!"

"It won't last forever." He increased the pressure on her hand. "Come on, Addy. Look at me. Focus."

She opened her eyes and bared her teeth. "I hate

you," she snarled. "You're mean and hateful and I wish you'd get the hell out of here and leave me alone."

Mack ignored her, knowing it was the pain talking. His wife had hurled similar accusations at him—and worse—while giving birth.

"Hate me all you want," he told her, "but I'm staying. We're going to get through this. Together. Now breathe."

She tried to wrench her hand away, then jackknifed to a sitting position, her eyes wide, her fingers clamped around his hard enough to crush bone. "It's coming!" she screamed. "Oh, God, get the nurse. The baby's coming!"

Mack grabbed the remote control clipped to the bed rail and punched the call button. Within seconds the door opened and a nurse strode into the room. She took one look at Addy's face and shouldered Mack aside, taking his place beside the bed.

"How far apart are the contractions?" she asked, as she checked Addy's pulse.

Mack dragged a shaky hand down his face, more than happy to relinquish control to the nurse. "Less than a minute."

The door opened again and a doctor sauntered in. "How's my favorite patient?"

Mack burned him with a look. "How do you think?" he snapped impatiently. "She's hurting like hell and needs something for the pain."

"No!" Addy cried and fell back against the pillows, holding her hands protectively over her stomach. "No drugs. I'm doing this naturally."

The doctor looked at Mac and shrugged as if to say

"you heard the woman," then stepped to the end of the bed and lifted the sheet to visibly check her progress.

"The head's crowned," he reported, then dropped the sheet and strode to the sink, his steps quicker now, his expression all business. As he squirted disinfectant on his hands, he glanced Mack's way. "If you're the father, you'll need to scrub up. Otherwise—" he tipped his head toward the door "—the waiting room's at the end of the hall."

Addy lunged, managing to catch Mack's sleeve. He glanced back and saw the fear in her eyes, the pleading. He set his jaw, knowing there was no way in hell he could leave her to face this birth alone.

"Where do I scrub?"

Mack sat in the chair by the window, his long legs stretched out in front of him and his head tipped back against the cushion, staring at the ceiling. Though exhausted, he couldn't sleep. His mind was racing, his body charged with adrenaline...and all because of the tiny bit of humanity, swaddled in a blue blanket and sleeping peacefully in the bassinet across the room.

He dropped his chin to look in that direction, and his heart did a slow flip. A boy, he thought, and had to swallow back the emotion that filled his throat, weighing in at a fraction over five pounds but healthy as a horse and with a set of lungs to prove it. Though there had been concerns that the baby wouldn't be fully developed, he'd passed all the tests like a champ, and wouldn't have to spend any time in an incubator, as most preemies were required to do.

Unable to resist, he heaved himself from the chair and crossed to peer down at the baby. Bundled up snug in the blue blanket, only the infant's face was visible, revealing rosy cheeks and a nose no bigger than a button. Dark fuzz covered his head, but Mack knew from experience that he'd probably lose it and what grew back might be a different color entirely. His own son's hair had been coal-black at birth, but by the age of two, it was cotton white. He wondered what color it would've been if he'd lived?

Stifling a groan, he dropped his chin to his chest. He didn't want to think about his son. Not now. Remembering made him hurt, and Mack had hurt for too many years.

Taking a deep breath, he lifted his head and stared hard, until he succeeded in shoving back the memory and was able to bring the baby into focus again.

His smile wistful, he reached to smooth the back of his fingers over the baby's cheek, marveling at its softness, the miniature features.

"You're one lucky guy," he whispered to the sleeping infant. "You've got a helluva mother. Even when the pain was really bad, she wouldn't let them give her anything to ease it, for fear it would hurt you." He smoothed a knuckle across the baby's opposite cheek. "Trust me. That kind of love is a rare thing."

The baby scrunched up his face, as if preparing to cry.

"Whoa, now," Mack warned and quickly lifted the baby from the bassinet. "None of that. You don't want to wake up your mom, now, do you?"

Cradling the baby in his arms, he tiptoed back to the

chair and eased down. The infant yawned, rooted around a moment, then settled back to sleep, holding one hand curled in a fist against his cheek.

Mack stared at the infant, and his heart seemed to stop, then kicked into a pounding beat. The baby's coloring and features mimicked those of his son so closely, he could be Mack's child. Unable to tear his gaze away, he stared, his heart thundering against his rib cage, as he wondered if this baby was an answer to the problem that had been troubling him lately.

Though he considered it morbid to think about his own death, that's exactly what he'd been doing for the better part of a year. He supposed it was a sign that he was getting old, for him to be having such thoughts—although he didn't consider forty-two all that old. But death was a fact of life, the same as living, and he was aware, especially with an estate the size of his, that he should have a will in place, no matter what his age or state of health. Having one drawn one up was easy enough. All he had to do was call his lawyer. What kept him from making the call was his lack of an heir. Most men named their wives or kids as their beneficiaries, or a combination of the two. But Mack didn't have a wife or children…at least, none that were living.

He'd lost his wife and son in a senseless car wreck twelve years before and had never remarried. For the first couple of years following their deaths, he'd found it hard enough to breathe, much less think about marrying again. But even after the pain of losing them had dulled somewhat, he still hadn't been able to work up the enthusiasm to ask a woman out on a date.

When asked, he claimed it was because he'd never met one that caught his eye. But the truth was, he'd never looked. Losing his wife and son had changed him, stripping him of the desire to develop attachments with anyone, especially a woman. As a result, he'd reached the ripe old age of forty-two with no family, other than his half brother, to name in a will.

He scowled at the reminder of Ty. Hell, if he left his estate to his half brother, everything Mack and Mack's father before him had worked and struggled to build would be lost in less than a year's time. Ty had the business acumen of a jackass and the attention span of a two-year-old. He looked at everything in terms of what he could turn it for and the fun it would buy him when he did.

No, he wouldn't leave his estate to Ty.

Mack focused his gaze on the baby again, wondering if the child could be the answer to his problem. He could adopt him, he told himself. Raise the boy as his own, ingrain in him the morals and integrity that the child would never learn if left up to Ty.

Ty didn't care about the kid, Mack told himself. If he did, he'd be here right now, instead of playing an adult version of hide and seek. If he'd felt any sense of responsibility at all, Ty would've been the one holding Addy's hand while the baby was born, not Mack. And it would've been Ty, not Mack, who the doctor had passed the scissors to and allowed to cut the umbilical cord, signifying the baby's official entry into the world.

The way Mack looked at it, his willingness to adopt

the baby was the perfect solution to everyone's problems. The child would have a father, Ty would be off the hook, and Mack would have an heir.

There was only one problem...the baby's mother.

In spite of the bond Mack and Addy had forged during the last fourteen-plus hours, he doubted she would embrace the idea if he were to suggest him adopting her baby. In fact, she'd probably think he'd lost his mind.

"Mack?"

He jumped at the sound of Addy's voice and glanced up to find her peering at him curiously.

"Is something wrong?" she asked in concern.

Fearing she would somehow read his thoughts and know what he'd been thinking, he dropped his gaze and tucked the blanket more snugly at the baby's chin. "No. He looked like he was going to start fussing, and I thought if I held him awhile, it would give you the chance to sleep a little longer."

Her smile tender, she eased herself to a sitting position and held out her arms. "Here. Give him to me. I'll bet he's hungry."

Rising, Mack carried the baby to the bed and settled the infant in her arms.

As if sensing his nearness to his milk supply, the baby twisted his head toward her breast, his mouth open like a baby's birds.

Addy placed a finger against the infant's lips and laughed when he began to suck. "See?" she said, and began to rearrange her nightgown. "He is hungry."

She stopped and glanced up at Mack, her cheeks

stained a deep rose, as if she'd just realized the intimacy of what she was preparing to do.

He immediately took a step back. "I'll wait outside," he said, and turned for the door.

"No! Wait."

He glanced over his shoulder, surprised by the panic in her voice.

Dropping her gaze, she fluttered a hand. "Just turn your back until I get him situated."

Mack did as instructed and waited until he heard her signal of "ready" before turning around. Finding her and the baby modestly covered by the blue blanket, he reached behind him to drag his chair closer to the bed.

"Its amazing how a baby instinctively knows how to nurse," he said softly, awed by the sight.

Her gaze on the infant, she smiled. "Yes, it is."

Moments passed in silence, both absorbed by the baby's movements.

"Mack?"

His attention focused on the nursing infant, he mumbled a distracted, "Yeah?"

"I'm sorry."

He angled his head to peer at her in puzzlement. "For what?"

"For all the mean things I said to you while I was in labor."

He waved away the apology. "I knew you didn't mean any of that stuff. That was the pain talking."

"Just the same, I'm sorry. I don't know what I would've done without you."

He choked out a laugh. "Heck, I had the easy part. You were the one who was doing all the work."

She looked down at the baby and smiled. "And look what I got for my trouble. A beautiful, healthy baby. I couldn't ask for anything more."

"He's a keeper, all right."

The door opened and Marjorie sailed in, trailing a balloon bouquet in her wake. Without so much as a how-do-you-do to Mack or Addy, she headed straight for the bed, her gaze on the baby.

"Oh, let me see that little tiger," she said eagerly, as she tethered the streamers of the balloon bouquet at the head of the bed.

Addy deftly separated the baby from her breast, rearranged her nightgown, then folded back the blanket, for Marjorie to see. "Isn't he beautiful?"

"Gorgeous," Marjorie agreed, then tipped her face up to Addy's. "Have you named him yet?"

Addy shook her head. "No. I had a girl's name picked out, but I hadn't settled on one for a boy."

"I thought you were going to use your father's name?" Marjorie said.

"Only his first name." She shrugged. "I haven't been able to come up with anything that sounds right with Antonio."

Marjorie pursed her lips thoughtfully, then swung her gaze to Mack. "What's your full name?"

Caught off-guard, Mack blinked, then stammered, "Uh, Jonathan Michael McGruder."

"What about Antonio Michael Rocci?" Marjorie suggested to Addy.

Frowning, Addy shook her head. "I want to use Antonio as his middle name."

"Then name him Jonathan Antonio Rocci. You could call him Johnny."

"Jonathan Antonio Rocci," Addy repeated, as if testing the sound of the name, then nodded. "It's a mouthful, but I like it." She glanced at Mack, her expression hopeful. "Would you mind if I gave my baby your name?"

Mind? Mack thought. Hell, he was hoping he could persuade her to give the baby his last name, as well. "I'd be honored."

The pager in Marjorie's pocket beeped and she pulled it out to check the display. "Those imbeciles," she muttered crossly. "You'd think they could run the ER for ten minutes without me." She slid the pager back into her pocket and offered Addy an apologetic smile. "Sorry, hon, but I've got to scoot. I'll try to come back later, when I'm on my dinner break."

"Call first," Addy warned. "I'm hoping I can persuade Dr. Wharton to release me."

Marjorie wagged a finger at her nose. "You listen to me, young lady. You've just had a baby. You have no business going home to an empty house. You stay right here where the nursing staff can take care of you and the baby."

Addy jutted her chin. "I can take care of myself."

"But—"

"No, Marjorie," she said, cutting her friend off. "I'm going home."

With a huff of disgust, Marjorie turned to leave. "*You* try talking some sense into that thick head of hers," she said to Mack. "She won't listen to me."

Mack had remained quiet during the exchange, absorbing the conversation and considering how he could use the situation to his own advantage. He knew the idea to adopt the baby was a crazy one and liable to send Addy into an apoplectic fit. But the more he thought about it, the more he was convinced it was the best solution to all their problems, both his and Addy's.

Now he just had to convince her of that.

He waited until the door closed behind Marjorie, then said quietly, "She's right, you know. It doesn't make sense for you to go home, when you have all the help you need right here."

Her lips pursed in annoyance, Addy bundled the sleeping baby back up into the blanket. "Marjorie's a buttinsky. She's forever sticking her nose in other people's business."

When he saw that she intended to carry the baby back to his bassinet, Mack stood. "Here. I'll take him." He took the baby from her and crossed to the bassinet. "She's only thinking of what's best for you," he said, refocusing the conversation on Marjorie's suggestion.

Addy folded her arms stubbornly across her chest. "I can take care of myself."

Mack glanced over his shoulder. "Like you were last night when I found you?"

She opened her mouth, then closed it, the blood slowly draining from her face.

Mack knew what he'd said was mean, even cruel, but he felt it was necessary, if he was going to convince Addy that she needed his help.

He crossed to sit beside the bed again. "Once you're able to return to work, what happens if you get sick? Who'll look after the baby then?"

She nervously wet her lips. "I...I'll manage."

"How, Addy?" he persisted. "Your mother certainly won't come to your rescue. I've talked to her. In fact, her last words to me were, 'she's the one who got herself into this mess, and she'll have to see it to its end.'"

She dropped her gaze, but not before he saw the tears that brimmed in her eyes.

He reached out a hand and laid it on her arm. "I'm not trying to hurt you, Addy," he said quietly. "I'm only trying to make you see that you can't do this alone."

She dragged a hand beneath her nose. "Like I have a choice."

It was the opening Mack had hoped for, needed. "I'd be willing to help you."

She snapped her gaze to his. "*You?* Why would you want to help me? You don't even know me."

He kept his gaze fixed on hers. "I know more than you might think."

When her forehead pleated in confusion, he decided it was time to tell all. "I know that the father of your baby isn't going to be around to take care of you and the baby."

Her jaw dropped, then closed with an angry click of teeth. "You don't know any such thing."

"Yes, I do," he replied calmly. "If his past actions are any indication, you'll never hear from Ty Bodean again."

Her eyes shot wide. "You…you know Ty?"

"He's my half brother."

"He's your…" She gulped, swallowed. "You mean, you knew about me and the baby, before…"

"Yes. The letters you sent to Ty in care of the post-master of Lampasas were delivered to my house."

If possible, her eyes widened even more. "You *read* them?"

"Yes," he admitted. "Though not at first. It wasn't until the third letter arrived that I decided I should open them, so I could find out what kind of trouble Ty had gotten himself into." He shook his head sadly. "You aren't the first person whose attempts to track Ty down have led to me. I had to read your letters so I'd know what I was dealing with."

She dropped her face to her hands. "Oh, my God," she moaned.

Mack laid a hand on her arm. "I'm not telling you this to embarrass you."

She snapped her head up to glare at him. "Then why are you? I may be slow, but I'm not stupid. I'd figured out that Ty was never coming back." She snatched her arm from beneath his hand. "You didn't need to drive all the way to Dallas to tell me *that*."

Sighing, Mack slowly drew his hand back to rest it on his thigh. "That's not why I went to your house. I went there to offer you money."

Steam all but came out of her ears. "Well, you can tell Ty Bodean to keep his damn money. I don't want it."

"The money's not Ty's. It's mine."

"Well, I don't want your money, either," she snapped. She pointed a stiff finger at the door. "Get out. And don't bother coming back. I never want to see you again. Ever."

Three

Mack figured he'd pretty much blown his chances of convincing Addy to allow him to adopt her baby…but that didn't mean he was ready to throw in the towel. It wasn't in his nature to concede defeat, not without first putting up a damn good fight.

And as far as Mack was concerned, the battle had only just begun.

In retrospect, he could see his mistakes…and he'd made some doozies. The first was blindsiding Addy with the news that he was Ty's half brother. Considering how she must feel toward Ty after he'd abandoned her, Mack should have suspected that she would want nothing to do with anyone even remotely related to his half brother.

His second mistake was in telling her he'd gone to her home to offer her money. In the less than twenty-four hours he'd known Addy, he had seen evidence of a strong pride, as well as a pretty wide stubborn streak. Offering a payoff to a woman like her would be an insult, a slap on the face. She wouldn't care about money or the lack thereof. A woman like her was ruled by her heart. She'd willingly sacrifice anything for those she loved…and she'd accept nothing as a replacement for it, not even money. How Mack knew that about her, he wasn't sure, but he'd bet his ranch that he'd pegged her right.

Since he was certain he'd destroyed whatever level of trust he'd managed to establish with her over the past twenty-four hours, he figured he would need some help winning it back, and that was going to require some fancy two-stepping. But Mack was prepared to wear out the soles of his boots, if that's what it took.

After checking into a hotel near the hospital, he made several phone calls, the first to his lawyer. He explained the situation and told his lawyer what he needed from him. Then he placed calls to his pastor, his banker and lastly to his best friend, who also happened to be a highly respected and well-known pediatrician in Mack's hometown.

After obtaining their assurance that they would do all they could to assist him, he then called Addy's doctor, knowing he would need the support and backing of people she knew and respected. The last call he made was to Marjorie. He quickly outlined his plan to Addy's friend and was relieved when she promised to do everything within her power to convince Addy to go along with it.

Satisfied that he'd done all that he could to ensure a positive outcome for the meeting he had arranged for the next morning, Mack fell into bed, exhausted, not realizing until the moment his head hit the pillow that he hadn't slept in more than forty-eight hours.

Addy checked the room one last time to make sure that she hadn't forgotten anything. Since her stay at the hospital had been brief and so few people had known about it, there wasn't much for her to worry about. Thanks to Marjorie, who had dropped by Addy's house the evening before and picked up a few of her things, she'd had a clean set of clothes to put on that morning and an outfit for the baby to wear home. Other than herself, the baby and a small overnight bag, the only personal items in the room were the balloon bouquet Marjorie had given her, a vase of long-stemmed roses from the hospital staff and a huge basket filled with baby gifts from her co-workers in the ER. Now all she needed was for Dr. Wharton to make his morning rounds and sign her release, and she could call a taxi and go home.

She glanced at her wristwatch and frowned, wondering what was taking her doctor so long. Normally he was finished with his rounds by eight, and it was already ten after. Impatient to be on her way, she checked the baby to make sure he was still sleeping, then headed for the door to peek into the hall to see if her doctor was still on the floor.

Before she reached it, the door opened and Dr. Wharton stepped inside.

Her smile sheepish, she lifted her hands, then dropped them to her sides. "I was just on my way to look for you. I was afraid you'd forgotten about me."

He slung an arm around her shoulders and walked with her toward the bassinet. "Forget about my favorite patient?" he teased. "No way." He dropped his arm from around her and stooped to peer down at the baby. "And how's our little man doing this morning?" he asked.

"Perfect. He only woke me up once last night for a feeding."

He nodded his approval. "Then your milk must be satisfying him."

"Seems like."

The door opened behind her, and Addy glanced over her shoulder. Her eyes shot wide open, when she saw it was Mack, then narrowed dangerously.

"What are you doing here?" she said from between clenched teeth.

Ignoring her, he glanced toward Dr. Wharton and nodded. "Tom," he said, by way of greeting. "I appreciate you arranging your schedule so that you could meet with us this morning."

Addy was so stunned by Mack's casual usage of her doctor's first name that it took her a moment to absorb what else he'd said.

"What meeting?" she demanded to know.

"The one I arranged," Mack replied.

The door opened again and Marjorie came in.

Addy turned to glare at Mack. "Did you ask *her* to attend this meeting, too?"

"Yes. I thought you'd want her input."

"Input on what?" Addy asked in growing frustration.

"On how best to resolve your problems."

"*You* are my only problem," she said furiously.

"Now, Addy," Marjorie scolded gently. "At least hear what Mack has to say."

Before Addy could tell Marjorie to mind her own business, Dr. Wharton spoke up. "Marjorie's right, Addy. You need to listen to Mack's suggestion."

Addy folded her arms across her chest and burned Mack with a look. "All right. You've got exactly two minutes and not a second more."

"I want you to marry me," he said simply.

"What?" she cried. "Are you crazy?"

"No, I assure you I'm perfectly sane. I'm a wealthy man, Addy. I can provide a lifestyle for you and the baby that you could never accomplish alone."

When she opened her mouth to tell him what he could with his lifestyle, as well as his proposal, he held up a hand.

"Please, hear me out. What I'm suggesting is not a traditional marriage. I would make no demands on you, sexual or emotional. My offer of marriage is simply a way to provide for you and give your baby a name. I'm prepared to legally adopt your child and raise him as my own son. My home is large enough to provide you with whatever privacy you deem necessary, plus it's staffed with a housekeeper and cook who will see to yours and the baby's needs.

"If at some time in the future," he went on, "you should find our arrangement confining or you feel threatened in any way, then I will grant you an annulment but will continue to provide financial support for the child."

"Why would you want to support him, if we're no longer living with you?"

His gaze remained steady on hers, his expression maddeningly calm in spite of her accusatory tone.

"For the same reason I'm offering you marriage," he said simply. "To ensure that he is always provided for. I take care of what's mine."

He held up a finger when she would have interrupted him. "When I adopt your son, I'll be assuming not only the legal and financial obligations associated with him but the moral ones, as well. Because of that commitment, I would place one stipulation on granting you an annulment, should you request one. I want the same rights awarded any father at the time of a divorce. Specifically, an equitable visitation schedule and the right to remain an active participant in his life. By remaining involved, I can be sure that he is instilled with the virtues necessary for him to develop into a man of honor and integrity."

Addy stared, part of her awed by what appeared to be his sincere concern for her son, and the other part unable to believe he would actually expect her to agree to such an outlandish arrangement.

"Do you have any idea what you're asking of me?" she said to him, then looked at Dr. Wharton and

Marjorie. "Do *you?*" she challenged. "I hardly know this man! Yes," she conceded, before either could remind her of the fact, "he probably saved my life and that of my baby, but prior to his coming to my rescue, I'd never seen him before! And you expect me to *marry* him?" she asked incredulously. "Are y'all crazy?"

"Mack has proven he's trustworthy," Marjorie argued. "He didn't have to follow the ambulance to the hospital, but he did. And he didn't have to turn around and drive back to Dallas when I called and told him that you'd gone into labor again. And, yes," she admitted, with a jut of her chin, when Addy narrowed her eyes at her, "I called him. So sue me."

"And he stayed with you throughout the delivery," Dr. Wharton interjected, taking over where Marjorie had left off. He dipped his chin and gave Addy a pointed look. "Which was at your request, as I recall."

She opened her hands. "I was delirious. Out of my mind with pain. Why else would I beg a complete stranger, and a man at that, to stay with me during the birth of my baby?"

"I can understand why you might be hesitant to accept my proposal," Mack said patiently.

"Hesitant?" she repeated, her voice rising as she whirled to face him. "How about violently opposed!"

Ignoring her, he continued. "In order to satisfy whatever concerns you might have, I've taken it upon myself to provide you with suitable references." He crossed to the door and opened it. "Gentlemen," he said, and spread an arm in invitation. "Would you please join us?"

Addy stared, wide-eyed, as four men filed into the room. The first to enter approached her, his hand held out in greeting.

"Leonard Boyles, Attorney-at-Law," he said by way of introduction. "I handle all Mack's legal needs and have for years. I can assure you that he has never been accused of any crime or sued in a court of law. His record, as well as his reputation, are both without blemish."

Speechless, Addy could only stare.

As soon as the lawyer moved aside, a second man—a clergyman judging by his white collar—stepped forward and gathered her hand between his.

"Pastor Nolan, my child," he said in a voice that invited trust. "I've served as Mack's spiritual advisor since he was a young boy and can honestly say that I've never known a finer man or one with a more generous heart. If you agree to marry him, it will be my honor to perform the ceremony."

Before Addy could think of a reply, a third man moved to stand before her.

"Jack Phelps," he said, and gave her a hand a brisk, no-nonsense shake. "President of Commerce Bank and Trust. Mack, as his father was before him, is a major stockholder in CB&T. As the bank's president, I can attest to Mack's financial soundness, and offer you my assurance that he's a well-respected leader in our community."

Numb, Addy could only nod.

The next man to step forward was large, both in girth and height, but the warmth and friendliness in his eyes thwarted any fear his size might've spawned.

"So you're Addy," he said, gripping her hand between bear-size paws. "Officially, I'm Dr. William Johnson," he said solemnly, then grinned. "But most folks just call me Dr. Bill." He glanced toward the bassinet, then shifted his gaze back to hers, his expression hopeful. "Mind if I hold the baby? I promise I won't wake him. I've had plenty of experience with little ones."

She lifted a hand, then dropped it helplessly to her side. "Why not?"

She watched as he lifted the baby from the bassinet and brought it to cradle against his chest.

"And aren't you just the cutest thing," he murmured to the baby, then looked up at her and smiled. "I know you must be proud."

She pressed a hand against her lips to stem an unexpected rush of tears. "Y-yes, I am," she managed to get out.

Clucking his tongue, he shifted the baby to one arm and moved to slip the other around her shoulder. "Now, now," he soothed, as he hugged her against his side. "It's okay to cry. Mood swings are to be expected in new mothers."

Addy had to fight the urge to turn her face against his chest and sob. "I know," she said, dabbing at her eyes. "I'm a nurse. I did a rotation in Labor and Delivery during my clinicals, so I know all about the baby blues."

He drew back to look at her in surprise. "You're a nurse? Then I guess I don't need to tell you how important it is for a new mother to take it easy the first couple of weeks, following childbirth. Takes time for a woman to heal properly and regain her strength. Did I mention that I'm a pediatrician?" he asked, then looked down at the baby before she could respond, and smiled broadly. "This little guy and I are going to get along just fine. After you get settled in at Mack's, bring him over to my office and we'll give him a complete checkup."

"But I'm—"

He hugged her again, nearly squeezing the breath out of her with his enthusiasm. "You're gonna just love living in Lampasas. I just know you are."

Addy twisted from his arms and balled her hands into fists at her sides. "Would someone please listen to me," she cried. "I'm *not* marrying Mack. Okay? *I'm not marrying Mack!*"

Marjorie rushed forward and caught her hand. "Oh, Addy," she whispered urgently. "Think what he's offering you. A worry-free life. You wouldn't have to work. You could stay at home with your baby, be the mother you've always wanted to be. And he's willing to adopt your son, give him his name. If you marry Mack, your baby will never be subjected to the embarrassment and humiliation you experienced growing up. He'll have a *name*. A father. People won't be able to whisper behind his back and call him ugly names like they did you."

Addy clamped her hand over her ears, sure that she could hear the jeers of the children who had taunted her on the playground, the whispered comments from adults. She didn't want her son to suffer as she had. Didn't want the same questions posed to him that were asked of her. *Where's your father? Who's your father? How come your mother's name isn't the same as yours?*

"Think, Addy," Marjorie begged her. "It's not as if you have to stay married to him. He's giving you an out, the offer of an annulment. What have you got to lose?"

Addy turned away, clamping her hands tighter over her ears. "Please," she begged. "Go. All of you. I need to think."

She heard the door open behind her and the shuffle of feet as the crowd of people in her room filed out. She felt a nudge on her shoulder, and glanced up to find Dr. Bill standing there.

He passed the baby to her, then braced a hand on her shoulder. "Mack's a good man," he said quietly. "Keep that in mind while you're doing your thinking."

He gave her shoulder a squeeze, then turned and left the room.

Blinking back tears, Addy hugged the baby to her breasts. "Oh, Johnny," she whispered tearfully. "What are we going to do?"

Holding the baby in her arms, Addy opened the door of her hospital room to find the group she'd ousted earlier standing in the hall. The lawyer, the banker, the preacher, Marjorie…and Mack. They were all there, except for Dr. Wharton, who she assumed had to leave because patients waited for him at his office.

Lined up as they were, those who remained presented a formidable wall of resistance.

She tipped up her chin, unwilling to show any sign of weakness. "You may come in," she informed them, then turned and led the way back into her room.

She waited until the door closed behind Mack, then directly addressed the lawyer. "If I agree to this, I want everything in writing, including Mack's promise of an annulment."

"Consider it done," he replied.

"And I want your assurance," she continued, "that my legal interests will be protected, as well as those of my son."

He held up a hand in a solemn pledge. "You have my word."

Satisfied, she shifted her gaze, meeting the eyes of each person in turn.

"You all heard what Mack said earlier, and I expect each and every one of you to serve as witnesses to the document the lawyer prepares. And be forewarned," she added sternly, "that I intend to hold each of you personally responsible for my welfare and that of my son, should Mack fail to honor the promises he's made to me. Understood?"

Each person nodded their agreement.

She drew in a deep breath and turned to face Mack. "I assume you want this marriage to take place as soon as possible."

"Now will do."

"Now?" she repeated. "But...won't we need a license?"

He nodded toward his lawyer, who was already drawing a document from the inside pocket of his jacket. "Lenny has taken care of that for us."

A bubble of panic rose in Addy's throat. She'd thought

she'd have more time to adjust, to plan…to come to her senses. "Blood tests," she said in a rush. "The state requires blood tests, before they'll issue a license."

Marjorie lifted a meek hand. "Um. That's been taken care of."

"How?" Addy asked incredulously. "I didn't give any blood."

"Dr. Wharton told Kenny, the phlebotomist, to use some of what he drew the night you were admitted to Emergency."

With nothing left to offer to delay the inevitable, Addy dropped her shoulders in defeat and turned to Pastor Nolan. "Looks like it your turn, Preacher. I suppose it would be foolish to ask if you have your Bible with you?"

He drew a small leather-bound book from his pocket and held it up for her to see. "I'm never without it."

Though she tried her best to hide it, Addy was totally blown away by Mack's home. The driveway he had turned onto was lined with massive oaks, their limbs twining overhead to create the canopy of shade they drove through. The house at the end of the drive reminded her of pictures she'd seen in magazines of Tuscan homes. Built from a combination of stucco and stone, angled wings jutted from either side of the central structure to form what could only be described as an exploding U. Beyond it, rolling hills covered with cedar, cactus and rock, served as a dramatic backdrop for his home.

Mack parked his car on the circle drive in front, then

climbed out and opened the rear door to remove the baby from the car seat. Her knees quaking, Addy followed Mack up the flagstone walkway to the front door.

Just as Mack reached to open it, the door flew back and two women rushed into the opening, their shoulders bumping, as they both tried to pass through at the same time.

Mack held up a hand. "Slow down, ladies. You'll both get a chance to hold him."

He reached back to catch Addy's hand and drew her to stand beside him. "Addy, I'd like you to meet, Zadie, my cook. She has an apartment at the rear of the house and pretty much rules the roost. Cross her and she'll come after you with a wooden spoon."

Shaking her head, the larger of the two women stepped forward. "Don't believe a word the man says," she warned Addy. "The only person I've ever chased with a wooden spoon was him, and that was because he cut into the pie I'd made for his supper." Smiling, she bobbed her chin in greeting. "Pleased to meet you, Ms. Addy."

"And this is Mary," Mack said, with a nod toward the second woman. "She's here from eight to five, six days a week, chasing the dust balls around the house."

Small in stature but fiery, Mary planted her hands on her hips. "If you can find a dust ball in this house, Mr. Mack, I'll eat it." With a sniff, she turned her gaze to Addy and smiled. "Welcome home, Ms. Addy. If you need anything, anything at all, you just come to me and I'll take care of it for you."

Mary's gaze shifted to the baby and she rubbed her

hands together in excitement, as if anxious to steal him away from Mack.

"Uh-uh," Zadie warned and stepped in front of her blocking her way. "Me first. You've got babies at home to hold. I ain't got any."

Her smile tender, Zadie eased the baby from Mack's arms into her own. "Ain't he just the prettiest thing," she said softly, then looked up at Mack in surprise. "Why, Mr. Mack, he looks just like those baby pictures of you that used to hang in your mama's front room."

"He's got Mack's nose," Mary said, peering down at the baby, then glanced at Addy. "What's his name?"

Shocked that the women thought her son looked like Mack, it took Addy a moment to find her voice. "Jonathan Antonio Roc—uh, I mean McGruder."

"Mighty big name for such a little tyke," Zadie said, chuckling. "What's you gonna call him?"

"Johnny," Addy replied.

"Johnny, huh?" Zadie studied him a moment, then turned for the house. "Well, come on, Johnny Mack. Let's get you inside and out of this heat."

Addy blinked in surprise. Johnny Mack?

Mary darted after Zadie. "You give Johnny Mack to me. You've had him long enough."

Addy turned to peer at Mack in disbelief. "Did you hear them? They called him Johnny Mack."

With a shrug, Mack turned for the car to retrieve her luggage. "Lots of people around here have double names."

She charged after him. "But I clearly told them his

name is Jonathan Antonio. Why would they stick Mack on the end? Why not Tony?"

Bent over the trunk, he dragged a suitcase out and set it on the drive. "I suppose because he looks like me." He straightened to face her. "Which shouldn't surprise you, since Ty and I have the same mother. We may not look like twins, but we both inherited our mother's nose and the shape of her mouth."

Addy gulped. Having had the resemblance pointed out to her, she could see it now.

Mack picked up the suitcase and turned for the house. "If you want, I'll tell Zadie and Mary to drop the Mack and just call him Johnny."

"No," Addy said slowly, deciding not to chance upsetting the women.

And what did it matter, anyway? she asked herself, as she followed Mack to the house. It was just a nickname.

Addy knew exactly what Dorothy must have felt like when she awakened to find herself in Oz. She definitely wasn't in Kansas anymore.

The suite of rooms Mary had left her to explore were larger than most people's homes. Besides the tastefully furnished bedroom, there was a private bath, with a garden-size tub and mile-long, marble-topped vanity. A sitting room connected her bedroom to Mack's and had been converted to a nursery prior to their arrival, complete with a crib, changing table and rocker.

She wondered how Mack had managed to have the room transformed so quickly, then shook her head at the absurdity of the question. As he'd already proven to her, he obviously had the resources and connections to accomplish anything he darn well pleased.

With a sigh of resignation, she slipped into the nursery to make sure the baby was sleeping peacefully, then stepped through the French doors that opened from her bedroom onto a private patio. Surrounded by a stone wall, the area was subtly lit by copper landscape lights and was lush with colorful plants and tall, lacy ferns. In the far corner, a waterfall tumbled over stacked rocks and spilled into a small pond, where koi swam lazily beneath lily pads. Finding the sound of tumbling water as soothing to the ear as the garden setting was to the eye, Addy sank onto a lounge chair and allowed the tension to seep from her body.

It had been an exhausting day, both mentally and physically. First there was the stressful confrontation at the hospital with the friends and business associates Mack had rounded up to plead his case, followed by the brief and impersonal marriage ceremony. Then the trip to her house and the almost-manic grabbing and packing of the few possessions she had chosen to bring with her. Mack had offered to hire a moving service to pack everything up and deliver it to his home in Lampasas, but Addy had refused. She wasn't at all sure that the arrangement she'd made with him was going to work, and she wanted her home intact and waiting for her in the event it didn't.

And then there had been the long drive from Dallas to Lampasas. Most of it had been made in silence, as

Addy was still too shell-shocked from the morning's events to make any attempt at conversation. What faculties she had remaining were stripped from her completely when she got her first glimpse of his home. In spite of his assurance that morning that his home was large and more than adequate to provide her whatever privacy she deemed necessary, it had in no way prepared her for the palatial mansion that had greeted her.

But her shock over his home's size and his obvious wealth was nothing compared to what she'd experienced when Zadie had called her son Johnny Mack. She supposed Mack's explanation made sense, but she still couldn't believe she hadn't noticed the facial features that Mack and Ty shared before Mack had pointed them out to her.

The thought of Ty put the tension right back in her shoulders. Though Mack had told her that she needn't worry about Ty, she couldn't shake free from the thought that he might come back to haunt her in some way.

For God's sake, she thought, her worry returning with a vengeance. The two men were brothers! What would keep Ty from unexpectedly dropping by for a visit? The very thought of seeing him made her shudder in revulsion. She *never* wanted to lay eyes on Ty Bodean again. She might have once thought herself in love with him, but that was before she'd discovered that he was a liar and a thief.

"I hope you've found your accommodations adequate."

She jumped at the sound of Mack's voice, then gulped and rose slowly to face him, twisting her hands at her waist. "This isn't going to work."

He peered at her in concern. "Is there a problem with your room? If so, there are several others to choose from."

She turned away to pace. "There's nothing wrong with the room. It's beautiful."

"Then what's the problem?"

She whirled to face him. "Have you forgotten that the father of my child is your brother?"

"Half brother," he corrected, then opened his hands. "What difference does that make?"

"What if he comes here? He could cause trouble. Even try to take the baby away from me."

He took her by the arm and guided her back to her chair. "Ty can't take the baby. Lenny is already preparing the adoption papers. Once they're filed, Johnny will be legally mine."

"But he could contest the adoption, couldn't he? Demand a blood test to prove that he's the natural father?"

With a sigh he released her arm and sank down onto the chair next to her. "I suppose he could, but why would he? He knew you were pregnant when he left you. Why would he want to claim the child, when your pregnancy was why he ran away in the first place?" He covered her hand with his. "But you're worrying about nothing, Addy. Ty won't come to Lampasas, much less to my house."

"You don't know that."

"Oh, but I do," he told her, and withdrew his hand. "Ty would do almost anything to avoid seeing me."

Frowning, she dragged the back of her hand across her stomach to ease the tingle his touch had left there. "You never talk to each other?"

"Rarely. And when we do, it's by phone, never in person."

He leaned back and stretched his legs out, his expression confident. "But even if he did come here, he'd never get past the front gate. He doesn't know the security code, and no one who works for me would let him in without asking my permission first." He angled his head to meet her gaze. "You're safe here, Addy. Both you and the baby. I'd never allow harm to come to either one of you."

She searched his face, wanting to believe him but afraid to let down her guard. Ty had looked her square in the eye and told her lie, after lie, after lie. Mack could be lying to her, too. Not only about his ability to protect her from Ty, but about his reasons for marrying her, as well. For all she knew, he could be planning to take advantage of her the same as Ty had.

But what could he possibly want from her? she asked herself honestly. Mack had no reason to steal from her, as Ty had. According to his banker, he was a wealthy man. And there was no way he'd want a physical relationship with her. For God's sake, she'd just had a baby! He'd seen her at her absolute worst, had even stood by her side while she'd given birth. If that wasn't a turn-off, she didn't know what was.

She supposed it was possible that he was telling the truth. The men he'd brought to the hospital to vouch for him had described him as a wealthy and generous man, and had sworn that he wasn't crazy, as she had accused him of being. And he seemed to genuinely care about her son.

"All right," she said reluctantly, then held up a finger in warning. "But if Ty should come here, I don't want him anywhere near me or my son. If you allow that to happen, I'll leave. Understood?"

"Fair enough." Flattening his hands against his thighs, he pushed to his feet with a sigh. "I have some paperwork I need to take care of in my office before I turn in. If you want, you can watch TV in the den."

She shook her head. "No. I think I'll go on to bed. It's been a long day."

He dropped a hand on her shoulder as he passed her and gave it a squeeze. "Good night, Addy."

Eyes wide, she murmured, "'Night," then listened to the sound of his footsteps, followed by the soft click of the door as it closed behind him. When she was sure she was alone, she tugged her shirt down over her shoulder and examined her skin, expecting to find a rash there, or at the very least a red mark. When she found neither, frowning, she dragged her shirt back into place, wondering what it was that made her skin tingle every time he touched her.

Four

Addy moaned, trying to block the voice that threatened her sleep.

"Addy," it persisted. "Wake up."

She slowly forced her eyes open and nearly jumped out of her skin when she found a man's shadowed face inches from her own. Recognizing it as Mack's, she went limp with relief. "You nearly scared the life out of me."

"Sorry, but the baby's hungry."

Instantly awake, she dragged herself up to a sitting position and held out her arms. "God, I'm sorry," she said guiltily. "I never heard him make so much as a peep."

He shifted the baby into her arms. "He didn't wake me. I heard him stirring when I got up to get a drink of water. Figured I'd rock him for a while, so you could sleep a little longer."

Grateful for the darkness, she quickly adjusted her nightgown so that the baby could nurse. "I appreciate the thought, but you didn't have to do that. I'm getting plenty of rest."

"I didn't mind."

Instead of leaving as she'd thought he would, he sank down on the edge of the bed and tucked the blanket around a bare foot the baby had managed to kick free. "In fact, I enjoyed rocking him," he added. "Brought back a few memories."

She heard the wistfulness in his voice and wondered about it. "Do you have children?"

"A son. He died when he was six."

"Oh, Mack," she said, her heart breaking for him at his loss. "I'm so sorry."

He lifted a shoulder. "It happened over twelve years ago. Time has a way of lessening the pain."

"Still…" She glanced down at her son, unable to imagine what it would do to her to lose him. As she considered that, it occurred to her that if Mack had a son, he probably had a wife, too.

"You're divorced?" she asked hesitantly.

"Widowed. My wife and son died together. A car wreck," he explained, saving her from asking.

She stared at his shadowed face, unable to fathom the magnitude of that kind of loss. "That must have been very hard for you."

"You have no idea."

Because she didn't, she turned her gaze to her son and said nothing.

They sat in silence while the baby nursed, the soft suckling noises the infant made the only sound in the room.

"Better change sides," Mack warned. "You don't want him to fill his tummy before he nurses your other breast."

"Right," she murmured, and placed a finger between her breast and the infant's mouth to separate him from her nipple. She started to shift him to her shoulder to burp, but on impulse, offered him to Mack. "Do you want to burp him?"

He sat up. "Yeah, I would."

With an ease that might've surprised her if she hadn't just learned that he'd once had a son, he placed the baby over his shoulder and began lightly patting his back. It wasn't until that moment that she realized Mack was wearing only a pair of jeans. Though she tried not to stare, she couldn't help but notice the dark hair that swirled around his nipples before plunging in a shadowed line down his abdomen to disappear behind the waist of his jeans, the bulge of muscles in his arms, as he held the baby.

The baby's loud burp made her start.

Chuckling, Mack said, "Good one," and passed the infant to Addy.

Amused, she guided the baby to her opposite breast. Though the darkness offered its own form of cover, she found it odd that she didn't feel more self-conscious about nursing in front of Mack. She supposed his presence during the birth had stripped her of whatever shyness she would ordinarily have experienced.

She lifted her head and looked at him curiously. "Do you consider this weird?"

His forehead pleated in confusion. "What?"

"This," she said, and lifted her arms slightly to indicate the baby. "Me nursing in front of you."

He pressed a palm against the mattress, as if about to rise. "If you want me to go—"

She laid a hand on his arm. "No. I was just thinking how odd it is to be doing this in front of a complete stranger."

"I'm hardly a stranger," he said wryly, as he settled back on the side of the bed. "I'm your husband."

Hearing him refer to himself as such was a little unsettling. "That may be true," she conceded, "but we've only known each other...what? Two days?"

He glanced at his wrist watch. "Two and a half," he corrected.

She sputtered a laugh. "Right. And that half day makes all the difference in the world."

"I've known people longer than I have you and know less about them."

She raised a brow, intrigued. "Oh? And what do you know about me?"

"You're stubborn as a mule."

"Well, that's certainly flattering," she said dryly.

Biting back a smile, he stretched out across the bed at her feet and braced himself up on an elbow. "I wasn't finished."

"I'm not sure my ego can stand hearing any more."

"You're brave, independent, resourceful."

She nodded smugly. "Now you're talking."

"And you're really good at hiding your feelings."

She looked at him in dismay. "Are you kidding? How can you say that, after all the fuss I kicked up about marrying you."

"I'm talking about the emotions you don't let anyone see."

"Oh? And exactly what emotions have I been hiding?"

"The ones concerning your mother. Her inattentiveness hurts you."

Embarrassed that he knew that about her, she averted her gaze but remained silent.

"She doesn't deserve you. You're a much better daughter to her than she is a mother to you."

The compliment, though sounding sincere, irritated her. "You don't know that. You've never even met her."

"I've talked to her. That was enough."

She rolled her eyes. "I disagree, but go on. Tell me what else you *think* you know about me."

"You're disappointed in yourself for letting a man like Ty get you pregnant."

Her embarrassment morphed to anger in the blink of an eye. "You make it sound as if I *tried* to get pregnant. I insisted he use condoms. Obviously one of them was flawed."

He patted the air, as if to calm her. "I worded that poorly. Let me try again. You're disappointed in yourself for becoming intimate with Ty. To be honest, I'm a bit surprised myself. You don't seem at all his type."

Though he was right about her regrets concerning Ty, she wasn't about to admit to her gullibility. "So what type am I?"

"The type who wants the whole package. Love, marriage, family. The whole ball of wax."

She stared, wondering if she was truly that transparent or if Marjorie had done more blabbing than Addy was aware. "And how did you arrive at that conclusion?"

"First, your house. The flowers along the walkway. The baskets of ferns on the porch. The bird feeder hanging from the tree out front."

"And from *that* you deduced that I'm Suzy Homemaker?" She tipped her head back and laughed. "You are *so* wrong."

"Am I?" he challenged. "Then why did you have the baby?"

She sputtered a laugh. "There was a choice?"

"Other single women in your situation have chosen to have abortions, rather than be saddled with a baby."

"So I'm pro-life. Shoot me."

"More like pro-family," he argued. "You may not have intended to get pregnant, but you weren't about to destroy your chance of having a family, even if it was missing one important element. The father."

Irritated that he was so close to the truth, she lifted the baby to her shoulder. "Okay, Freud. That's enough psychoanalysis for one night. I want to go to sleep."

He stood and held out his arms. "I'll put him to bed."

She resisted a moment, tempted to tell him that she was more than capable of putting her own child to bed, then decided why argue, when he had to pass through the nursery on the way to his room, anyway.

After handing over Johnny, she slid down and pulled the covers to her chin. "Don't forget to cover him up," she called to him.

"I know the drill."

In spite of her irritation with him, a smile tugged at the corners of her mouth. She could get used to this, she thought, as she nestled her cheek against the pillow.

It was kind of nice having someone wait on her for a change…even if the someone who was doing the waiting was a bossy know-it-all.

From the rocking chair, Addy watched Mary bustle from the bedroom to the nursery and back, putting away the baby's things. After over a week in Mack's house, she still couldn't get used to people waiting on her.

"Mary, really," she scolded gently. "You don't need to put those things away. It's enough that you're doing our laundry. Just leave the basket on the bed, and I'll put everything away later."

"It's no trouble," Mary insisted. Dipping into the basket again, she pulled out a sleeper from the pile of clothes she'd laundered and held it up to admire. "Oh, and isn't this just the sweetest thing," she said, and couldn't resist pressing the sleeper against her cheek. "Reminds of me when my kids were babies."

"How many children do you have?"

"Four."

"Four?" Addy repeated, then glanced down at the

baby placidly nursing at her breast and wondered how on earth a mother took care of that many children, when one seemed to her a full-time job. "How do you do it?"

Chuckling, Mary plucked out a blanket to fold. "Didn't you know? Mothers come equipped with an extra pair of hands."

Addy glanced down at her own and frowned. "I was cheated."

"How?"

Addy looked up to find Mack standing in the door-way…and had to blink twice to make sure it was him. Dressed in scuffed boots, faded jeans and with his hair mussed from the wind, he looked younger and much less imposing than the stone-faced man who, less than a week before, had promised to love and cherish her until death did them part.

She averted her gaze, still finding it hard to think of him as her husband.

"Mary says that mothers are given an extra set of hands," she explained. "I told her I was cheated, because I only have one."

He gestured toward the baby. "Little thing like that? One set is all you need." He started toward her. "Give him to me. You women have had him all morning. It's my turn."

Daddy's home! That wasn't at all what he'd said, but those were the words that shot into Addy's mind as he strode toward her, wiping his hands across the seat of his pants and wearing a grin that stretched from ear to ear.

Rising, she passed him the baby, then stepped aside, letting him have the rocker.

As Mack sat down, Johnny began to fuss, and Mack looked up at Addy in alarm. "Did I do something wrong?"

"Probably needs burping." She pulled the burp pad from her shoulder and draped it over Mack's. "He just finished nursing."

He shifted the baby up high on his chest and began to rub his back. "Come on little guy," he murmured, pressing a kiss to the top of the baby's head. "Give ol' Mack a big burp."

Johnny Mack complied almost instantly.

Laughing, Mary picked up the empty laundry basket. "Looks like you haven't lost your touch," she called to Mack, as she left the room.

Addy saw the shadow that passed over Mack's eyes and knew Mary's comment must have reminded him of his son. Hoping to distract him from what must be a sad memory, Addy sat down on the side of the bed opposite the rocker.

"Mary is determined to spoil me. She did Johnny's laundry this morning, then insisted on putting it all away."

Mack shifted the baby to cradle in his arms, but kept his gaze averted. "She's crazy about kids. Always has been."

Addy racked her mind for something else to say. "Has she worked for you a long time?"

"Fourteen years. Worked for my mother before that. I hired her on after Mom passed away."

"Did Zadie work for your mother, too?"

"Yes, but she went to work for a restaurant in town after my mother passed away. After my wife died, I realized I needed a cook, so I stole her away from the restaurant. She's been with me now about six years I guess."

Reminded of the delicious meals Zadie had prepared, she pressed a hand against her stomach. "I can understand why you'd want to steal her, but how on earth do you keep from getting fat? Much more of her cooking, and I'll have to revert to wearing maternity clothes again."

"Zadie says you eat like a bird."

Her jaw dropped. "You've seen how much I eat! We share every meal. I clean my plate."

"But refuse seconds."

She thought of the second helping of coconut cake Zadie had waved beneath her nose the night before, with its thick, creamy filling and the sprinkles of toasted coconut on the icing, and moaned pitifully. "The woman should be shot. How am I supposed to lose weight, when she keeps shoving those fabulous desserts in my face?"

"I'll tell her to cut out the sweets."

Fearing that she had just cut off her nose to spite her face, Addy said, "Uh, maybe you shouldn't say anything. I wouldn't want to take a chance on hurting Zadie's feelings."

He shot her a sideways glance. "Is it Zadie's feelings you're worried about or satisfying your sweet tooth?"

Pursing her lips, she snatched the burp pad from his shoulder and slapped his arm with it. "Jerk."

He ducked, chuckling. "That's what I thought."

He looked down at the baby and his smile slowly

faded. He caught a dribble of milky drool with his thumb and wiped it on the leg of his jeans. "Thanks," he said quietly.

She frowned at him in confusion. "For what?"

"For pulling me back." He angled his head to look at her. "Remembering hurts."

Addy sucked in a breath, stunned by the pain she saw in his blue eyes, the years of sorrow she saw stacked behind it. More than anything, she wanted to cup a hand at his cheek and soothe away the sadness, take away the hurt.

Before she could give in to the urge, she stood abruptly and held out her arms. "I better take him so you can get back to work. I'm sure you've got things to do."

He turned his shoulder to block her. "Nothing that can't wait. Go on and relax while you can." He glanced down at the baby and smiled. "Johnny Mack and I need us some man time."

Addy lay on a chaise lounge on her private patio, her eyes closed, the sun warm on her skin. A ring of condensation pooled around the tall glass of lemonade that stood within easy reach of her hand, while the magazine she'd been reading lay open over her stomach, marking her page. She felt relaxed, lazy even, and sinfully content.

To say she had landed in heaven wouldn't be much of an exaggeration, she thought with a sigh. Mack's home was lavish, the food five-star-restaurant quality, her every need met before she could voice it. And she never had to lift so much as a finger. Zadie cooked all the meals, while Mary took care of the cleaning and laundry. All Addy was allowed to do was care for the baby, and even that small task was lightened by the three other adults in the house, who were constantly looking for an excuse to steal Johnny away from her. New mothers need their rest, Mary would claim and disappear with the baby. Babies need constant stimulation, Zadie would say and whisk the baby off to the kitchen where a playpen had been set up by a wide set of French doors.

Then there was Mack. And of the three, he was the absolute worst. If Addy didn't know better, she'd swear he slept on the floor beside the crib at night. Before the baby could open his mouth to cry, Mack was in the nursery changing his diaper. He would rock him a while to make sure he was hungry and not just lonely, before delivering him to Addy. And he seldom left after bringing her the baby. He would usually stretch out across the bed at her feet and keep her company while the baby nursed.

She knew it was foolish, but she'd begun to look forward to that time with Mack. She found him easy to talk to and their conversations as intellectually stimulating as they were entertaining. Equally enjoyable were the times when they didn't speak at all. The peacefulness of the hour and the shadowed darkness of her room added an intimacy to their time together, giving it an almost dreamlike quality.

During the short time she'd been in his home, they had developed a friendship of sorts, one that she had grown to cherish. They talked, laughed, watched television together. He'd even invited her to take a few walks with him—to the barn to check on a mare or to the front gate to collect the daily mail. She knew the short jaunts were his way of getting her out of the house for a while and away from the baby, something she was reluctant to do. To Addy, it was yet another indication of his thoughtfulness, his consideration.

"Look what I found?"

Addy jolted at the sound of Mack's voice, then turned to find him standing in the doorway, holding the baby.

She gave him a stern look. "Mack McGruder, if you woke that baby up, I'm going to be really mad."

"Didn't have to. He was already awake." Using the toe of his boot, he dragged a chair next to hers and dropped down, stretching out his legs, while he shifted the baby to cradle in the crook of one arm.

Addy watched, impressed at the ease with which he handled the infant.

"I'll bet you were a good father."

The thought was out of her mouth before she realized she'd spoken it out loud.

She laid a hand on his arm, regretting the thoughtless comment. "I'm sorry. It's just that you look so natural holding Johnny, so at ease."

He shook his head. "Being reminded I was a father doesn't bother me." He angled his head to look at her. "But I don't know that I was a good one. Sometimes it takes losing something before you realize how precious it is."

She nodded solemnly, thinking of all the regrets he might have, the if-I-could-only-do-it-overs he probably lived with every day. "What was your father like?" she asked impulsively.

He raised a brow, as if wondering where the question had come from, then shrugged. "Fun." Chuckling, he shook his head. "My mother swore that I could ride a horse before I could walk, and I imagine there was more truth in that statement than exaggeration. My father took me with him everywhere he went. Checking cattle, riding fence line, hunting, fishing." He shrugged again. "Whether it was work or play, he dragged me along."

Addy smiled, envying the relationship he'd described. "You were lucky."

"Yeah, I was," he agreed, then glanced her way. "What about your father? What was he like?"

"I never knew my dad. He was killed in Vietnam."

"That's tough," he said sympathetically.

She shrugged. "You can't miss what you never had."

"What about your stepfather? Were you close to him?"

"Which one?" she asked wryly.

He looked at her askance. "You have more than one?"

"Four to be exact."

His eyes rounded in amazement. "Four?"

"Yes, four. And, no, I wasn't close to any of them." She wrinkled her nose. "To be honest, the first three weren't around long enough for me to develop any kind of a relationship with them, and by the time the fourth came along, I really wasn't interested in trying."

"Four," he said again, as if having a hard time getting past that number.

She hesitated a moment, then figured he might as

well know her whole sordid past. "That's how many times my mother's been married. Four."

He frowned thoughtfully, as if mentally completing the steps to solve a complicated math problem, then gaped. "Your mother and father never—"

"No. They never married. When she told him she was pregnant, he ran off and joined the army, rather than make an honest woman of her. She's never forgiven him that slight."

He blew a silent whistle. "Well, that certainly explains some of the things she said on the phone."

"I can just imagine what all she had to say about my father. She never forgave Tony Rocci for what he did to her. And after he died, she shifted the blame to me."

"Well, that's just plain wrong," he said indignantly. "You can't be faulted for something you had no control over."

"Yeah? Well, try telling my mother that."

He stifled a shudder. "I think I'll pass." Frowning, he shifted the baby to his other arm. "Do you have any contact with your father's family?"

"No. My mother refused to have anything to do with the Roccis. I guess she blamed them for him abandoning her, as much as she did their son."

"But she gave you his name," he said in confusion.

"That wasn't a courtesy, I assure you. It was revenge. She wanted the world to know what a rotten SOB he was, that he'd gotten her pregnant, then skipped out on her."

He gave her a pointed look.

She drew back with a frown. "What?"

"Does this story sound at all familiar?"

She pursed her lips and looked away. "Parts of it maybe. But I'm nothing like my mother. I may detest your brother—"

"*Half* brother," he reminded her.

She flapped a hand. "Whatever. The only similarity between my mother's situation and mine is that we both got pregnant out of wedlock. I didn't give my baby his father's name, I gave him mine. Or would have," she added, and sent him a glance, "if you hadn't adopted him. And I will never blame Johnny for what happened. Getting pregnant was my fault and I accept full responsibility."

She dropped her gaze to the baby, and her face softened. "But I'll never regret having him," she said, and reached to take the infant from Mack. Cupping a hand at the back of the baby's head, she nuzzled his cheek with her nose. "How could I regret something as sweet as this?"

Settling back, she patted the baby absently, her thoughts growing reflective. "The weirdest thing happened the day I went into labor."

"A strange man showed up at your house?"

She shot him a look. "Besides that." Turning her gaze to the distance again, she frowned, remembering. "This lady called. She said that our fathers served together in Vietnam. Her call caught me totally off guard, because I seldom think about my father."

"I'd imagine it was a jolt to hear his name."

"Yeah. But what was weird was that she called to ask me about a piece of paper she found while going through her father's belongings. She wanted to know if my father had sent something similar to my mother."

"Did he?"

She lifted a shoulder. "Beats me. If he did and Mom kept it, it's probably in her trunk. When she moved to Hawaii, she left it in my garage. It's filled with all kinds of junk. Things she saved from her high school years, previous marriages, that kind of thing. Things she didn't want her husband to know she'd kept."

"If you know that's where you'd find it, why didn't you look?"

"I never had a chance. I went into labor." She slid her back down the chair, continuing to pat the baby's back, while letting her mind run with the possibilities. "Wouldn't it be something if it was valuable?" she said, thinking out loud. "I could get rid of my old sled and buy a new one."

"Sled?"

"My car. All that's holding it together are baling wire and duct tape."

He dropped his head back and laughed.

She gave him a quelling look, and he quickly sobered.

"Sorry," he murmured. "It was the duct tape and wire. I thought only country folk used that kind of stuff for repairs."

She jutted her chin. "Necessity and creativity know no boundaries."

He tipped his head, conceding the point. "No, I don't suppose they do."

She waved a hand. "Doesn't matter. It's foolish to put any hope in something that doesn't exist."

"You don't know that it doesn't," he reminded her. "It could be in the trunk."

"I doubt it. Even if he did send it to her, she wouldn't have kept it. She hated him. She wouldn't have wanted anything around that would remind her of him."

"He's smiling."

She blinked in confusion. "What?"

"The baby. He's smiling."

She lowered her son to her lap to see for herself. "He is!" she said in excitement, then laughed and lifted him to press a kiss on his cheek. "Johnny Mack, you are the sweetest baby ever," she cooed. "Your mommy loves you so much."

"Guess that makes it official," Mack said.

She looked at him in puzzlement. "What?"

He gestured at the baby. "You called him Johnny Mack. Makes it official."

Five

A woman could stand being waited on hand and foot just so long. After a month in Mack's house, Addy had reached her limit.

The kitchen was Zadie's domain, and she guarded it like a chicken would her eggs, refusing to allow Addy to so much as boil water. Mary, though much kinder when declining Addy's offers of help, was just as territorial about her household duties.

At first, Addy had enjoyed being spoiled, had considered the women's concern for her thoughtful, even sweet. Now it grated on her nerves, and she was determined to put an end to it before she went stark raving mad.

Thinking it best to discuss the situation with Mack before saying anything to the women, Addy went in search of him. Not finding him in his bedroom or office, she headed to the kitchen, where she found Zadie busily kneading dough. Steam rose from a large pot simmering on the stove, and the scent that emanated from it momentarily distracted her from her mission.

"What's cooking?" she asked, as she crossed to peer into the pot.

"Stew. Mr. Mack requested it special." Chuckling, Zadie rounded the island. "That man does like my stew."

Addy dipped her head over the pot and inhaled deeply. "I can see why. It smells delicious." She reached for the wooden spoon, intending to give it a quick stir.

Before she could, Zadie snatched the spoon from her hand.

"I does the cookin' 'round here," Zadie said, wagging the spoon in her face, like a stern finger, "not you."

Something in Addy snapped, and she snatched the spoon right back. "I'm the woman of this house and I can stir the damn stew anytime I want."

Zadie fell back a step, her eyes round as saucers, then flattened her lips. "Well, fine then," she said and returned to her dough. "Stir. But mind you do it gentle like," she warned. "Mr. Mack likes his taters in chunks, not shredded to bits."

Addy released a long, shaky breath, as surprised by her fit of temper as Zadie obviously was.

Dipping the spoon into the pot, she began to stir, careful to keep her strokes slow and easy.

Remembering her purpose in coming to the kitchen, she asked, "Where is Mack?"

"Don't know. Left 'bout an hour go. Got a call and took off like the devil hisself was chasing him."

Addy looked up in alarm. "Was something wrong?"

Zadie pushed a fist into the ball of dough, flattening it. "Didn't say. Just hung up the phone and lit out of here like his tail was on fire."

Addy's stomach knotted in dread. "Do you know who called?" she asked, trying to hide the fear in her voice.

Zadie pursed her lips and kept right on kneading. "Who Mr. Mack talks to is *his* business, ain't no business of mine."

Addy dropped the spoon, sure that she knew who the caller was. "It was Ty, wasn't it?"

"Ty Bodean?" With a humph, Zadie slapped the rolling pin down on the dough. "Mr. Mack wouldn't give that no-good boy the time of day. He done wore his welcome out here a long time ago. Always comin' 'round demandin' money." She humphed again. "Just like his daddy, that's what I says. But Mr. Mack made that promise to his mama, so he kept givin' it to 'im, knowin' as well I did that the boy would have it spent 'for he was out the door good." She shook her head sadly. "Went on for years till Mr. Mack finally got a stomachful of his foolishness and told him he wudn't gonna give him no more. Made Ty madder than a hornet, it did. Stormed outta here cussin' and yellin' and tellin' Mr. Mack how he'd get even with him."

"When?"

Zadie looked up, her brow pleated in confusion. "You mean about Ty leavin'?"

Addy nodded, not trusting her voice.

Zadie puckered her lips thoughtfully, then shrugged and went back to rolling out the dough. "Goin' on two years, I'd guess. Hadn't heard so much as his name mentioned 'round here, till the postmaster called and told Mr. Mack about those letters you sent. Stormed around for days, 'for he decided he'd best do something 'for Ty found hisself stuck with another paternity suit."

Her hands froze on the rolling pin and she glanced up, her expression stricken. "I didn't mean no disrespect, Miss Addy. Just 'cause Ty can't keep his zipper up, that ain't no reflection on you."

Even though she feared it was, Addy shook her head. "None taken."

Seemingly relieved, Zadie went back to rolling out the dough. "Marryin' you and bringin' you and the baby home with him wasn't what Mr. Mack had in mind that day he left for Dallas, and that's a fact. He was plannin' to pay you off, the same as he did the others." Chuckling, she set aside the rolling pin and wiped her palms down the front of her apron. "But I guess the Good Lord had somethin' else in mind for him this time around."

"What was that?"

Zadie looked up at her in surprise. "Why, Mr. Mack marryin' you and bringin' you and the baby back home with him, that's what." She picked up the biscuit cutter and sank it into the dough, frowning thoughtfully as she gave it a turn. "Now, I know it ain't none of my business," she began hesitantly. "But I think it's high time you was sharing Mr. Mack's bed. I know you had a hard time with the birth, and all. Mr. Mack tol' me about that. But that baby's a month old or more and you need to be doin' your duty to Mr. Mack and not sleepin' in that room by yourself."

Addy stared, stunned by Zadie's suggestion, then turned and all but ran for the door, her cheeks flaming in embarrassment.

"Where you goin' in such a rush?" Zadie called after her. "I thought you was gonna stir that stew?"

Anxious to show Addy the surprise he'd bought for her, Mack tossed his hat onto the kitchen counter. "Hey, Zadie. Where's Addy?"

Scowling, Zadie slammed the oven door. "How would I know?" she snapped, tossing up her hands. "Nobody tells me nothin', jist zip in and outta my kitchen like they was bees chasin' honey."

Mack lifted a brow, surprised by her sour mood. "If you're upset with me because I didn't tell you where I was going, I'm sorry. I was in hurry. Had some business in town I needed to take care of."

She spun to face him and planted her hands on her hips. "Did I ask you where you was?" Before he could answer, she marched to the refrigerator, her nose in the air, and yanked open the door. "Everybody askin' where everybody else is," she muttered under her breath, as she dug around inside. "A person would think I's a secretary instead of the cook."

When she turned from the refrigerator and nearly bumped into Mack, she scowled again. "I thought you was in an all-fired hurry to find Miss Addy." She pushed out a hand, shooing him away. "Well, get on with you. I've got dinner to cook."

Deciding it was safer to leave than question her further, he went in search of Addy. He found her in her bedroom, standing before the French doors, staring out.

"Addy?"

She jumped but didn't turn around. "Yes?" she said uneasily.

He noticed that she was wringing her hands and wondered if it had anything to do with Zadie's sour mood.

"Did you and Zadie have an argument or something?" he asked.

She tensed. "Did she say that we did?"

He bit down on his frustration, wondering if the women in the house had conspired during his absence to drive him crazy. "No. But she nearly bit my head off when I asked her where you were."

"What else did she tell you?"

Puzzled, he shook his head. "Nothing. Just chased me out of her kitchen."

She turned then, and he saw the tears that brimmed in her eyes.

"What's wrong?" he asked in concern.

"It's my fault she's in a bad mood. I yelled at her. Zadie," she clarified, then sniffed and dragged a hand beneath her nose. "I just wanted to stir the stew, and she snatched the spoon away from me, and I...I—" She lifted her hands, then let them drop helplessly to her sides, tears welling in her eyes again. "Something inside me just snapped. I'm so bored," she said miserably. "Nobody will let me do anything. Zadie. Mary. They treat me like I'm an invalid or an idiot, and I don't know which is worse."

"They just don't want you to overdo."

"Overdo?" she repeated, her tears instantly drying. "Much more of this sedentary lifestyle and I'll atrophy! I'm used to being busy. At home and at work. Eight-hour shifts of nonstop action in an Emergency Room in no way prepares a person for this kind of inactivity. Much more and I'm going to go crazy."

"Do you want me to talk to them?"

"Yes. No." Groaning, she dropped her face to her hands. "I don't know. I just want to do something, *any*thing, and they won't let me."

Though it was a struggle, Mack managed not to laugh. "I'll talk to them. Tell them to let you help when you want."

She dropped her hands, her face stricken. "Promise you won't tell them that I said anything. I mean... well—" She began to wring her hands again. "They've been so nice to me. I don't want them to think I'm ungrateful."

He drew a cross over his heart. "You have my word. They'll never know this discussion took place."

She sagged her shoulders. "Thank you."

Hiding a smile, he draped an arm around her and headed her for the door. "Come outside with me. I want to show you something."

She hung back, her gaze on the nursery door behind them. "But what if Johnny Mack wakes up?"

He urged her on. "There are monitors all over the house. Mary or Zadie will tend to him if he does."

When they reached the front porch, he stopped. "Well?" he asked, indicating the vehicle parked on the drive. "What do you think?"

She stared, her jaw going slack, then whipped her gaze to his. "You bought a new car? But you already have a Mercedes and a truck. What do you need with another vehicle?"

Before he could explain that the car was for her, she took off at a run. When he caught up with her, she was behind the wheel, her head tipped back against the leather headrest, her eyes closed.

She inhaled deeply, her expression rapturous. "Smell that? New car. Nothing in the world compares."

Chuckling, he circled the hood and climbed into the passenger seat.

Flipping open her eyes, she leaned forward to examine the controls. "Oh, my gosh. Satellite Radio! That is beyond awesome."

"So you like the car?"

"Like it?" She sank back against the seat with a dramatic sigh. "This is the original lustmobile."

He dug the keys from his pocket and offered them to her. "Give it a try."

She tucked her hands beneath her thighs. "Uh-uh. No way. What if I wrecked it?"

"Don't worry. It's insured." He nudged the key against her arm. "Go on. Try it out."

Worrying her lip, she eyed the key like a druggie

would his next fix, then snatched it from his hand. "Okay. But if I wreck it, it's your fault."

She started the engine, then fell back against the seat, her body limp. "Oh, my God," she said weakly. "I don't think I can stand it."

"Stand what?"

"It started on the first try."

Laughing, Mack pulled the seat belt across his chest and clicked it into place. "I take it the sled doesn't."

She rolled her head to the side and gave him a bland look. "I'm lucky if it starts at all."

"Well, you won't have to worry about that anymore," he assured her.

She snorted a laugh. "Yeah, right. The sled has to last a couple more years, at the least."

Mack laid a hand on her arm. "This is yours, Addy."

She stared, her face going slack. "Mine?"

He laughed. "Yes, yours."

She switched off the ignition and shook her head. "I can't accept something like this."

"Why not? You need something to drive."

"Well, yeah. But I've got my sled."

"Which is in Dallas," he reminded her.

She opened her arms, indicating the car. "But I can't afford something like this."

"Yes, you can. I told you. I'm a wealthy man."

She shook her head again. "You may be, but I'm not."

"You're my wife," he reminded her. "What's mine is yours."

She stared, eyes wide, then gulped. "You mean you're just...giving this to me?"

"Seems like." Smiling, he reached to turn the key. "Now how about taking us for a ride?"

Later that night Addy lay in bed listening to the sounds coming from the nursery. The wooden creak of the rocking chair; the low, husky rumble of Mack's voice as he talked to Johnny Mack. Any minute now she knew he would be bringing the baby to her to feed. She could've easily climbed from her bed and saved him the trip, but she hated to deny him this special time with Johnny Mack when he seemed to enjoy it so much.

So she lay there listening, while Mack carried on a one-sided conversation with her son, and let her thoughts drift back over the day.

She still couldn't believe Mack had bought her a car. And not just any car, she thought with a shiver of excitement. A Lexus SUV. How had he known that was the vehicle she'd always wanted, the one she'd lusted over, dreamed of owning? To her, it was the perfect mommy car. Luxurious enough to satisfy even the most discriminating woman's need for extravagance, yet roomy and durable enough to use for driving carpools and hauling groceries. It was the perfect car for a family.

Family?

She stared wide-eyed, considering. But that's exactly what she had begun to think of them as, she realized. A family. She knew it was wrong for her to think of them as such. It wasn't at all the arrangement she had made with Mack. He had offered her a marriage of convenience, without any sexual or emotional obligations, a name for her baby. So why would she allow herself think of them as a family, when it was clear that wasn't what Mack had wanted or what she had agreed to?

Growing pensive, she glanced toward the nursery. She couldn't see Mack and the baby, but she could hear the creak of the rocker, Mack's low crooning, and knew they were there in the darkness. Did he think of them as a family? she wondered. He was definitely crazy about Johnny Mack, spent as much time with the baby as he possibly could. And he seemed to genuinely like Addy. He was kind to her, generous, thoughtful. But he seldom touched her. Not like a husband would his wife. He treated her more like a...a sister or perhaps a close friend.

You need to be doin' your duty to Mr. Mack and not sleepin' in that room by yourself.

Heat crawled up her neck as she remembered Zadie's comment. What on earth would possess Zadie to say such a thing? Surely she knew that Mack and Addy's marriage wasn't a real one, not in the traditional sense. Heavens, how could she *not* know? Mack and Addy had been strangers prior to him coming to Dallas. And they'd married less than forty-eight hours after they'd met! Strangers didn't marry for love—those kinds of feelings developed over time—and Addy wouldn't sleep with a man she didn't love...or at least think she was in love with.

And duty? She rolled her eyes. She would *never* sleep with a man out of any sense of duty. There had to be something stronger before she'd ever consider giving herself to a man. She had to *feel* something for him, an emotion, a connection of some kind. Definitely something more than a sense of duty.

The rocker creaked to a stop, and she mentally slammed the door on her thoughts, knowing that Mack would be bringing her the baby. Hearing the pad of his feet on the carpet, she quickly scooted up to a sitting position and held out her arms. "Is he hungry?" she asked, forcing a smile.

He leaned to give her the baby. "Starving."

Chuckling, she looked down at her son and arranged her nightgown for him to nurse. "He's turning into a little pig."

Yawning, Mack stretched out across the foot of her bed. "He's definitely putting on some weight."

She folded back the blanket to trail a finger down a dimpled thigh. "Three, maybe four pounds would be my guess."

"Bill can tell us for sure when we take him to his appointment tomorrow."

She glanced up in surprise. "You made Johnny Mack a doctor's appointment?"

"Yeah. I saw Bill in town this afternoon, or rather yesterday afternoon," he corrected, with a glance at his wristwatch. "He said we could bring him in around noon, if that's all right with you."

She looked down at the baby and swallowed hard, knowing he would be receiving his first series of shots and dreading it for him. "He won't hurt him, will he?"

He choked a laugh. "Bill's been taking care of babies for years. He knows what he's doing."

She tucked the blanket protectively around Johnny Mack's legs. "I know. It's just that—"

"He's your baby," he finished for her.

She gave him a sheepish look. "You probably think I'm one of those crazy, overprotective mothers."

"No, I think you're a mother who loves her son very much. There's nothing wrong with that."

She started to reply, but a cramp knotted in her foot. "Ow," she cried and drew up her knee.

Mack pushed up higher on his elbow. "What's wrong?"

With the baby in her arms, it was impossible for her to reach her foot, so she kicked her leg free from the covers and flexed her toes hard. "I've got a cramp."

"Here. Let me."

He gripped her foot between his hands, pressed his thumb deeply into the arch and began massaging. After a few minutes the cramp began to ease.

"Better?" he asked.

"Yes," she said in relief. "Thank you."

He sank back down to his elbow again, but kept a hand curved around her foot, his fingers stroking up and down its length.

He didn't seem conscious of the action, but Addy was. Heat radiated up her leg, gathered in her stomach.

She knew she should break the contact, but she couldn't. The silky glide of his fingers was mesmerizing, sensual, erotic. The heat that had gathered in her stomach churned hot and molten, climbing higher and higher until it parched her mouth, burned behind her eyes. She was aroused, she realized slowly, and was stunned that Mack could bring her to such a level with something as simple as a foot massage.

She stole a glance at him and was relieved that the shadowed darkness kept him from seeing her face clearly and possibly knowing her thoughts. She knew it was crazy, insane, but the desire to make love with him was there in her mind, a yearning that throbbed deep in her womb.

"We could grab a bite to eat after we see Bill," Mack said, continuing the conversation. "Give you an opportunity to see a little bit more of Lampasas."

She stared, wondering how he could talk about something as mundane as lunch, when all she could think about was undressing him. Did he not *feel* what she was feeling, *want* what she wanted? How could he *not,* when it was all she could do to breathe?

Because he wasn't attracted to her.

The answer was so obvious and so brutally humbling, it was like having cold water thrown in the face.

And why would he be attracted to her? she asked herself miserably. She'd just given birth. She still had a good ten pounds to lose, her breasts were as big as melons and her scent—if she had one—was Eau de Baby. What man in his right mind would find her in the least bit alluring?

Disheartened, she eased her foot from his grip and lifted the baby to her shoulder to burp.

"I don't know," she said evasively. "Maybe we should wait and see how Johnny Mack feels after he gets his shots."

* * *

Bill appeared in the doorway to the reception area and waved them back. Since Mack had the baby, Addy was left to gather up the diaper bag and her purse and follow.

By the time she reached the exam room, Bill had the baby and was cooing to him. He glanced up as she entered. "Hey, Addy. How are you feeling?"

His warm smile put her immediately at ease. "Fine, thank you."

"Have you had your checkup yet?"

She shook her head. "No. I thought I'd go to Dallas and see my own doctor."

"Why wait?" Bill plucked the phone from its cradle on the wall.

"Oh, no, really," she said, panicking at the thought of being examined by a stranger. "That's not ne—"

Bill held up a finger. "Hey, Sally," he said into the receiver. "Mack and Addy are here with the baby. Do you think Kathy could squeeze Addy in for a postpartum exam?" He listened a moment, then nodded. "Good. I'll send her right over."

He hung up the phone and turned to Addy. "Kathy— she's my wife, by the way, and a darn good OB-GYN— can see you right now, if you hurry." With the baby cradled in the crook of one arm, he opened the door and pointed to a second set of doors at the end of the hall. "Right through there," he said. "Just tell Sally—the lady behind the reception desk—that you're Addy, and she'll fix you right up."

"But what about Johnny Mack?" Addy shot a terrified look at Mack. "I can't just leave him."

Mack placed a hand at the small of her back and urged her out the door. "Don't worry about Johnny Mack. I'll be here with him."

"But, Mack—"

"Better hurry," Bill warned. "Kathy runs a tight ship. Put her behind schedule and she gets in a hell of a mood."

Before Addy could argue further, the door closed in her face.

Following the physical portion of her exam, Addy followed Sally to the doctor's office, thinking that having a female OB-GYN wasn't such a bad idea. She'd felt more comfortable and a whole lot less self-conscious being examined by a woman than she ever had with Dr. Wharton.

As she took a seat opposite the doctor's desk, the office door opened and Kathy strode in.

"Everything looked fine," she reported, as she sat down behind her desk. "The stitches from the episiotomy have all dissolved and the incision has healed nicely." She flipped open the file the nurse had left on her desk and scanned the lab reports. "Blood count looks good," she said. "Iron level more than sufficient." She closed the file and beamed a smile at Addy. "I'd say you're good to boogie."

Addy blinked. "Excuse me?"

Chuckling, Kathy sank back in her chair. "Sorry. I'll translate. You can resume your normal sexual activities."

Heat crawled up Addy's neck. "Oh. Well…I, uh… Mack and I…well, you see…"

Kathy did her best to hide a smile. "I'm not saying that you have to have sex tonight. I'm merely telling you that you're physically ready, if the situation should present itself."

If possible, Addy's face heated even more. "Yes. Right. Of course."

Smiling openly now, Kathy stood and extended her hand. "It's been a pleasure meeting you, Addy. You're everything Mack said you were and more."

Addy gaped. "Mack talked to you about me?"

Kathy rounded her desk to escort Addy to the door. "Not directly. But Mack and Bill have been joined at the hip since they were kids. If something is going on in one's life, the other knows about it." She stopped in the doorway and shrugged. "What Bill knows, I know. The man couldn't keep a secret if his life depended on it." She gave Addy an assessing look, then nodded. "And I have to agree. You're perfect."

You're perfect.

Addy played Kathy's comment over and over through her mind as she folded the clothes Mary had laundered, trying to figure out what the woman had meant. Since Kathy had just confessed that Bill told her everything, she had to assume that by "I agree" it was Bill she agreed with. But about what? she asked herself in confusion.

"How's he feeling?"

Addy jumped at the sound of Mack's voice and turned to find him in the doorway. Unbidden, another of Kathy's comments popped into her mind...her verdict of "you're good to boogie."

Mortified that she would think of *that*, she whipped her head back around, praying her cheeks weren't as red as they felt. "Fine," she said, and gulped to steady her voice. "He hasn't had any fever or been fussy."

Mack crossed the room to peek into the nursery where the baby slept. Her heart hammering in her chest, Addy watched him through the corner of her eye, wondering why, more and more often, her thoughts seemed to turn to sex whenever he was near. Six months ago she wouldn't have given him a second look. Older men were a turnoff for her, and Mack was at least ten years her senior. He failed in the physical department, too, as she was usually drawn to taller, lankier men, and though there was no question that Mack was tall—a good six feet, if not more—he definitely wasn't lanky. He was built more like a brick wall—and about as impregnable as one. From day one, he'd been bossy to the point of overbearing, and that was a relationship killer in her book, as she tended to bow her back when told what to do.

He turned away from the nursery, and she quickly busied herself folding clothes, so he wouldn't catch her staring.

"He looks like he weathered the shots okay," he said, as he moved to stand beside her.

"I thought so, too."

He picked up a bib and rubbed a thumb over the teddy bear appliqué on its front. "Did you enjoy having lunch in town yesterday?"

She glanced his way, surprised that he'd ask when she specifically remembered telling him she had, as well as thanking him for the meal. "Yes. I told you I did."

Nodding, he dropped the bib and picked up a bootie and slipped two fingers inside. "What do you think of Lampasas?"

Though he was obviously talking to her, he didn't look at her, which struck her as odd. He kept his gaze on the bootie and the puppetlike movements he was making with his fingers.

"It's nice," she replied, frowning slightly. "Much smaller than Dallas, but small towns have their own special charm." Unable to stem her curiosity, she asked bluntly, "Why all the questions?"

With a shrug he tossed the bootie back into the basket and turned away. "No reason. Just curious."

Addy stared after him, as bewildered by his questions as she was by his obvious reluctance to meet her gaze.

It was hormonal.

Addy had reached the conclusion during the night, while unable to sleep. It was the only explanation she could come up with that made any sense for her sudden attraction to Mack. She knew hormonal changes were common in pregnant women, both during and after a pregnancy. She'd experienced a few herself while carrying Johnny Mack. The sudden, unexplainable rush of tears; the drastic swings in her internal thermostat, leaving her freezing cold one minute and sweating profusely the next.

Hormones, she thought decisively. That had to be it.

She stole a glance at Mack, sitting opposite her at the table, his attention on the folded newspaper propped beside his plate. He'd barely acknowledged her presence when she had joined him at the table for breakfast, and had kept his gaze fixed on the newspaper throughout the meal.

Grimacing, she stabbed her fork into a triangle of pancake. It wasn't fair, she thought miserably, as she dragged it through the puddle of syrup on her plate. Why should she suddenly be stricken with an acute attack of lust, while his interest in her seemed to be dwindling with each passing day?

Not that he ever had been interested, she thought glumly. But he'd at least been nicer to her, more friendly. Keeping her company at night while she fed the baby. Sitting with her in the evening and watching TV. Insisting she take walks with him to the barns where he stabled his horses or to the pastures to see his cattle, in order to get her out of the house for a while and away from the baby.

She stole another look at him and felt the now-familiar stir of desire in her womb. The streaks of gray at his temples were nothing if not sexy. And the creases at the corner of his eyes and those between his brows when he concentrated, added an air of sophistication to an already handsome face. And that chest... She covered her mouth with her napkin to smother a lustful moan, imagining what it would be like to have it bare beneath her hands, pressed against her breasts.

"Mr. Mack?"

At the sound of Zadie's voice, Addy snatched her napkin from her mouth and balled it guiltily in her lap.

"Yes?" Mack replied to Zadie, his gaze still on his newspaper.

"I gonna need a couple days off."

He lifted his head to peer at her, his forehead creased in concern. "Is there a problem?"

She twisted her hands in her apron. "It's my sister Mabel. Her boy Willie just called. Said Mabel fell and broke her leg last night."

He set the newspaper down, giving her his full attention. "I'm sorry to hear that. Is she going to be all right?"

She gulped, nodded. "They put in a steel pin to hold it together. Done the surgery early this morning. But I needs to go and tend to her. Make sure she don't overdo none."

Mack nodded gravely. "Stay as long as you need. Do you want me to drive you?"

"I 'preciate that, but I can drive myself." She wrung her hands. "I jest hate to up and leave y'all so sudden like. If I'd know'd, I'd've cooked up a bunch of food to see y'all through till I get back."

Mack glanced at Addy. "I'm sure Addy wouldn't mind doing a little cooking."

Addy brightened at the suggestion. "Not at all. I love to cook."

"I suppose she could handle things," Zadie said doubtfully. "I could leave some recipes for her to follow."

Mack rose and placed a hand on Zadie's shoulder. "Don't you worry about us. It's Mabel you need to concern yourself with. Addy will see that we don't starve."

Addy stood before the mirror in her bathroom, naked as the day she was born, giving her body a last brutal assessment. Her face appeared somewhat thinner, she decided, her waist more defined, her stomach almost as flat as it had been before she had become pregnant. She cupped her hands beneath her breasts and tipped her head to the side to study them. They were definitely bigger than her prepregnant state, but they had lost that "melon" look and appeared almost…well, normal.

Relieved, she leaned close to examine her face and smoothed a finger over her cheek, searching for the dark spot that had appeared several months ago, "pregnancy mask" as Dr. Wharton had referred to it. She was pleased to find that it had faded, and knew that with a little makeup it wouldn't be noticeable at all.

Stepping back, she lowered her gaze to look at her abdomen and spotted a couple of stretch marks. Wincing, she traced a nail over the most obvious one that lay along her bikini line, then sputtered a laugh. Bikini line, she thought, rolling her eyes. As if she'd be caught dead in a bikini, postpregnancy or not.

Telling herself that a couple of stretch marks were small payment for the gift of her son, she stepped into the tub and, with a sigh, slid into the chin-deep bubbles.

Lined along the edge of the tub were everything she'd need to make herself beautiful…or, at the very least, presentable. A razor and shaving cream, an avocado mask for her face, perfumed oils to scent her body, lavender bath salts to help her relax. Frowning, she sprinkled the salts generously over the water, knowing she was going to need all the help she could get in the relaxation department.

As she'd discovered, planning a seduction was hell on a woman's nerves.

The idea to seduce Mack had come to her shortly after Mary had left at five o'clock and with her departure the realization that, with Mary gone for the day and Zadie in Austin taking care of her sister, Addy and Mack would have the house to themselves for the first time ever—with the exception of Johnny Mack, of course, but she had already put him down for the night and was praying he would sleep until morning.

Although the idea had come unbidden and in a flash of what could only be described as divine inspiration, she hadn't embraced it immediately. She'd stewed and fretted, worrying that Mack wouldn't find her physically attractive. After a good ten minutes of hand wringing, she'd decided to hell with it. What makeup and candle-light couldn't hide, she wouldn't worry about. He'd accept her as she was or not all. No big deal.

Yeah, right, she thought wryly.

Ignoring the tremble in her fingers, she smeared the mask over her face and let it set while she lathered and shaved her legs. Next came a full-body scrub with the loofah sponge and the scented oils, followed by a brisk shampoo and conditioner for her hair.

Once she was sure her hair was clean, her body smooth and seductively scented, she stepped from the bath. After drying off, she looked around for her clothes and hissed a breath when she realized she'd forgotten to bring them in with her.

With a sigh of resignation, she wrapped the towel around her and opened the bathroom door, tucking the ends to secure the towel between her breasts. Halfway across the room, she heard a noise behind her and glanced over her shoulder to find Mack backing from the nursery. Her heart skipped a beat, then kicked hard against the wall of her chest. She looked toward the closet, then back at the bathroom, mentally calculating the distance to each…and realized she'd never make it to either without being seen.

Standing with a damp towel draped around her, her hair hanging in wet clumps to her shoulders, her face freshly scrubbed, but minus the concealing makeup she'd intended to apply, she could all but see her plans for a seduction going up in smoke before her very eyes.

Mack turned. "Hey," he said, smiling. "I was just about to—" He stopped short, his smile melting as he slid his gaze slid down her front. "You're wearing a towel," he said dully, then lifted his gaze to hers.

She jerked up her chin, refusing to let her embarrassment show. "I forgot to take my clothes into the bathroom with me."

His gaze skimmed down her front again, and his Adam's apple bobbed convulsively. When he lifted his eyes to meet hers a second time, she saw the heat that burned there, would swear she felt it sizzle and pop against her damp skin.

Praying she wasn't reading him wrong, she inhaled deeply...and dropped the towel.

SIX

Six

It wasn't until the towel hit the floor that Addy remembered candlelight and the fact that she'd been counting on it, as well as the makeup, to conceal some of the flaws on her body. Thankfully, the overhead light was off, but the bedside lamp wasn't, which meant Mack had a fairly clear view of her every imperfection, if he were to look closely enough.

And he was definitely looking.

At the moment, his gaze was riveted on her breasts. Though she wanted more than anything to grab the towel and make a run for it, she squared her shoulders and thrust out her chin.

She heard what she thought was a moan come from him, and a shiver of response skated down her spine. *In for a penny, in for a pound,* she told herself, and forced herself to take that first bold step.

His gaze shot to hers. "Addy…"

She heard the warning in his voice…or was it a plea? Praying it was the latter, she stopped in front of him and laid her hand on his chest. She felt him jolt at her touch, the thunder of his heart beneath her palm, but his gaze remained steady on hers, his eyes turning a dark, smoldering blue.

"Do you know what you're doing?"

This time the warning in his tone was clear. She gulped, nodded. "Yes."

His chest swelled beneath her palm as he hauled in a breath, then deflated, as he released it. "You have exactly two seconds to change your mind."

She lifted a brow in challenge. "And if I don't?"

"One…two."

Before she had time to draw a breath, his mouth came down on hers, fierce and demanding, his arms wrapping around her like a vise. She felt the need in him, tasted it, even as a part of her mind marveled that she had the power to evoke that level of emotion in a man.

His hands burned like brands on her back, searing her flesh, as he forced her body up hard against his. She felt the swell of his erection against her abdomen, the heat of it spreading through her in wave after dizzying wave, and wondered why she'd waited so long to seduce him.

He was a marvelous kisser. She was surprised she still had the presence of mind to form the thought. His lips were possessive, demanding, arousing, as were the hands that stroked her bare back, urging her ever closer. When her breath began to burn in her lungs, her knees to grow weak, he slowly softened the kiss, his impatience giving way to a sensual exploration she found no less arousing.

The desire to touch him, to have her hands on his bare skin, as his were on hers, was too strong to ignore any longer.

"Your clothes," she said breathlessly, and reached for the buttons of his shirt.

Though he loosened his hold on her enough to give her access, he kept his arms looped low on her waist, holding her groin against his. She'd released three when she sensed his gaze. She glanced up and found him looking at her, his expression...curious? Questioning? Confused?

Unsure, she stilled her hands, fearing she'd done something wrong. "What?"

Shaking his head, he dipped his head to nuzzle her neck. "Nothing."

Though his reply did nothing to allay the doubts that suddenly crowded her mind, his mouth did the trick, as he nibbled his way up her neck and over her chin. She freed the last button on his shirt, just as he found her mouth again. Her breath stolen, she braced her hands against his chest, as much to steady herself as to satisfy her need to touch him. Warmth, strength...she sensed both beneath her palms, as she swept them up his chest and over his shoulders to strip away his shirt.

With a groan he cupped her buttocks and brought her up hard against him. "Bed."

His request was one-word simple, leaving no doubt in her mind as to his meaning, his needs. Before she could tell him that's what she'd had in mind from the start, he scooped her up into his arms.

She might've shivered deliciously at his caveman tactics, perhaps even lifted a brow at the finesse with which he stripped back the bedcovers while holding her in his arms. But she had time for neither, as he immediately began to undress.

Lying on her back in the center of her bed, she followed his movements like a voyeur, watching as he toed off his boots and peeled down his jeans. But when he straightened, her gaze refused to budge from the stiff shaft jutting from a nest of dark hair at the juncture of his legs. She didn't want to compare. That seemed so tawdry, so high schoolish. But she couldn't help but notice that he was better equipped than Ty. Gulping, she lifted her gaze to his.

With his eyes fixed on hers, he sank a knee into the mattress and stretched out over her, until his mouth covered hers again. His body was like a blanket, warm and comforting, his kiss so tender, so gentle, it drew tears to her eyes.

He lifted his head and combed her hair back to search her face, saw her tears. "It's okay for us to do this, isn't it?" he asked hesitantly.

She didn't need for him to tell her what he meant by *this*. She gulped, nodded. "According to Kathy, I'm good to boogie."

He blinked, then hooted a laugh and fell to his back at her side. "God, that sounds just like her."

She felt a moment's panic, fearing that she'd somehow ruined the mood by telling him what Kathy had said. But then his gaze slid to her breasts and his smile slowly faded. He rolled to his side and reached to cup one in the palm of his hand, his expression soft.

"When I'd watch you nurse Johnny Mack, I'd wonder what your breasts looked like, how they might feel." He rubbed the ball of his thumb over the nipple, then leaned to flick his tongue over the budded tip and said, "How they'd taste."

Prickles of desire danced to life beneath her skin at his tongue's urging, and shot to quiver like plucked strings in her womb. Trembling, she squeezed her knees together, fearing she would come apart right then and there.

He glanced up, and she saw that the heat had returned to his eyes. Holding her in place with nothing more than his gaze, he pushed up to an elbow and pressed his lips to hers. A shiver shook her, as he hooked an arm around her neck and pulled her over on top of him, holding her face to his between his broad hands. He deepened the kiss by degrees, while shifting his hands to stroke up and down her back. Heat radiated from her, beading her skin, slicking her hands. Sure that he intended to drive her mad before he made love to her, she rocked her hips impatiently against his.

His response was to grip her buttocks firmly within his hands, holding her against him. He thrust his tongue between her lips, an oral teasing that shot heat through her, a bolt of lightning that blinded and seared. Never in her life had she experienced anything like this, she thought desperately. Never such urgency, such need.

"I want you," she whispered, pressing herself against him.

He drew back to look at her, his expression uncertain. "I don't want to hurt you."

"You won't," she told him, even as she slipped a hand between their bodies to guide him to her. The tip of his erection slid across her opening, and she nearly wept in frustration.

"Mack," she gasped, straining toward him.

He tightened his hands on her buttocks to still her. "Easy," he murmured. "Let's take this slow."

She shook her head wildly. "No. Please. *Now.*"

In spite of her demand for urgency, he entered her slowly, inch by slow inch. The tremble of his hands on her hips, the quiver of his legs against hers, told her how much his restraint cost him. Though touched by his concern for her, she didn't want slow. What she wanted, needed, was *him.*

Pushing up to her knees, she clamped her legs at his hips. "You can't hurt me," she told him again, as she lowered her hips to his groin. Taking him in to his hilt, she dropped her head back with a groan, glorying in the sheer, sensual pleasure of having him fill her completely, of feeling his hips ground against hers. After a moment, she began to rock slowly back and forth, absorbing each sensation, while the pressure built inside her.

She felt the change in his body, even as her own body readied. The gathering and bunching of muscle, the quiver of flesh, the almost desperate dig of his fingers into her buttocks. Wanting, needing to share that ultimate experience with him, she braced her hands against his chest and thrust her hips back hard against his groin. She held herself there, on that pinnacle of pleasure, her head thrown back, her lungs heaving, accepting the gift of his passion, while her body exploded around him with her own.

Until that moment she'd never truly understood the meaning of rapture, what it was to experience it first-hand. But she knew now. The pleasure, the intensity of it, was blinding, liberating, spellbinding, humbling.

She drew in a breath through her nostrils, held it a moment, then opened her eyes and released it on a sigh…and found Mack watching her, his eyes a soft, translucent blue. His face was damp with perspiration, a dark stubble shadowed his jaw. With his gaze on hers, he reached up to stroke a hand over her belly, and a soft smile curved his lips.

She tensed, remembering the stretch mark that trailed along her bikini line. Wishing she could melt into the mattress or, at the very least, switch off the bedside lamp, she placed a hand over her stomach, trying to hide it.

"Don't," he scolded gently. "That's nothing to be ashamed of."

As if to prove it, he hitched himself up on an elbow, then bent his head to press a kiss against the mark. Lifting his head, he met her gaze, as he dragged his thumb through the moisture he'd left there. "That's a medal of motherhood. Wear it with pride."

Her heart seemed to stop a moment, then kicked against her ribs. She was falling in love with him, she realized, as she stared into his eyes. How could she feel anything less for a man who could say such an outrageously sweet thing and obviously mean it?

Before she had time to completely absorb the notion, consider it, he caught her arms and pulled her down to his chest. Their faces only inches apart, he searched her gaze.

"Addy…"

He caught her face between his hands and drew it down to touch his lips to hers. The kiss was so tender, so incredibly sweet, it brought tears to her eyes.

Drawing back, he swept a finger across her damp lashes. "Hey," he said softly. "Why the tears?"

She gulped, shook her head. "I…I don't know."

"I didn't hurt you, did I?"

She shook her head again, then tucked her face into the curve of his neck. "No. I'm fine."

Cupping a hand at the back of her head, he pressed his lips to her hair. "Regrets?"

She sputtered a watery laugh. "How can I regret something I planned?"

He drew back to search her face. "You planned this?"

Realizing how awful she must look, she touched a hand to her hair and grimaced. "Well, not *this* exactly. I had it all thought out. Candlelight. Soft music. A bottle of wine. A totally irresistible *me*." She wrinkled her nose. "Unfortunately you caught me before the transformation was complete."

"I don't know about that." He swept her hair back from her face, held it there. "I wasn't able to resist you."

He lifted his head and touched his lips to hers. "You knocked me completely off my feet." Dipping his head, he nuzzled her neck, then inhaled deeply. "What's that scent you're wearing?"

She closed her eyes and arched her neck, giving him better access. "Seduction. It seemed appropriate."

Zadie would have a fit if she could see her kitchen. Cracked eggshells littered the island, a pound of bacon lay in a heap beside the range ready to add to the skillet warming there, and flour dusted every surface within a five-foot span of the dough board where biscuits were lined up like soldiers preparing for battle.

But Addy didn't care about the mess she'd made. What Zadie couldn't see couldn't hurt her, and Addy was having the time of her life.

She'd spent an unbelievable night in bed with Mack, making love, cuddling and finally sleeping, only to wake and do it all again. And now, while he showered, she was cooking his breakfast, which she considered the perfect way to celebrate what had proven to be an unforgettable night.

And if her stomach was a little jittery about facing him in the bright light of day, she supposed that was to be expected. It was one thing to make wild, passionate love with a man in the dark of night, and quite another to sit across the breakfast table from him afterward and share a meal she'd prepared, as if nothing had changed between them.

"Smells good."

She jumped, nearly burning her hand on the skillet, then wilted, as Mack looped his arms around her waist from behind and buried his nose in the curve of her neck.

"Me or what's cooking?" she asked coyly.

Chuckling, he nipped her neck, then moved to stand beside her, keeping an arm looped at her waist. "Both. What's for breakfast?"

"Biscuits, omelets and bacon. Hungry?"

"As a bear." He gave her bottom a playful pat and turned away. "I checked on Johnny Mack," he said, as he crossed to the refrigerator. "He's still asleep." He poured orange juice into glasses and brought one to her. Sliding an arm around her waist again, he rested his hip against hers and sipped his juice, while she fried bacon.

To Addy the whole scene screamed family. In fact, if it were any more so, she feared she would explode with happiness.

"What have you got planned for today?" he asked.

She lifted a shoulder as she turned the bacon. "Nothing special. Do a few loads of laundry. Maybe help Mary around the house. What about you?"

"I need to go into town and take care of some business. Later I thought we might do something. Just the two of us. I bet Mary would jump at the chance to babysit Johnny Mack."

She looked up at him in surprise. "You mean, like a date?"

His smile sheepish, he rubbed a hand across the back of his neck. "Yeah. Something like that. Marriage first, then lovers. Somewhere along the way, seems we missed a step or two."

Addy spent an insane amount of time agonizing over what to wear on her "date" with Mack. It wasn't as if she needed to impress him, she told herself, as she flipped through the closet for the third time, searching for something appropriate to wear. He'd seen her at her absolute worst more times than she cared to think about, and he hadn't run yet, so what difference did it make what she wore?

"Because it's our first date," she reminded herself, "and I want everything to be perfect." She pulled a sundress from the closet and held it up to her, as she crossed to the bed. "What do you think?" she asked the baby, who sat propped up in an infant carrier on her bed. "Too casual? Too revealing?"

Johnny Mack kicked his feet and cooed, obviously excited at the attention he was receiving.

"So you think I'd look good in this, huh?" Laughing, she bent to drop a kiss on his cheek. "You're just saying that because I'm your mommy."

Straightening, she held up the dress, frowning as she studied her reflection in the dresser mirror. "Okay," she conceded. "I'll wear it." She glanced toward the baby and raised a brow in warning. "But if Mack doesn't go all google-eyed when he sees me in it, the blame is all yours."

In answer, Johnny Mack blew a bubble of spit.

Laughing, Addy bussed him another kiss. "You are just too darn cute."

Addy crossed and uncrossed her legs for the third time since they'd left the house.

"Did I tell Mary that I left bottles of breast milk in the refrigerator?"

"Twice," Mack replied patiently, then reached to pat her hand. "He'll be fine. Mary has four kids of her own. She knows how to take care of a baby."

She caught her lower lip between her teeth. "But her children are older, aren't they? She may have forgotten that she needs to warm his bottle before giving it to him."

Shaking his head, he pulled his cell phone from the holster at his waist and offered it to her. "Call her. You aren't going to be able to relax until you do."

She eyed the phone a moment, then pushed his hand away. "No. Mary knows how to take care of a baby."

Chuckling, he slid the phone back into the holster. "Seems as if I've heard that before."

She made a face at him, then turned to peer out the passenger window, watching the scenery that swept past. "Where are we going?" she asked, after a moment.

"Austin. I thought I'd show you some of the sights." He glanced her way. "Have you ever seen the State Capitol?"

She shook her head. "No. In fact, I've never been to Austin, other than driving through, of course, but that doesn't count."

"I'll give you the five-dollar tour some other time. Today we'll just hit the high spots."

The high spots, it seemed, included a drive down Sixth Street, which, according to Mack, was Austin's version of New Orleans's Bourbon Street. From there, he drove her by the state capitol and shared with her the story of how some men full of Texas pride had schemed to construct a building, without breaking any laws, that would exceed the height of the U.S. Capitol in Washington, D.C., by choosing a hill as their building site. They enjoyed a relaxing stroll through Lady Bird Johnson's Wildflower Center, where Mack insisted on buying her a huge bag of bluebonnet seeds she stopped to admire. Then, late that afternoon, he rented a canoe on Town Lake, situated in the heart of downtown Austin, and gave her an entirely different perspective of the city, this time from the water.

The sun was just beginning its descent, turning the horizon blood red, when he pulled the oar from the water and rested it across his thighs, letting the canoe drift.

"A penny for your thoughts," he teased.

More relaxed than she'd been in what seemed like ages, Addy hid a smile as she leaned to trail her fingers through the water. "I'd take you up on that, if I had any."

Catching her hand, he set aside the oar and tugged her over to sit on his lap.

She gasped, clinging to his neck, as the canoe rocked precariously from side to side. "What are you trying to do?" she cried. "Drown us?"

Chuckling, he wrapped his arms around her waist. "No. Just wanted you closer."

She melted at his response and smiled, as she stroked his windswept hair back from his face. "You could've just asked, you know. What if I'd fallen in?"

Since his face was even with her breasts, he was unable to resist nipping at her nipple. "I'd have jumped in and saved you."

She sucked in a breath, then released it with a shiver. "Watch it, buster," she warned and pressed the tip of her finger against the center of his forehead to push him back. "There are laws against public groping."

"That wasn't groping." His gaze on hers, he slipped a hand beneath her dress and stroked his fingers up her thigh. "This is groping."

Even as his fingers molded her mound, he took her mouth with his, stealing her breath. The heat was instantaneous, bone melting.

"Mack," she begged, her breath hot against his lips. "You shouldn't. Someone might see."

He swung her legs around, bunching her dress up around her waist, until she was straddling him. "Who?" he challenged. "There's nobody out here but you and me."

She stole an uneasy glance around and discovered that he was right. They truly were alone. The canoe had drifted into a narrow inlet, darkened by the canopy of trees whose limbs draped overhead. In the far distance, lights gleamed from businesses that lined the opposite shoreline, but the area immediately around them was webbed with shadows of dusk, creating a private spot perfect for lovers.

He tugged on the string that crisscrossed her breasts, loosening it and pressed his lips in the valley he exposed.

"Ever made love in a canoe?" he asked, as he swept his tongue up her chest toward her chin.

She dropped her head back and closed her eyes. "N-no," she said breathlessly. "I don't think so."

He drew her hips up against his. "Good. Then this'll be a first for us both."

That night Addy lay with Mack spooned at her back, her head pillowed by one of his arms, the other hooked loosely over her waist. The fit was near perfect, the peace that filled her beyond anything she'd ever known, ever imagined.

She supposed she owed Ty a debt of gratitude—although she'd cut out her tongue before she'd ever tell him so. If not for Ty, she never would've met Mack.

Realizing how different her life would be without Mack a part of it, how empty, she linked her fingers with his, finding reassurance and comfort even in that slight connection.

So this is what it feels like to be in love, she thought with a shiver. She glanced over her shoulder to peer at the man responsible for her making the fall, and her heart turned to mush. He looked so boyish, with his hair all tousled and his face relaxed in sleep. So peaceful. Did he love her? she wondered uncertainly. He hadn't said the *L* word. But then, neither had she.

Setting her jaw, she turned her face away and settled her head on the pillow in front of his again. Don't get ahead of yourself, she lectured silently. It was like Mack had said earlier that day, when she'd asked if he was taking her on a date. They'd missed a few steps along the way. Virtual strangers, they'd married, become lovers. Now they would have to take the time to explore the possibilities, get to know each other, see where their feelings took them.

Gulping, she crossed her fingers and sent up a silent prayer that he would discover that he had fallen in love with her, too.

Johnny Mack let out a wail, and Addy flung back the covers, but Mack tightened his arm around her waist, stopping her before she could rise.

He pushed himself up to an elbow and pressed a sleepy kiss to the back of her neck. "Stay in bed. I'll check on him."

Though she was more awake than he, she lay back down and watched his shadowed form disappear into the nursery.

"Hey, little buddy," she heard him whisper to the baby. "What are you doing awake at this hour?"

Smiling, she closed her eyes, able to monitor his movements by the sounds coming from the nursery. The light metallic grate of the crib's guard rail being lowered. The wooden creak of the rocker accepting Mack's weight. The husky croon of Mack's voice as he soothed the baby. She grew sleepy, listening, as comforted by the sound of his voice as Johnny Mack seemed to be.

How lucky her son was to have Mack, she thought as sleep tugged her toward the brink. She'd never had a father to soothe her tears or rock her to sleep. But her son would always have Mack.

Seven

Mack sat before his lawyer's desk, listening carefully as Lenny explained the legal requirements of the request he'd made.

When Lenny was finished, Mack absorbed the information a moment, then said, "Let me see if I understand this correctly. You prepare the document necessary for Ty to forfeit all paternity rights and once he signs them, that's it? Johnny Mack is legally mine?"

"Legally he's already yours. The adoption papers we filed took care of that. Addy's refusal to name the father on the birth certificate simplified the process." He lifted his hands. "But since we both know Ty is the baby's biological father and are aware of his propensity to cause trouble for you, the forfeiture of paternity rights adds further protection should he ever choose to challenge the adoption."

"Then let's do it. I don't want Ty to have any legal claim on my son."

Lenny nodded. "All right. But I feel I should warn you. This is going to cost you, and I'm not talking about my legal fees. Ty will use this an opportunity to squeeze more money from you."

Mack stood and snugged on his hat, preparing to leave. "We'll worry about that if and when it happens. What we need to focus on now is locating Ty. Hire a private investigator. Ty usually leaves a trail of destruction a mile wide in his wake, so locating him shouldn't be too hard."

"Will do." Lenny rose and followed him to the door. "You didn't mention Addy. How are the two of you getting along?"

Mack ducked his head to hide a smile, nodded. "Good. Real good."

Lenny looked at Mack closely. "Well, I'll be damned," he murmured, then laughed and clapped Mack on the back. "Who'd have thought that an old coot like you would ever fall in love again?"

Zadie was gone four days, nine hours and twenty-two minutes. Addy knew, because she'd thoroughly enjoyed each and every second she'd spent in the kitchen during her absence. But that freedom was soon coming to an end, as Zadie was due to return that afternoon.

"You scrub that sink much more," Mary warned, "you're going to rub a hole in it."

With a sigh, Addy dropped the dishcloth in the sink, then glanced around the kitchen, looking for anything out of place. "It looks the same, doesn't it?" she asked uneasily. "I've put everything back just the way she had it."

"Would you quit worrying?" Mary fussed. "It's *your* kitchen, not Zadie's. You can paint the walls fire engine red, if you want. You don't need her permission."

"Yeah, right," Addy said dryly. "Zadie would hang me by my toes if I so much as moved the dust mop, without asking her first."

Mary wagged her head. "I can't believe you've let that woman bully you into believing she's the boss around here. *You're* the boss. Mr. Mack's wife. Remind her of that, and I'll bet she'll sing a different tune."

"You really think so?" Addy asked doubtfully.

"Wouldn't say it, if I didn't consider it the gospel truth."

"I don't want to make her mad. I really do like her." She wrinkled her nose. "It's just that she's so possessive about the kitchen."

"Stand up to her," Mary advised. "She's had the run of this place long enough."

Addy squared her shoulders. "All right. But you have to promise me one thing."

"What's that?"

"After they bury me, you have to paint the kitchen fire-engine red."

Mary blinked, then hooted a laugh. "Girl, you've got yourself a deal."

In spite of her brave talk, Addy made another sweep

through the kitchen, checking to make sure she'd returned everything to its proper place.

She was standing in the pantry, straightening the canned goods on the shelf, when she heard the back door open. Sure that it was Zadie returning, she was tempted to pull the door closed and hide. All but trembling in fear, she listened as Zadie shuffled into the kitchen and set down her overnight bag.

"Would you look at that," she heard Zadie mutter under her breath. "Somebody left the dishcloth in the sink to sour."

Addy winced, remembering too late that she'd failed to spread the dishcloth out over the drainboard to dry, as was Zadie's habit.

"Well, hi, Zadie," she heard Mary say, as the housekeeper entered the kitchen. "How's Mabel doing?"

"Good as can be expected, I guess."

"I'm surprised you didn't stay with her longer."

"Her daughter came from Tyler to see after her. Just as well. I 'bout worked myself to death cleanin' that house. I swear that woman lives like a pig. Had to scrub down the kitchen 'for I could even cook a meal."

As Mary passed by the pantry, she reached to close the door. When she saw Addy cowering inside, she pressed her lips together to smother a laugh and walked on, leaving the door open a crack.

"I 'magine Mr. Mack will be glad to see I'm home," Zadie said. "Poor man's probably half-starved by now."

Addy curled her nose in a snarl at the jab at her cooking abilities.

"Actually," Mary replied, quick to come to Addy's defense, "he's fit as a fiddle. Addy's cooked him three squares a day."

Addy beamed a smile. It quickly morphed to a scowl, when she heard Zadie's "humph."

Deciding it was high time she put Zadie in her place, she pushed open the pantry door and stepped out.

"Well, hello, Zadie," she said in surprise, as if she was unaware Zadie had returned and hadn't heard every word the woman had uttered since entering the house. "How's Mabel feeling?"

Zadie's eyes went round as saucers. "Uh—" she shot Mary a panicked look "—she's gettin' along real good. Real good."

Smiling sweetly, Addy braced a hip against the island and folded her arms across her chest. "I'm glad to hear that. Being waited on hand and foot gets old after a while."

"Yeah," Zadie agreed, and shot Mary another look. "I 'magine it do."

Addy looked around the room, considering. "You know," she said thoughtfully. "These walls could use freshening up."

Zadie swelled her chest in indignation. "Why, ain't nothin' wrong with these walls."

"Not the walls, per se," Addy conceded. "It's the color that needs sprucing."

"Ain't nothin' wrong with the color, either."

"But it's so…drab." She glanced at Mary, who was struggling not to laugh. "What do you think, Mary? Don't you think the walls need some color?"

"I like color," Mary agreed, playing along with Addy. "Brings life to a room."

Zadie looked as if she were about to explode. "This room's got enough life in it. Don't need no more."

"What color were you thinking of painting it, Addy?" Mary asked, egging her on.

Addy puckered her lips thoughtfully. "I don't know. Something strong. Vibrant. Maybe red."

"Red!" Zadie cried. "You ain't turnin' my kitchen into no whorehouse."

The back door opened and Mack strode in, stopped short. "Well, hi, Zadie," he said, in surprise. "I wasn't expecting you back so soon. Welcome home."

"Thank you, Mr. Mack," she replied, and shot Addy a frown. "Looks like I got back jist in the nick of time."

He tossed his hat onto the counter and looked at her curiously. "In time for what?"

Zadie tossed up her hands. "To save my kitchen, that's what. She's wantin' to paint it red."

Mack glanced at Addy. "Red?"

She smiled weakly. "Maybe not red. I just thought the kitchen could use some freshening up."

Mack glanced around the room, as if considering, then nodded. "You're right. It could stand to be re-painted. Let me know when you decide on a color, and I'll hire a crew to come in and do the work." He glanced at his watch. "I need to make a couple of phone calls." He stopped in front of Addy and gave her a kiss full on the lips, then headed for the door. "If you ladies need me," he called over his shoulder, "I'll be in my office."

Zadie stood staring, her mouth open wide enough to catch flies, obviously shocked by the kiss she'd just witnessed.

Addy lifted a brow. "Problem?"

Zadie pursed her lips. "Well, I guess I don't need to be askin' who's sleepin' where," she muttered. "And here I was thinkin' I was gonna have to lock the two of you up in a room together, 'fore y'all figured out what a man and woman was created to do."

Addy pushed herself up to an elbow and swept her hair back from her face. "And then she said she was afraid she was going to have to lock us up in a room together so we could figure out what a woman and a man were created to do."

Chuckling, Mack stroked a hand along the curve of her waist. "She probably would've, too."

Addy snuggled close to his side, folding her hands between her head and his chest. "It's weird. Creepy even."

He drew back to look at her. "What?"

"Having someone living in the same house with us and her knowing what we're doing every second of the day, even where we're sleeping."

A laugh rumbled in his chest. "It's not as if we're doing something illegal."

She lifted her head to frown at him, then laid it back on his chest. "You know what I mean." She stifled a shudder. "It's creepy. Makes me feel like I'm on camera or something."

He stroked his fingertips lazily down her side. "Her

apartment is on the other end of the house," he reminded her. "She seldom comes to this wing of the house."

"Yeah, but still…"

Chuckling, he rolled to his side and gathered her into his arms. "Would it make you feel better if I had an apartment built for her separate from the house?"

She hid a smile, secretly pleased that he would go to such lengths just to make her happy. "No. But you might consider getting her ear plugs."

He lifted a brow. "You're a screamer?"

She drew a circle on his chest with a nail and shrugged. "If properly aroused."

"Since I've never heard you scream, am I supposed to take that as an insult?"

She gave him a coy look. "Or a challenge."

Laughing, he pulled her over on top of him and gripped her buttocks in his hands. "Nobody enjoys a challenge more than I do."

Smiling, she inched up his chest until her mouth was a breath away from his. "Lucky you. It just so happens I'm in the mood to scream."

"Found him in Houston," Lenny told Mack, then spun the file around on his desk for Mack to read. "He's shacked up with a woman in a condo near the Galleria. Been there about five months, best the P.I. can figure."

Mack studied the picture of the leggy blonde captured on film walking down the sidewalk, her arm linked through Ty's. "Looks like his type," he commented, then pushed the file back toward Lenny and sank into his chair. "Have you made contact with him?"

"This morning." Lenny shook his head sadly. "Ten o'clock in the morning and I woke him out of a dead sleep."

"I take it he's unemployed."

"Appears that way. The P.I. said when he leaves the condo, he has the woman in tow."

"Is she wealthy?"

"Lives off a trust fund set up by her grandfather. From her financials, if she's careful, she'll never have to work a day in her life."

Mack snorted. "A year, two at the latest, and Ty will drain her dry."

Lenny tipped his head in acknowledgment. "If his past spending habits are any indication, you're probably right."

"So, what have you got planned?"

Lenny pulled a file from the drawer on his left. "The document is prepared and ready for his signature. I've arranged for a notary public to meet you at the Houston airport at three o'clock tomorrow afternoon to witness Ty signing, and advised Ty of the same."

"He agreed to meet me?"

Lenny gave him a droll look. "What do you think? All I had to say was the word *paternity* and he was scrambling for a pen."

Mack shook his head. "He'll never grow up."

"Oh, he grew up, all right," Lenny said, then added dryly, "Too bad his brain didn't develop at the same rate."

* * *

Mack tossed his toiletry bag into his suitcase and crossed to the closet to pull out a shirt. "It's fairly cut-and-dried," he explained to Addy. "I give Ty the document Lenny prepared, he signs it, the notary stamps it with his seal, and we're done."

He stripped the shirt from the hanger, as he walked back to the bed. Addy took it from him and carefully folded it, her forehead pleated with worry.

"And that's the end of it?" she asked uncertainly, as she tucked the shirt into his suitcase. "He can never challenge his parental right to Johnny Mack?"

"Nope. Once he signs the document, he gives up all rights to our son."

Addy pressed a hand against her chest, touched by Mack's reference to Johnny Mack as their son, rather than just hers. Blinking back tears, she dropped her hand to reach for his and linked her fingers with his. "You'll be careful, won't you?"

His gaze on hers, he brought their joined hands to his lips and pressed a kiss against her knuckles. "Ty might be many things, but he's not violent. He won't hurt me."

Though she'd never seen any evidence of violence in Ty, she couldn't shake free from the premonition of doom that had shadowed her thoughts ever since Mack had returned from the lawyer's office and told her of his plans to go to Houston.

Forcing a smile, she gave his hand a squeeze and released it. "Just the same, be careful. I don't want anything happening to you."

"I'll be fine." He zipped his bag closed and hefted it from the bed.

It was all she could do to keep from throwing herself at his feet and begging him not to go.

"Do you really need to leave tonight?" she asked, trying to think of a way to delay his departure. "You're not scheduled to meet him until tomorrow afternoon."

"I don't want to take a chance on traffic or car trouble keeping me from getting to the airport by three."

"But you could leave early in the morning and make it to the airport with time to spare."

Shaking his head, he slung an arm around her shoulders and hugged her against his side, as he walked with her to the nursery door. "Would you stop worrying? I'm going to be fine."

She pressed her head against his shoulder as they entered the nursery, then eased from his embrace as he stopped before the crib and set his suitcase on the floor. Tears filled her eyes as he leaned over the crib and brushed his fingers over Johnny Mack's cheek.

"You be good while I'm gone," he whispered to the sleeping baby. "And take good care of your mommy for me." He bent over and pressed a kiss to Johnny Mack's forehead, then straightened and simply looked at him, a hand cupped at the top of the infant's head.

After a moment he picked up his suitcase and hooked an arm around Addy's waist. "If he wakes up in the night," he whispered as he guided her from the nursery, "try singing to him. He seems to favor country-western.

Two verses of a George Strait song usually puts him right back to sleep."

He stopped in the doorway of what she had come to think of as "their" room and placed a hand on her cheek. "Let's say our goodbyes here," he suggested quietly. "If I kiss you 'bye at the door, Zadie might expect one, too."

Laughing through the tears that filled her eyes, she wrapped her arms around his neck and hugged him tight. "Be safe," she whispered.

"You, too."

He kissed her, lingering a moment, then sealed it with another quick kiss and turned away. "See you tomorrow."

She lifted a hand as he walked away. When he reached the turn in the hallway that led to the front of the house, panic seized her. "Mack! Wait!"

He stopped, turned. "Yes?"

With tears blurring her vision, she pressed a hand to her lips to hold back the three words her heart screamed for her to say.

Dropping her hand to her side, she said instead, "Don't forget to put on your seatbelt."

The smile he offered her was soft, the look in his eyes warm. "I won't forget. 'Night, Addy."

He turned and rounded the corner, disappearing from sight.

"'Night, Mack," she whispered.

Mack offered his hand to the notary public seated at the table at the airport bar. "Mack McGruder," he said, by way of introduction.

The man stood, his grip firm as he shook Mack's hand. "Glen Powell."

Mack juggled the briefcase nervously in his hand, as he looked around. "Ty hasn't made it yet?"

Glen sat back down. "Not so far as I know." He glanced at his wrist watch. "It's not quite three, though. He's got some time."

Releasing a nervous breath, Mack propped the briefcase on a chair, then sat down opposite the notary public. A waitress appeared at his side and he ordered a beer, hoping it would calm his nerves. He hadn't slept much the night before, which is why he'd insisted on going to Houston a day early. He'd known if he'd stayed at home, he wouldn't have been able to hide his nervousness from Addy, and he didn't want his uneasiness to infect her. She was worried enough as it was.

Not that there was anything to worry about, he reminded himself. There was no reason to think that Ty would balk at signing the papers. He'd signed the other paternal releases Mack had presented him with without batting an eye.

The waitress arrived with Mack's beer and he gulped a swallow, then glanced toward the wide aisle beyond the bar's entrance, where passengers hustled past in both directions, hurrying to meet their flights. Not a sign of Ty, though.

He rolled his wrist, checked the time: 3:05. He set his jaw, refusing to accept Ty's tardiness as a sign his half brother wasn't going to show. Ty was always late, he reminded himself. Time meant nothing to a man who had nothing to do, nowhere to go.

* * *

Addy ran out the front door, clutching the baby in one arm and waving the other frantically over her head. "Zadie! Wait!"

Her lips pursed in disgust, Zadie cranked down her window. "What'd you forget this time?" she asked sourly.

"A bottle of champagne. Mack will be home tonight and we'll want to celebrate."

Rolling her eyes, Zadie cranked the window back up and drove away.

"Hag," Addy muttered under her breath, then nuzzled her nose against Johnny Mack's cheek. "She really loves us," she told him. "She just has a hard time showing her feelings."

He pumped his legs and arms as if trying to fly, and made Addy laugh. "You little doll," she said, hugging him to her, as she stepped back into the house. "How about a bath?" she asked him, as she headed back to her suite of rooms. "You can blow bubbles and splash all you want."

He pumped his legs again in excitement, as if he understood exactly what she was saying.

"You are way too smart," she informed him, as she set out the items needed for his bath on the bathroom vanity. Placing him on the elevated platform of his tub, she began removing his clothes. "Mack will be home tonight," she told him, then couldn't resist tickling him under his chin. "I'll bet he missed you. Did you miss him?"

He stared at her, his eyes round, listening intently.

She turned on the tap and waved her fingers beneath the stream of water, testing the temperature. "Mack's a good man," she went on. "You're lucky to have a father who loves you so much." Slipping the bath mitt over her hand, she squirted soap over her palm. "I never knew my father. Did you know that? He died before I was born."

She wrinkled her nose and leaned to bump it against the baby's. "Sad, huh? Not having a father?" Smiling, she began to rub the soapy mitt over his stomach. "But you'll always have Mack. He loves you so much. And he's a good father," she assured him, as she worked her way down his stomach to his legs. "Not many daddies would get up in the night like he does with you. Let's scrub your back," she said, and slipped a hand beneath him to lift him up far enough to soap his back side.

"There," she said, after rinsing him off. "All clean." Taking the hooded towel she'd laid out, she picked him up and wrapped it around him. "Ready for a diaper and some clean clothes?" she asked, continuing the one-sided conversation.

Entering the nursery, she balanced him in the crook of her arm, while plucking a romper from his chest of drawers. Cooing to him, she quickly diapered him and fumbled him into his clothes. "There," she said, at last. "All dressed for the day. How about if we rock while you nurse?" she asked as she sat down in the chair. Settling Johnny Mack in her arms, she opened her blouse and offered him her breast. A loving smile curved her lips, as he latched on to the nipple and began to suckle.

She pushed her foot against the floor to set the rocker into motion and began to hum. As he nursed, her mind drifted to the worries that had huddled on the edge of her mind since Mack had left the night before. Specifically Mack's meeting with Ty.

Closing her eyes, she laid her head back, silently praying that all would go well and Mack would return with Ty's signature on the document. With the tune of the George Strait song she hummed serving as background music, she let images of Mack sift through her mind. Mack standing beside her bed during Johnny Mack's birth, his hand gripped tightly around hers, his forehead creased in concentration, his blue eyes fixed on hers. Mack standing at her side in her hospital room, her arm looped through the crook of his, his hand folded over hers, as Pastor Nolan had pronounced them man and wife. Mack sitting in the rocking chair, his smile tender, his gaze on Johnny Mack as he rocked Johnny Mack to sleep. Mack asleep in her bed, his legs twined with hers, his arms around her, his breath warm on her cheek.

"Well, look who we have here."

She jumped, flipped open her eyes to find Ty standing in the doorway that opened to her bedroom. She gulped, instinctively tightening her arms around Johnny Mack. "Wh-what are you doing here?"

"I think that would be obvious." Smiling broadly, he opened his arms in an expansive gesture. "I came to see my family."

She turned a shoulder, as if to protect Johnny Mack from him. "Mack's not here."

"Addy, Addy," he scolded gently, as he stepped into the nursery. "I didn't come to see Mack. I came to see you. Our baby."

She curled herself further around her son. "He isn't yours."

Stopping in front of the rocker, he lifted a brow. "Do you really expect me to believe that baby is Mack's? Well, it's easy enough to do the math." He gestured to the baby. "He's, what? A month old? Let's see, the last time I saw you was in December, which was about five or six months ago, give or take a week. At the time, you claimed to be two months pregnant, and we'd been living together at least four months prior to that." His smile turned smug. "So, yes, the baby is definitely mine."

"He's not yours!" she cried. "He's Mack's. Mack adopted him."

"And why would Mack want to adopt a baby? A man his age? What would he hope to gain by taking on the responsibility of raising another man's child?"

When she only glared at him, he hunkered down in front of his chair. "You're no fool, Addy. Think. Mack's forty-two years old. A widower. He lost his wife and son in an automobile accident."

She swung her knees to the side, angling her body away from him. "No. I'm not listening to you."

"Oh, but you are," he replied calmly. "And your mind's working, isn't it? You're wondering why Mack would want the child of the half brother he openly admits he despises."

He laid a hand on her knee, and she knocked it away.

"Don't touch me! Don't you dare touch me ever again."

He shrugged and stood. "No skin off my back. You never were much fun in bed."

Repulsed by the sight of him, she turned her face away, refusing to look at him any longer. "Leave. Get out of this house or I'll call the police."

"Oh, I wouldn't do that, if I were you. Just think of all the gossip that would create. Everyone in town would know that I'm the baby's father, not Mack."

She glared at him, hate radiating from her eyes. "If it's money you want, I don't have any."

A slow smile spread across his face. "Mack does. Buckets of it. And I bet he'd pay a pretty price for my son. He thought he could get him for nothing. Have me sign the papers and give up my rights." He bent over, bracing his hands on his knees to put his face level with hers.

"That's why he went to Houston, wasn't it? To have me sign my rights away? He wanted my signature on the dotted line before I found out he wanted my kid for himself. But guess what, Addy? I'm smarter than my brother thinks. The P.I. he hired to find me was sloppy. I made him the first day he was on the job. I suspected Mack was the one who'd hired him. Then I get the call from Lenny, asking me to meet Mack to sign a paternity release, and my suspicions were confirmed.

"Call me paranoid, but something just didn't feel right about the whole setup. So I made a few calls to some old friends of mine in Lampasas. Imagine my surprise, when I learned that Mack had recently got married, and to a woman with a newborn, no less. A woman from Dallas. Since I'd left a pregnant woman in Dallas, it made me wonder. What I couldn't figure out was how the two of you got together.

"Then I remembered how anal Mack's always been about tying up loose ends, especially those that pertain to me. Considers it his God-given duty to protect the family name, his precious estate. So I put two and two together. Figured he'd somehow heard about you, knew you were pregnant and went to Dallas to buy you off." He lifted a brow in question. "Have I got the story right so far?"

She gulped, unable to tear her gaze from his, but refused to answer.

Straightening, he looked down at her and smiled. "No need to reply, Addy. I got the answer I wanted. You never could keep a poker face." He hunkered down again, holding his hand against the side of his mouth, as if about to share a secret. "Just between you and me, Addy," he said confidentially. "I don't give a rat's ass about the baby." He dropped his hand and grinned. "But Mack's going to pay for the right to call the kid his. I don't give away anything for free. Not even something I don't want."

Seething, Addy bared her teeth. "You have no right. You never wanted the baby. You ran so that you wouldn't have to accept responsibility for him."

He shrugged, unfazed by her accusations. "Why would I want the brat? But what you should be asking yourself is why *Mack* would want him. Do you suppose it's out of pity?" he asked curiously. "He felt sorry for the poor, defenseless unwed mother, left to raise a baby on her own, and decided to step in like the white knight he likes to think he is and save the day." He leaned a little closer. "Or maybe his reason was purely selfish. Mack needs an heir. His son is dead. He doesn't have anyone to leave all his money to, his estate."

"That's a lie," she cried angrily. "Mack isn't selfish. He's good and honest and generous."

Ty straightened to his full height and lifted a brow. "Oh, really? Has he ever mentioned how he feels about me?"

Addy gulped, remembering the things Mack had shared with her about his and his half brother's relationship. "Only that your relationship is...strained."

"Strained?" He tipped back his head and hooted a laugh. "Well, I guess that's one way of describing it. Mack hates me," he said bluntly. "Resented me from the day I was born, because our mother favored me over him."

She didn't believe him for a minute, but held her tongue, fearing that if she challenged his claim it would make him angry and he might do something rash.

"That's why he wanted to marry you and adopt my son," he went on. "Not because he's generous and kind. But because he'll do anything to keep me from getting a penny of what he considers his. Even marry a complete stranger and adopt her son. A son," he added, lifting a brow, "who shares some of the same blood that runs through Mack's veins."

Addy went as still as death. "Mack didn't adopt my baby because of any blood-tie. He loves Johnny Mack as if he were his own."

He snorted a laugh. "Don't kid yourself, Addy. Mack McGruder loves only one person. Himself."

"That's not true! He loves us."

"*Us?*" he repeated, then gave her a pitying look.

"Please tell me that you don't think Mack's in love with you just because he's slept with you? Hell, he's a man, Addy! One woman is the same as any other."

She felt tears burning behind her eyes and fought them back.

He shook his head in wonder. "Man, oh man. I've got to give my big brother credit for pulling off the perfect coup. He not only got himself an heir, he gets sex on demand."

He opened his hands. "But, hey. What does all this really matter? Whatever Mack's reasons for marrying you and adopting your brat, you're still the winner, right? You've landed yourself in high cotton." He spread his arms, indicating the house. "Not bad, huh? And quite a step up from that cracker box you were living in in Dallas. Of course, there's all his money, too. He's got tons of it socked away. But I'm sure you already know that."

He hunkered down in front of her again, bracing an arm on his thigh, and looked her square in the eye. "Now here's the deal, Addy. I want some of that money, too. A lot of it, in fact. And you're going to help me get it. If you do, you get to keep the brat and live a life of luxury as Mack's wife." He lifted a finger in warning. "But try cutting me out of the winnings, and I'll stake my claim on the baby and you'll be back in Dallas scrubbing out bed pans again."

"Git your hands up and your ass out of Mr. Mack's house."

Addy snapped up her head to find Zadie standing in

the doorway, the stock of Mack's rifle braced against her shoulder, the barrel aimed at Ty's back.

Ty stood. "Now, Zadie," he scolded in a voice that all but dripped sugar. "You know as well as I do that you'd never shoot me. Hell, you helped raise me."

She flipped off the safety, but kept the barrel aimed at Ty's chest. "Should'a drowned you when you was a baby and saved us all the shame you brung to this family."

"Now, Zadie," he began, and took a step toward her.

The metallic click of the rifle being cocked silenced him and had him throwing up his hands.

"Don't think for a minute I won't pull this trigger," she warned. "Now, git outta this house. And don't think 'bout coming back and terrorizing this family anymore. If you do, I'll fill your heart with lead."

Ty obviously believed her, because he skirted a wide path around Zadie, as he made his way to the door, his hands high over his head. Zadie followed at a safe distance, keeping the rifle aimed at his back.

Trembling, Addy sank back in the rocking chair, her arms locked around Johnny Mack. She was still sitting there when Zadie returned a few moments later, the rifle now at her side, its barrel pointed at the floor.

"You okay, Miss Addy?" she asked hesitantly.

Addy drew what felt like the first real breath she'd drawn since she'd looked up and found Ty standing in the doorway. "Y-yes. He didn't hurt me."

"And won't. He's gone now. I made sure of that, and locked the doors up tight when I came back inside."

Numb, Addy nodded. "Thank you, Zadie."

Frowning, Zadie propped the rifle against the door. "Why'd you let that no-count boy in this house, in the first place?" she fussed. "You shoulda knowed he was up to no good."

Addy shook her head. "I didn't let him in. He just… appeared."

Zadie's frown deepened. "Must have sneaked through the gates when I left for the grocery store." Shaking her head, she crossed to Addy. "Here, honey. Give me that baby. You're shakin' like a leaf."

Addy tightened her arms around Johnny Mack. "No."

Zadie planted her hands on her hips. "Well, you can't jist sit in that rocker all day and hold him."

When Addy refused to relinquish her hold on Johnny Mack, Zadie heaved a sigh of defeat. "All right, honey. You go on and rock that baby all you want. I 'magine your nerves are near shot. I know mine are." She forced a smile. "I know what we need. A good cup of strong tea. And I'll toss in a shot of whiskey. Just for medicinal purposes, mind you." She turned for the door. "You just sit right there and collect yourself. I'll bring the tea in here, once I've brewed it."

After Zadie left, Addy remained in the rocker, her body stiff, her eyes unblinking. She was numb, paralyzed, unable to move or think. Thoughts whirled through her mind too fast for her to grasp, while others seemed to scream obscenely for her attention.

He was lying, she told herself, fighting the doubts Ty had planted in her mind. Mack wasn't a mean person or a selfish one, as Ty had claimed. Mack was loving and giving. And he hadn't adopted Johnny Mack simply to get an heir. Mack genuinely loved Johnny Mack. Nothing Ty could say would ever convince her differently.

Sure, he loves the baby. But does he love you? Or does he just want sex from you, as Ty had claimed?

She gulped, unsure of the answer. Mack had never told her that he loved her. Not in so many words. He was kind to her, unbelievably generous, and the most extraordinary lover. But did he *love* her? As much as she loved him?

Tears filled her eyes. Oh, God, how she wanted him to. She wanted family so badly, yearned for what she had never known, been denied throughout her life. She thought she'd found that with Mack, had begun to believe that they could create a family. Not in the sense that she wanted it. She needed his love, his heart. She'd already lost hers to him and would accept nothing less in return, not even the semblance of family he'd offered to her when he'd married her.

Time, she reminded herself stubbornly. She and Mack were still feeling their way, just beginning to get to know each other. She knew he card for her. In time he would grow to love her as much as she loved him.

But what if they ran out of time?

Fear gripped her chest at the thought, its icy fingers winding their way up to her throat and squeezing. What if they ran out of time? What if Ty made good his threat? He'd claimed that if she didn't help him get money from Mack, he'd take her baby. She couldn't bear to lose her son. Nor could she bear the thought of Mack losing him.

And that's what frightened her most, she realized, at

last able to single out the true source of her fear. She was afraid that Ty would succeed in taking Johnny Mack away from Mack.

She had to do something to stop him, she told herself, her fear giving way to anger. She wouldn't be a part of Ty's scheme to blackmail Mack. She would never do anything to purposely hurt Mack.

But if she didn't do as Ty had told her, he would drag them all through an ugly court battle, suing for custody of a child he'd openly admitted he didn't want.

She gulped, barely able to swallow past the fear that rose to crowd her throat again. Without Ty's signature on the paternity release Lenny had prepared, he still possessed the rights accorded any natural father, rights that would supersede any that Mack was awarded when he'd adopted Johnny Mack. It was in the news all the time. Judges ruling in favor of a natural parent's right to a child and taking the child away from its adoptive parents.

She shot up from the rocker. She had to leave, she thought, her heart hammering wildly in her chest. With her gone, she would render Ty powerless, taking away the one bargaining chip he thought he had. Fool that he was, he thought she was as greedy as he, that she would be willing to do anything in order to live the life of luxury afforded her as Mack's wife. But he was wrong. Mack meant more to her than money. She would willingly sacrifice anything for his happiness and that of her son.

* * *

By the time Zadie returned with the promised cup of tea, Johnny Mack was bundled up in his car seat in the center of Addy's bed and Addy was packing.

Zadie froze in the doorway. "What are you doin'?" she cried in dismay.

Addy stuffed a stack of clothing into the suitcase. "I'm leaving."

Zadie's eyes shot wide. "What you mean, you's leaving?"

Addy crossed back to the dresser and scooped another stack of clothing from the drawer. "I'm going home. To Dallas."

Zadie bustled into the room and set the tea tray onto the top of the dresser. "Dallas ain't your home. This here is where you live now. Right here with Mr. Mack. What's he gonna think when he comes home and finds you gone? What's I supposed to tell him?"

Addy dumped the clothing into the suitcase and slammed the lid, locking it into place, then turned to face Zadie with a calm that would surprise her later.

"You can tell him to file for the annulment he promised me."

Eight

Fury burned through Mack's blood as he braked his car to a tire-squealing stop in front of his house. What a colossal waste of time, he thought angrily and shoved the gearshift into Park. And it was just like Ty to pull a stunt like this. Agreeing to a meeting, then not showing up. Wasting people's time. It was so like his half brother, Mack was amazed he hadn't expected it from the beginning.

With a weary sigh, he dropped his forehead to rest against the steering wheel. The hell of it was, now he had to go in and face Addy, tell her that he'd failed, that he'd come home empty-handed. She was going to be upset. Hell, *he* was upset! And she'd worry. No more than he would, but he'd hoped he could put to rest once and for all her fears that Ty would somehow cause trouble for them.

Heaving another sigh, he shouldered open the car door and climbed out. He paused a moment to stretch his arms above his head, straightening out the kinks sitting all day had put in his back, then dropped them to his sides and headed for the house.

He opened the door and stepped inside, closing it behind him. "Anybody home?" he called.

Zadie rushed from the kitchen and met him in the hallway, wringing her hands. "Oh, Mr. Mack," she said tearfully. "They's gone. Packed up and left."

His gut tightened in dread. "Addy's gone?"

"Yessir. Soon as Ty left, she packed up and lit out."

His heart seemed to stop. "Ty? He was here?"

"Yessir. When I left this mornin' to do the grocery shoppin', he must'a sneaked through the gate while it was still open. I didn't see him, but he was here at the house when I came back to get the grocery list I left sittin' on the kitchen counter." She pulled her apron up and buried her face in it. "It's all my fault," she wailed. "I shoulda never left her here by herself. I shoulda knowed that boy would do somethin' bad."

He grabbed her arms and gave her a shake. "He hurt her?"

She wiped her face on the apron and shook her head. "Not so you could see. But he musta said somethin' to make her run like she did."

"Where did she go?"

"Dallas. Said she was goin' home. I tried to make her

wait till you got back, but she wouldn't listen to nothin' I said. Talkin' crazy, she was. Said for me to tell you to file for that annulment you promised her."

Mack dropped his arms to his side. "No," he whispered, then spun away and dug his fists against his eyes. "Oh God, please, no."

Mack wasn't about to lose Addy. He was going to Dallas and he was bringing her and the baby back home with him where they belonged.

But before he could do that, he had to settle some business with Ty.

He didn't know what Ty had said to Addy, and really didn't care. What he *did* know was that Ty was the one who was responsible for her leaving, and Mack was going to make damn sure that his half brother never had the power to interfere in his life again.

Since his last attempt to meet with Ty had failed miserably, he decided to try a different tactic this time around.

At 9:00 a.m. sharp, two days after Addy's departure, he pulled into the parking lot of the condo in Houston where Ty was currently living and gathered the bulky file the P.I. had prepared for him under his arm, along with the thinner and neater file of documents Lenny had prepared, and climbed from his car. He shot a glance at the car that pulled into the slot next to his, then headed up the walk toward the condo.

Hoping that his half brother was true to form, he leaned on the doorbell. He could hear the continuous musical peel through the wooden door and smiled, knowing there was no way Ty could ignore the irritating sound for very long.

Within minutes, he heard the angry stomp of footsteps approaching from the other side of the door, and his half brother's muttered curses. He quickly stepped out of view, so that Ty couldn't see him through the peep hole, and waited.

The door was yanked open and Ty stepped out, wearing nothing but a pair of silk pajama pants and a scowl.

Mack pulled his finger from the doorbell. "Good morning, Ty."

"Go to hell," Ty growled and gave the door an angry shove.

Mack stuck his boot in the opening, before the door could slam in his face, and stepped inside.

"Nice place," he commented as he looked around.

Ty whirled, his face flushed an angry red. "What the hell do you want?"

Calmly Mack drew the folders from beneath his arm. "Since you missed our previous appointment, I thought I'd save us both the frustration of attempting to schedule another by dropping by unannounced."

"If that's a paternity release you've got, you're wasting your time. I'm not signing it."

"You might want to reconsider that decision," Mack suggested mildly.

Ty folded his arms across his bare chest, his stance cocky. "If you think you can waltz in here and bulldoze me into signing away my rights to the kid, you're wrong.

I'm a step ahead of you, big brother. I figured out your little scheme. That baby's mine and you're going to pay dearly to have it."

Unfazed, Mack flipped open the file folder Lenny had prepared for him. "Speaking of money, I have some financial statements that might interest you."

Ty eyed him suspiciously. "What financial statements?"

Ignoring the question, Mack peered around him. "Is there a place where we can sit down and discuss this more comfortably?"

Ty hesitated a moment, then dropped his arms with a sigh and turned away. "In here," he said and led the way into a living area that opened off the entry.

He gestured to a chair opposite the sofa. "Make it quick," he told Mack, before sprawling on the sofa. "I want to get back to bed."

Mack perched on the edge of the chair and opened Lenny's file on the coffee table in front of him. He picked up the first set of clipped documents and tossed them onto the coffee table in front of Ty.

"As you can see," he said, tipping his head to indicate the papers. "That is the Year-to-Date statement of the trust Mom set up for you, prior to her death."

Ty didn't so much as glance at the document. "So? I get one from the accountant every quarter."

"Do you ever read it?" Mack asked.

Ty shifted uncomfortably. "What's the use? It's just a bunch of numbers."

Mack leaned over and picked up the document. "If you'd bothered to read the report," he said as he flipped to the last page, "you'd know that the balance of your trust is zero, and has been for almost two years."

He had the satisfaction of watching Ty pale.

"That can't be right," Ty blustered. "Funds are deposited to my personal account every month, same as always."

Mack sank back in his chair. "Yes," he agreed. "But the funds haven't been coming from your trust. As I mentioned, that account bottomed out almost two years ago."

Ty shot to his feet. "That's bull!" he cried. "There was a million and a half in that trust."

Mack nodded. "And you managed to blow it all in a little over twelve years."

Ty dragged a hand over his hair, shooting it into spikes, as he paced away. "No way. There's no way in hell I spent all that money."

"Oh, but you did. And then some."

Ty whirled. "But I'm still getting money every month. I must have investments left that are paying dividends."

Mack shook his head. "You don't have any assets left. If you'll remember, you had the accountant turn all your assets into cash on your thirtieth birthday. Against my advice, I might add. As I recall, you wanted the cash to purchase a boat of some kind. A small yacht, wasn't it?"

Mack could see that his half brother was beginning to sweat, and knew he had him where he wanted him.

He dismissed the boat with a wave of his hand. "But that's old history," he said. "Out of respect to our mother," he went on, "I continued to make deposits to your account, using my own personal funds, to support you."

Wanting to give Ty a moment to absorb that information, before hitting him with the final blow, he leaned forward and picked up the statement. After placing it carefully back in the file, he sank back in the chair again and met Ty's gaze. "But I won't be making those deposits in the future."

The blood drained from Ty's face. "But how am I supposed to live? How will I pay my bills?"

Mack shrugged. "I suppose you could sell your yacht. That ought to be enough to keep you going until you can find employment."

Ty sagged down on the sofa with a groan and dropped his face into his hands.

It was all Mack could do to appear concerned. "Is there a problem?"

"The yacht's gone," Ty mumbled.

"Gone?" Mack repeated in confusion, though he'd already known Ty was no longer in possession of the yacht. The coastguard had confiscated it during a drug raid over a year ago, a bit of information the P.I. Mack had hired had discovered.

Ty dropped his hands and fell back against the sofa with a weary sigh. "Yeah, gone," he said miserably. "I loaned it to a buddy of mine, and he…well, he got into a little bit of trouble on his return from Mexico and the feds ended up with it."

Mack shook his head sadly. "That's a shame, Ty. A real shame." He glanced around the room, noting the expensive furniture and accessories. "Maybe the woman you're living with would be willing to support you, until you can find a job. Looks as if she could afford to."

Ty dropped his head back and dragged his hands down his face. "Not for long. She's already harping about me chipping in more."

"Well, gee," Mack said sympathetically, "that kind of puts you between a rock and a hard place, doesn't it?"

Ty lowered his chin to narrow an eye at Mack. "You knew all along, didn't you? All this talk about my finances was a set up, so you can get the kid."

Mack reached again for the file Lenny had prepared. "I'd rather think of it as laying all the cards on the table. Sounds much more civil, don't you think?"

He drew the second set of clipped pages from the file and tossed them onto the coffee table in front of Ty. "Those are the papers you were supposed to sign yesterday at the airport. To save you the time of fighting your way through all the legalese, it is a legal document Lenny prepared in which you forfeit all paternal rights to Addy's baby." A slow smile spread across his face. "But I guess you probably know what a Forfeiture of Paternity Rights consists of. You've signed enough of them over the years to know the verbiage by heart."

Scowling, Ty sat up and dragged the document closer. "So what do I get out of this?" he asked as he scanned it. "I deserve something out of this deal. I am the kid's father, after all."

"A responsibility you ran from," Mack reminded him.

Ty lifted his head and grinned. "Your gain, though, right? Come on, Mack, let's cut to the chase. How much is the kid worth to you?"

The world. But Mack wasn't about to let Ty know how much he loved Johnny Mack.

"You can't put a value on human life," he informed Ty wryly. He pulled the last set of clipped pages from the file, tossed them on top of the papers of forfeiture, then sank back in his chair and templed his fingers before his chest. "But I do feel a moral obligation to our mother. Before she died, she made me promise that I would look after you, a promise that I've honored for fourteen years. But I'm done, Ty. I won't be depositing any more money into your account, and I won't be bailing you out of trouble any longer. Your life is yours to live, and you'll have to deal with the consequences of how you choose to live it all on your own. I refuse to serve as your safety net any more."

He dipped his chin, indicating the last document he'd tossed to Ty. "I'm sure Lenny found a much more complicated way in which to state it, but that's pretty much what that document says. Your signature on the last page will acknowledge your understanding of what I've just explained to you. The same is needed on the Parental Forfeiture document, which will relieve you of any financial support required by the state and its courts now and any time in the future."

Ty quickly flipped to the last page, where a thin black line awaited his signature. "And if I don't sign?" he asked.

"As far as the document that spells out my financial responsibility to you in the future is concerned, it doesn't matter one way or the other. You've spent your trust, and what money I have is mine to spend as I see fit and I no longer feel an obligation to give any of it to you.

"But the document concerning your parental rights is a different matter. If you insist upon retaining your parental rights, then you will also be responsible for the child's support, which will be decided by a judge."

Ty snorted. "Hard to get blood out of a turnip. A judge can't order me to turn over money I don't have."

Mack flapped a hand, indicating the document Ty still held. "If you'll look at paragraph three on page one, you'll find that you do have some money. Not much, considering the amount you've blown, but enough to clear my conscience and give you the time you'll need to find yourself a job."

Ty quickly flipped back to the first page and scanned until he found paragraph three. "A hundred thousand dollars," he read in disbelief, then lifted his gaze to Mack's. "You're giving me a hundred thousand dollars?"

"If you'll read a little further, you'll discover that the gift is contingent on you signing the document."

Ty glanced down at the paper again. After a moment, he choked a laugh. "Oh, I get it now. This is a trick. A smooth one, I have to admit, but a trick nonetheless. If I sign this, but refuse to sign away my paternal rights, then I'm setting myself up to be stripped clean by some judge, who'll garnish a healthy portion of the funds as support for the kid."

Mack plucked a pen from the pocket of his shirt and tossed it onto the table. "In the eyes of the court, a child is entitled to support from his father."

Shaking his head, Ty picked up the pen.

"Wait just a second," Mack said, stopping him before he could sign his name. He rose and headed toward the front door.

"Where are you going?" Ty asked in frustration. "Let's get this over with."

"I intend to," Mack replied, then opened the door and waved a hand, signaling the men parked in the car beside his to come inside.

Ty stared, slack-jawed, as Mack's lawyer, preacher, banker, and childhood friend, Bill Johnson, followed him back into the room.

"Just to make everything legal," he explained to Ty, as he took his seat opposite his half brother again, then smiled. "I don't like leaving any loose ends."

"It's not that we're destitute," Addy assured Johnny Mack, as she cranked the handle of the infant swing she'd placed him in. "But having a little nest egg to fall back on for those little emergencies that tend to crop up certainly wouldn't hurt."

She set the swing in motion, then approached the trunk, dragging her sweaty palms across her rear end to dry them.

"Cross your fingers," she said to the baby and lifted the lid. Sinking to her knees, she began to pull out items.

"Good heavens," she fussed. "Would you look at all this junk?" Curling her nose in disgust, she pulled a dried corsage from inside, its flattened flowers yellow and brittle with age. "Why on earth did Mom save all this stuff?"

After ten minutes spent sorting and discarding without finding anything that closely resembled the torn piece of paper that had supposedly belonged to her father, Addy grew discouraged.

"I don't know why I'm wasting my time," she told the baby crossly as she pawed through the scattered items remaining on the bottom of the trunk. "If he really did send it to Mom, she would've thrown it away."

She froze when she caught a glimpse of an air mail envelope, its red and blue markings faded with time, but distinctive enough to recognize. Her fingers trembling, she pulled it from the trunk and sat down on the floor.

"It's stamped 'Vietnam,'" she told Johnny Mack, as she smoothed a hand over the front of the envelope. "But there's no name on the return address. Just an APO." She closed her eyes, promising herself she wouldn't be disappointed by whatever she found inside.

Bracing herself, she flipped up the flap and pulled out the letter enclosed. She said a quick prayer, then opened the folds. As she did, a piece of paper fell out. Her heart seemed to stop, as she watched it float to her lap.

"Johnny Mack," she whispered, as if the sound of her voice might cause the piece of paper to disintegrate if she spoke too loudly. "I found it. Oh, my God, I really found it!"

With her heart beating wildly in her chest, she lifted the scrap of paper to examine it. She frowned as she scanned the handwritten words, unable to make heads or tails of their meaning from the fragmented words. She quickly turned the paper over and looked at the back side. There she found a notary public's seal, a woman's name and what must be Antonio Rocci's signature.

She traced the tip of her finger along the scrawled letters of his name, awed that the signature was obviously written by her father's hand. "It's like touching him," she said to Johnny Mack, then gulped back the emotion that crowded her throat. "I never knew him, never saw him. He died before I was born."

She glanced up at her son, his image blurred by her tears. "He was your grandfather. Antonio Rocci was my father and your grandfather. This is his signature."

Johnny Mack kicked his feet and cooed, making the swing dance. Wanting, needing to share this moment with her son, Addy gathered the letter up and moved to sit in front of the swing.

"Let's see what the letter says," she told him and opened it to read aloud.

Dear Mary Claire,
You don't know me, so I feel I should introduce myself. My name is Larry Blair and I served alongside Tony in Vietnam. I was with him the day he died.

She lifted her head to peer wide-eyed at Johnny Mack. "The letter's not from him," she told Johnny Mack, then gulped and dropped her gaze to read on.

I know that what I'm about to tell you will in no way make up for the loss you have suffered, but I feel a tremendous burden to share my impressions of Tony with you.

I first met Tony in Austin the day we shipped out for San Francisco, the first leg in our journey to Vietnam. I didn't know his real name at the time, as the guys who'd attended boot camp with him had given him the nickname "Romeo." I guess it isn't much of a stretch for you to understand why they'd tag him as such. His Italian good looks and those dark eyes of his were hard for any woman to resist.

But Tony was a lot more than a pretty face. He had a heart as big as the state he called home and the kind of personality that made him a favorite with all the guys. Here in Vietnam, there are times when it's hard to find anything to laugh about. But when morale was low and everybody was suffering a bad case of the blues, we could always count on Tony to do or say something to pull us out of the muck.

He was a good friend to the guys he served with. One in particular, Preacher, Tony treated like a kid brother. He'd argue and fight with him some, kind of like brothers do, I guess. But when push came to shove, Tony was first in line to defend Preacher. Some of the men give Preacher a hard time because he is—well, I guess you'd say he is tender-hearted. The thought of shooting another human being, enemy or not, is something he can't bring himself to do. But Tony didn't hold that against Preacher the way the others did. In fact, he bloodied the noses of a few who dared call Preacher a coward.

As I said before, I was with Tony the day he was killed. The mission we were on was supposed to be "safe," but I guess there's no such thing in times of war. I won't go into the details of the battle, but I do want to tell you this. Tony was a brave soldier and gave his life to protect the men he served with.

The night before he was killed, Tony told me about the baby you carry. His baby. He said that he felt bad about running off and leaving you alone to take care of everything and wanted to do something to make things right. His plan was to send you a portion of his check each month. When he returned home, he hoped to find a job that paid more than a soldier's pay and be able to send you a larger sum for child support. I guess it goes without saying that he won't be able to do that now.

He made me promise him something that night, while we were talking. He made me promise that I would send you the piece of paper I've enclosed. Maybe I had better explain how he came to have this piece of paper. The night before we left for Vietnam, we were in a bar in Austin having a few drinks. We met a man there who had lost a son in the war. Since he no longer had anyone to leave his ranch to, he said he wanted to give it to us. He wrote out a bill of sale and tore it into pieces, giving each one a piece, then had a notary public witness each of our signatures.

I don't know if this will ever be worth anything, but Tony said he had nothing of any value to leave you, if something should happen to him, and wanted me to send you this.

I had hoped that I'd never have to fulfill my promise to him, and it grieves me that I have to now. I found your address among Tony's personal effects, and I'll hang on to it. I'll contact you after I get home and tell you what you need to do in order to get Tony's share of the ranch. Like I said before, there's no guarantees, but for Tony's sake, and that of his child, I hope this piece of paper turns out to be the inheritance he would've wanted his child to have.

Sincerely,

Sgt. Larry Blair

With tears streaming down her face, Addy stared at the letter, a hand pressed over the ache in her heart.

"Do you think this means he loved me?" Swiping a hand over her cheek, she lifted her head to look at the baby. "I mean, think about it. He told this Larry person he felt bad about leaving Mom to raise me alone and wanted to help support me. Even asked him to send Mom the piece of paper, in case he was killed, because it was all he had to give me."

Johnny Mack's lower lip quivered and he let out a wail.

Addy jumped up, stuffing the paper and envelope into the pocket of her robe. "Oh, baby, don't cry," she soothed, as she pulled him from the swing. "Just because Mommy's sad, doesn't mean you have to be sad, too." She tucked his head in the curve of her neck and pressed a kiss to his forehead. "You've got a daddy," she told him. "There's no need for you to cry. You've got Mack, and you'll always know that he loves you."

Mack parked his car in front of Addy's, then sat there for a minute, studying her house. The front windows were dark, but there was a light on in the rear of the house. It was late, probably too late to be making a social call, but he hadn't come this far to turn back now.

Drawing in a deep breath to steady his nerves, he climbed from his car and smoothed a hand over his hair, as he strode up the walk, knowing he probably looked like something the cat dragged in, after driving all day, first to Houston, then to Dallas. But he hadn't wanted to stop and shower and clean up. He'd wanted only to see Addy. He rapped his knuckles twice on the door, then waited. Unlike the last time he'd knocked on Addy's front door, her response was almost immediate. The porch light blinked on, nearly blinding him, and he heard her uneasy call of "Who's there?" from the other side of the thick wooden door.

"It's Mack. I need to talk to you."

A long stretch of silence followed his pronouncement, making him doubt his chances of getting inside. But then the door opened a crack, revealing a narrow slice of her face.

"Mack? Why are you here? It's late."

"I know and I'm sorry, but we need to talk."

She hesitated a moment, then asked, "About what?"

He bit down on his frustration. "Addy, would you please just let me in."

Though he could tell she'd rather not, she opened the door wider.

Relieved, he stepped inside and closed the door behind him. When he turned, he saw that her feet were bare and she wore a robe cinched at the waist. He glanced at his wristwatch and bit back a groan when he saw that it was past midnight. "I woke you," he said with real regret.

She eased back, as if wanting to keep a safe distance from him, and shook her head. "I wasn't asleep."

Biting down on his frustration, he glanced around. "Is there somewhere we can sit down? It's been a long day."

She hesitated a moment, then gestured to a doorway at her left. "In here." She led the way into the living room that opened off the entry, paused to switch on a lamp, then sat down in the chair opposite the sofa.

Willing to honor her need for distance—for the moment, anyway—he seated himself on the sofa.

"Did Zadie give you my message?"

He lifted a brow. "About the annulment?"

"Yes."

"Yeah. She told me."

"Have you notified Lenny?"

"Didn't see the point."

Her jaw sagged. "But you promised! You said if I ever wanted to end our agreement, you'd grant me an annulment."

"Annulment is no longer an option," he informed her. "If you'll remember, we consummated our marriage. An act that was your idea, if I recall."

She dropped her gaze, her cheeks reddening.

He wondered if she was remembering the night she seduced him. He did. Every detail. From the damp towel she'd dropped to the floor to the exquisite feel of her tight warmth surrounding him to the peace and contentment of having her body curled against his, as they'd slept.

"Why did you leave, Addy?" he asked quietly.

She snapped up her head, her eyes wide with surprise, then dropped her gaze to her lap again and began nervously pleating the ends of the sash that cinched her robe. "I...I thought it would be best."

"For who? You? The baby? It sure as hell wasn't for me."

She caught her lip between her teeth, but kept her head down. "F-for everyone."

"Come on, Addy," he chided. "I deserve more of an explanation than that."

She whipped up her head, her eyes filled with anger.

"What is it you want from me?" she cried. "You got the heir you wanted. That's why you married me."

He wanted to deny her claim, but to do so would be a lie. He had wanted an heir, had offered her marriage, in order to get one.

"That's true," he admitted. "Or at least it was in the beginning. But things changed. *I* changed."

Desperate to convince her, he slid from the sofa and knelt at her feet, closing a hand over those she gripped so tightly on her lap. "You were happy living with me, weren't you?"

She squeezed her eyes shut and turned her face away. "Mack, please," she begged. "Don't do this."

The tears in her eyes, her inability to answer his question proved to him that she loved him.

"Addy, look at me." When she stubbornly kept her face turned away, he cupped a hand at her cheek and forced her to face him. "Addy," he ordered gently. "Look at me and tell me that you weren't happy with me."

She flipped open her eyes. "Yes, I was happy with you!" she cried, tears now streaming down her face. "I fell in love with you! That's why I left. I couldn't let him hurt you, and if I'd stayed, he would."

He peered at her in confusion. "You mean Ty? Addy, Ty can't hurt me."

"He could've if I'd stayed!" She swept an angry hand across her wet cheeks. "He was going to use Johnny Mack as bait to extort money from you. He said that if I didn't help him get what he wanted, he would claim

Johnny Mack and I'd be back in Dallas scrubbing bed pans again."

He blinked, unable to make the leap from extortion to bed pans. "But how did you think your leaving was going to protect me from him?"

"Don't you see?" she cried in frustration. "It isn't Johnny Mack Ty wants, it's your money! If I'd stayed, Ty would have taken you to court and proven his paternity and you would've lost everything you've worked so hard for. By leaving and ending our marriage, I take you out of the picture and there's only me for him to deal with. Once he realizes the only thing he can gain out of a child custody battle with me is a child, he'll back off quick enough.

"And if he did try to fight me for custody, he'd lose. No judge in his right mind would turn a child over to a loser like Ty. Either way, I'll have full custody of Johnny Mack, and you can see him as often as you want. I know how much you love him, and he loves you. You're his *father,* Mack. I'd never try to keep the two of you apart."

Though he didn't understand her logic and found it impossible to follow, he wasn't about to question her further. She'd told him all he needed to know to convince him that she still loved him.

His smile tender, he cupped a hand at her cheek. "Oh, Addy. Though I appreciate the sacrifice you were willing to make, it isn't necessary. Ty can't hurt us. Not you, or me, or Johnny Mack. I've seen to that."

She went as still as death. "But…how?"

"He signed the papers."

She shook her head, refusing to believe him. "No. That's impossible. He was at the house with me when he was supposed to be meeting you in Houston."

"That's true, though I didn't know why he didn't show up until later. When I returned home and found you gone, I figured he had something to do with your leaving. I wanted more than anything to leave right then and there and come after you, bring you and the baby back home, but I knew I couldn't do it until I'd settled things with Ty once and for all. I spent yesterday getting all the legal documents ready that would sever my relationship with him, then drove to Houston this morning and had him sign them."

Eyes wide, she stared, as if afraid to believe what he was telling her was true. "And that's enough? His signature, I mean. That makes it all legal? He can't ever challenge the documents' validity?"

Mack snorted a laugh. "I'd like to see him try, considering he'd be questioning the integrity of the men I brought along to witness his signature."

She gulped, swallowed. "I...I don't know what to say," she said helplessly. "What to do."

He shifted to gather her face between his hands. "I do," he assured her. "Remember earlier when you asked me what more I wanted from you?"

She gulped again, nodded.

He swept a thumb beneath her lashes, catching a tear that shimmered there. "You, Addy. Only you. I love you more than life itself."

She closed her hands over his, going all but limp with relief. "Oh, Mack. I didn't know. You never said."

He looked at her curiously. "That I love you?"

She sniffed, nodded.

"Well, shame on me, then, although I'd swear I had."

She shook her head. "No. I'd remember something as important as that."

Chuckling, he bussed her a quick kiss. "Yeah, I'd imagine you would." He frowned thoughtfully, then shook his head. "I don't recall the exact moment I realized I'd fallen in love with you. It was before the night you seduced me, that much I know for sure. But I can't put my finger on exactly when, as it kind of slipped up on me, unexpected like. Kind of like the way we met. Unexpected, I mean. Seems we've done everything bass-akwards. Having a baby. Getting married. Falling in love."

He hauled in a breath. Released it, wanting to do this right. "When I proposed to you before, I offered you a marriage of convenience. I'd like to propose again, but this time I want the whole ball of wax. I want us to be husband and wife, in every sense of the word. I want us to be a real family."

"Oh, Mack," she whispered tearfully.

"Wait a minute," he said and stood, catching her hand to draw her to her feet, as well. "I nearly forgot something."

He stuffed his hand into his pocket and fished around for the ring he'd taken from the safe in his office before he'd left home that morning. Finding it, he took her left hand and placed the ring at the tip of her finger, then held it there while he met her gaze.

"This was my mother's wedding ring. The one my father gave her," he clarified, "not the one she wore when she was married to Jacob Bodean. After my mother passed away, I put the ring in my safe and that's where it has remained until this morning. Though it seems odd, now that I think about it, I never thought about giving it to my first wife. Maybe I somehow knew that it was meant for someone else. You."

He drew in a shuddery breath to steady his voice, then went on. "The love my parents felt for each other was strong, so strong that sometimes I was jealous of it. Mostly, though, I envied the relationship they shared. Especially after I became an adult. That's the kind of love I feel for you, Addy, the kind of relationship I want you and I to have. This ring symbolizes family for me, the love a man holds for his wife. Will you wear it as a physical reminder of my love for you?"

"Oh, Mack." She glanced down at the ring. "It's beautiful." When she looked up at him, her eyes were filled with tears. "I'd be honored to wear your mother's ring."

In her eyes he saw the same depth of love he'd seen in his mother's eyes when she'd looked at his father, the promise of a lifetime together. As he looked deeply into her eyes, he felt a distinct quiver in his heart, then a flood of warmth that spread slowly throughout his body, and knew it was a sign from the wife and son he'd lost, letting him know that they were glad that he'd found happiness again. At that moment he knew that his life had come full circle. An ending of one, a new beginning…and a son to carry on his family's legacy.

He pushed the ring all the way onto her finger, then raised her hand and pressed his lips to it, sealing the promise of his love. "I love you, Addy."

She lifted her face to his. "And I love you, Mack."

He kissed her deeply, wanting to show her with more than words the depth of his love. When he withdrew, he gripped her hand tightly in his. "I want more children. Sisters and brothers for Johnny Mack to grow up with."

She released a shuddery breath, then, laughing, threw her arms around his neck. "Me, too. I want that, too."

Hearing the crinkle of paper between them, frowning, Mack pushed her to arms' length and looked down. "What's that?"

She followed his gaze to the slight bulge in the pocket of her robe. "Oh, my gosh!" she cried and stuffed her hand into the pocket. "I forgot to tell you." She pulled out an envelope and held it up for him to see. "I found it! The piece of paper that my father sent my mother. It was inside the trunk, all along."

He took it from her to examine it. "This is from your father?" he asked, scanning the return address.

"No, it's from a soldier he served with. In fact, it's from the father of the woman who called and told me about the piece of paper."

He lifted his gaze to hers. "And…" he prodded.

She looked at him in confusion. "What?"

"Is it valuable?"

Taking the envelope from him, she slipped it back into the pocket of her robe and shook her head. "Not like you'd think." Smiling, she wrapped her arms around his neck again. "But to me it's worth millions."

* * * * *

*This mini-series continues with
Peggy Moreland's*
The Honour Bound Promise,
available in August from Desire.

REUNION OF REVENGE

by
Kathie DeNosky

KATHIE DeNOSKY

lives in her native southern Illinois with her husband and one very spoiled Jack Russell terrier. She writes highly sensual stories with a generous amount of humour. Kathie's books have appeared on the Waldenbooks bestseller list and received the Write Touch Readers' Award from WisRWA and the National Readers' Choice Award. Kathie enjoys going to rodeos, travelling to research settings for her books and listening to country music. Readers may contact Kathie at: PO Box 2064, Herrin, Illinois 62948-5264, USA or e-mail her at kathie@ kathiedenosky.com.

For Charlie, Bryan, David and Angie,
for loving me in spite of my eccentricities.

From the desk of Emerald Larson, owner and CEO of Emerald, Inc.

To: My personal assistant, Luther Freemont
Re: My grandson Nick Daniels

My grandson, Nick, will be leaving at the end of the week to take over running the Sugar Creek Cattle Company in Wyoming. Please be advised that he won't be particularly happy when he discovers that his ranch foreman is the woman he was to have married thirteen years ago. To ensure the success of my plan and to avoid the fallout of his displeasure, I am instructing you to intercept all calls from him until further notice.

As always I am relying on your complete discretion in this matter.

Emerald Larson

One

"**D**rop that roll of wire and back away from your truck."

Nick Daniels took a deep breath and tried to ignore the jolt of awareness that shot from the top of his head all the way to his feet. It had been thirteen long years since he'd heard that soft, feminine voice. But if he lived to be a hundred, he knew he'd recognize it anywhere, anytime. The melodic sound had haunted his dreams and left his body aching with unfathomable need too many nights for him to ever forget.

"I told you to put that down and step away from the truck."

At the sound of a shotgun being pumped, Nick slowly lowered the coil of barbed wire to the tailgate of his new truck and raised his gloved hands to show he was complying with her command. Then, turning to face the reason he'd left Wyoming one step ahead of the law, he smiled sardonically. "It's been a long time, Cheyenne."

The widening of her eyes and the slight wavering of the double-barrel shotgun she pointed at him were the only indications that she was the least bit surprised to see him after all this time. "I don't know what you think you're doing out here, Nick Daniels, but I'd advise you to get in your truck and go back to wherever you came from. Otherwise, I'll call the law."

He took a deep breath as he stared at her. Damned if she wasn't more beautiful now than she'd been at sixteen. Her long brown hair, streaked with golden highlights, complemented the healthy glow of her sun-kissed skin and her aqua-green eyes to perfection.

His gaze drifted lower. Her pink tank top caressed her torso, fascinating the hell out of him and giving him more than a fair idea about the size and shape of her breasts. He swallowed hard as his gaze drifted even lower. She'd always been a knockout in a pair of jeans, but the well-worn denim hugged her hips and thighs like a second skin and emphasized how long and shapely her legs were.

He diverted his gaze back to the gun in her hands. He'd do well to forget how good she looked after all this time and concentrate on the fact that she was ready to blow his ass to kingdom come.

"Go ahead and call the sheriff. Last time I heard, it wasn't against the law for a man to mend a fence on his own property."

"It's not your land. It belongs to the Sugar Creek Cattle Company. And you're trespassing."

He shook his head as he took a step toward her. "No, I'm not."

"I swear I'll shoot you if you don't stop right there, Nick."

"That wouldn't be very neighborly of you, sweetheart."

"Don't call me that." She released the safety on the shotgun when he moved forward.

From the sharp edge he'd heard in her voice, he knew he'd hit a nerve. He inched a little closer. "You used to like when I called you sweetheart."

She shook her head. "That's past history. Now, get in your truck and disappear like you did thirteen years ago."

"Why would I want to do that? This is my home." With the gun barrel still pointed at the middle of his chest, he wisely chose not to point out that her father had been behind his disappearing act back then, or that he was damned tired of a Holbrook trying to run him off his own land. "If you'll remember, the Sugar Creek ranch has been in my family for over a hundred and twenty-five years."

"If *you'll* remember, you gave up the right to this land a long time ago." Was that bitterness he detected in her voice?

"That's where you're wrong, Cheyenne." Easing forward a bit more, he was almost close enough to reach the shotgun. "I still own this place, lock, stock…" He lunged forward and, grabbing the shotgun, shoved it away with one hand at the same time he reached out to wrap his arm around her waist. "…and barrel," he finished, pulling her to him.

"Turn me loose." She pushed at his chest as she tried to wiggle from his grasp.

"Not until we get a few things straight." The feel of her soft body squirming against his was heaven and hell rolled into one shapely little five-foot-two-inch package. He did his best to ignore it. "When you point a gun at a man, you'd better be prepared to use it, sweetheart."

"I was." She sounded breathless and if he didn't know better, he'd swear he felt a slight tremor pass through her.

Shaking his head as much in answer to her statement as in an attempt to clear his mind, he whispered close to her ear, "You and I both know you could never shoot me, Cheyenne."

"Let me have my gun back...and I'll show you." There was no doubt that she shivered against him this time.

He couldn't resist teasing the side of her neck with his lips. "Not until you calm down."

Her labored breathing quickly reminded him of the changes in her body since the last time he'd held her. At sixteen, Cheyenne Holbrook had had a figure that sent his hormones racing around like the steel bearings in a pinball machine. But that had only been a hint of the woman she would become. Her breasts were fuller now and her hips had a slight flare that promised to cradle a man and take him to paradise when he sank himself deep inside her.

When his lower body tightened, he cursed himself as the biggest fool God ever blessed with the breath of life. He wasn't an eighteen-year-old kid anymore. He was a thirty-one-year-old man and should have mastered at least a modicum of restraint.

"Turn me loose."

When she pushed against him this time, he let her go, but held on to the gun. He shook his head when she reached for it. "I'll hang on to this for a while longer."

"Suit yourself." She reached for the cell phone clipped to her belt. "It's not going to stop me from calling Sheriff Turner and having you arrested for trespassing."

"You do that."

Her finger hovered over the phone's dial pad as she glanced up at him. "You aren't worried about being arrested?"

"Why should I be? I own the Sugar Creek." He shrugged as he placed the shotgun on the tailgate of his truck, well out of her reach. "You, on the other hand, are on my land." He stopped short of adding that her father and the sheriff would have a hell of a time getting him to leave again.

"I don't think so." She impatiently brushed a silky strand of hair from her cheek as she glared at him. "Emerald, Inc. is the corporation that bought your ranch after you and your mother left."

"The hell you say." He removed his leather work gloves, then, tucking them into the waistband of his jeans, he folded his arms across his chest. "And just how would you know that?"

She looked hesitant a moment before taking a deep breath and defiantly looking him square in the eye. "I'm the foreman of the Sugar Creek Cattle Company. Don't you think I'd know who my employer is?"

Nick couldn't believe it. Cheyenne's father, the judge, had actually allowed his precious daughter to work? And at a job where she might actually get her hands dirty? Interesting.

It appeared that Emerald Larson had omitted a couple of important details when she told him she was his grandmother and gave him back the ranch. She'd explained her reasoning behind having his mother sign documents stating that the identity of his father would remain a secret until she deemed he was ready to learn the truth. She'd even solved the mystery of who had tipped his mother off about his impending arrest the night they left Wyoming when she told him that she'd had a private investigator reporting his every move from the time he was born. But she hadn't mentioned anything about Cheyenne Holbrook being the ranch foreman. And as soon as he went back to the house, he was going to call Wichita and find out what other surprises the old gal had in store for him.

"I know this is going to come as a shock to you, but I really am the owner of this spread," Nick said.

Cheyenne paled, then stubbornly shook her head. "I don't believe you. When Luther Freemont from the corporate office called me just last week to discuss my quarterly report, he didn't mention anything about Emerald, Inc. selling the Sugar Creek."

Nick wasn't surprised to hear the name of Emerald's personal assistant. She trusted the man implicitly and relied on him to be the liaison between her and most of the managers of the companies she owned.

"I'll tell you what, Cheyenne." He picked up the shotgun and emptied the shells from its chamber before handing it to her. Then, pocketing the ammunition, he pointed to the truck she'd parked several yards away. "Why don't you go back to your father's ranch and give old Luther a call?"

"Don't think I won't," she said, raising her stubborn little chin a notch.

"After you hear what he has to say, we'll go from there." Nick pulled his work gloves from the waistband of his jeans and prepared to finish mending the section of fence he'd thought looked weak before he went back home to call Emerald. "Be over at my house tomorrow morning at nine."

"Why?"

She didn't look at all happy about having to see him again. And he knew as surely as he knew his own name that she didn't for a minute believe he was telling the truth about owning the Sugar Creek.

"We'll have to discuss the terms of your contract." He grinned. "And the last I heard, it's pretty common for a rancher and his foreman to work together running a ranch."

In an obvious test of wills, she glared at him for

several more seconds before turning to stalk back to her truck.

As Nick watched her leave, he couldn't stop himself from noticing the gentle sway of her delightful little backside as she walked away. She still had the ability to take his breath away with her beauty and with no more than a touch she could make him harder than hell in less than two seconds flat.

But he'd do well to remember that her father was the mighty Judge Bertram Holbrook, the most ill-tempered, acrimonious son of a bitch on two legs. A man who had half the county officials in his pocket and the other half scared to death he'd turn his wrath their way.

And if Holbrook had his way about it, Nick would still be rotting away in jail, simply because he'd tried to marry the man's only daughter.

The next morning, as Cheyenne drove the five miles between the Flying H and the Sugar Creek ranch houses, she wondered for at least the hundredth time what she could do about the situation. When she'd talked to Luther Freemont after her confrontation with Nick, she'd developed a splitting headache. He'd confirmed everything Nick had told her and, feeling as if her world had once again been turned completely upside down, she'd ended up lying awake the entire night, reliving the past and worrying about what the future held for her and her father.

It had taken her years to get over the devastation when Nick walked away from their relationship—from her—without so much as a backward glance, and seeing him after all this time had shaken her more than she could have ever imagined. But when he'd grabbed her to take away her gun, she couldn't believe the awareness that coursed through her traitorous body. At the feel of his rock-hard muscles surrounding her, she'd grown warm from the top of her head all the way to her toes and drawing her next breath had taken supreme effort. It had also scared her as little else could.

When they'd been teenagers, she'd thought the sun rose and set around Nick. He'd been two years ahead of her in school and the best-looking boy in the county. With his dark blond hair, charming smile and tall, muscular build, he'd been every sixteen-year-old girl's dream and every father's worst nightmare. Her pulse sped up as she remembered the heart-pounding excitement she'd felt the first time Nick had turned his sky-blue eyes and charming smile her way. She'd instantly fallen head over heels in love.

But her father wouldn't hear of her having anything to do with Nick. He'd told her the boy was nothing but bad news and a heartache waiting to happen. He'd never explained why he felt that way about

Nick, but unfortunately, she'd found out the hard way that her father had been been right.

When he and the sheriff had stopped her and Nick from getting married the summer between her junior and senior year of high school, Nick had disappeared that very night. She'd waited for months, hoping for a phone call, a letter—anything that would explain why he'd abandoned her. But there had been no word from him at all and she'd finally come to the conclusion that just as her father had said, Nick Daniels was trouble with a great big capital *T*. He hadn't even had the common courtesy or the courage to face her and tell her it was over between them.

But now he was back. And worse yet, he was her boss. How could fate be so cruel?

Seeing him again had been more than a little disturbing. But when he'd announced that he owned the Sugar Creek Cattle Company, the situation had become downright impossible.

She'd hoped when she questioned Mr. Freemont he would tell her that it was all a lie and that she had corporate's blessing in having Nick thrown off the property. But without elaborating on the details, Luther Freemont had verified that Nick Daniels did indeed own the Sugar Creek and that, in accordance with her contract, she was locked into working for the cattle company for the next four years, no matter who the owner was.

Parking her truck at the side of the big, white two-story Victorian house, she swallowed around the lump clogging her throat. She hadn't dared tell her father about the latest development. He wasn't well and hearing about Nick's return would only upset him and possibly cause more problems. And until she figured out what she could do about the situation there was no reason to worry him unnecessarily. Besides, she was doing enough stressing for the both of them.

As she grabbed the manila folder on the seat beside her and got out of the truck, she prayed for a miracle. She didn't really expect one, but at this point, divine intervention seemed to be her only hope of escaping the current mess she found herself in.

When she climbed the steps of the wide wrap-around porch and knocked on the door frame, instead of Nick, a heavy-set woman of about sixty opened the screen. "You must be Cheyenne Holbrook." She stepped back for Cheyenne to enter the foyer. "I'm Greta Foster. My husband, Carl, and I have been the caretakers here at the Sugar Creek for several years, but I don't believe we've had the pleasure of meeting."

Cheyenne wasn't surprised that they hadn't met. Before Nick left, her father had forbidden her to go anywhere near the place. And after she'd become the ranch foreman a little over six years ago, she hadn't ventured this far onto the Daniels property because it only reminded her of the shattered dream she'd had when she was sixteen.

She was supposed to have been Nick's wife and lived here with him and his mother in this big, wonderful house. While he ran the ranch, she was going to teach school and together they were going to raise a houseful of children and live happily ever after.

Removing her red ball cap, she shook her head to dispel the last traces of her troubling thoughts. "I've talked to Carl on the phone several times to let him know some of the men I supervise would be working close by, but I've never actually been here."

"Well, now that you have, you'll have to drop by more often." Greta's smile was friendly as she motioned toward a closed door across from the great room. "Nick's waiting for you in his office. Would you like something to eat or drink? I just took an apple pie out of the oven and made a fresh pot of coffee."

"No, thank you." Cheyenne smiled and raised her hand to knock on the office door. "I'm hoping this meeting won't take long." At Greta's surprised expression, Cheyenne hastily added, "I need to make a trip to the feed store for some supplies before Harry closes for lunch."

Apparently satisfied with her explanation, Greta nodded. "If you change your mind, I'll be in the kitchen."

As the woman moved down the hall toward the back of the house, Cheyenne took a moment to settle her jangled nerves. The last thing she wanted to do was go through with this meeting, but the choice had been taken out of her hands.

Before she could change her mind and run as far away as her old Ford truck could take her, she knocked, then opened the door. "Nick?"

He was sitting at a large oak desk, talking on the phone. "I'm glad to hear that you and Alyssa had a good time on your honeymoon in the Bahamas." Nodding for Cheyenne to come in and sit in the chair in front of his desk, Nick laughed at something the person on the other end of the line said. "Let me know when you hear more from Hunter about his E.M.T. courses. Talk to you later, Caleb."

When Nick hung up the phone and turned his attention on her, his easy expression faded. "I take it you spoke with Luther Freemont?"

Unable to relax, she sat on the edge of the leather armchair and pushed the folder across his desk. "Mr. Freemont told me that you were the owner of the Sugar Creek now and that I should discuss the terms of my contract with you."

His expression unreadable, he stared at her for several tense seconds before he picked up the file and flipped it open.

Cheyenne's cheeks grew increasingly warmer the longer he scanned the contents of the file. When she'd signed the contract to work for the cattle company, Mr. Freemont had assured her that the terms of their agreement would be handled with complete discretion and only a handful of people would know the real reason she'd signed away ten years of her life.

When Nick finally looked at her, his questioning expression had her wishing the floor would open up and swallow her. "Would you like to explain all this, Cheyenne?"

Humiliated beyond belief, she bit her lower lip to keep it from trembling. When she felt in control enough to get the words out, she proudly raised her head to meet his gaze head on.

"I think it's pretty self-explanatory." She took a deep breath. "Not only do you own the Sugar Creek, you own my father's ranch, as well."

Two

Nick couldn't have been more shocked if he'd been zapped by a juiced-up cattle prod. How ironic that the eighteen-year-old boy Judge Bertram Holbrook had tried his best to ruin all those years ago had not only returned to reclaim his ranch, he owned the good judge's ranch as well. If what the man had tried to do to him hadn't been so low and vindictive, Nick might have laughed out loud. But one look at Cheyenne's pretty face told him there was more behind the story than met the eye.

"All this contract tells me is that I own the Flying H and you have four more years left on a ten-year work agreement." Shoving the folder aside, he sat back in the leather desk chair. "Why don't you fill me in on the details?"

He could tell that was the last thing she wanted to do. But when she raised her eyes to meet his, there was a defiant pride in their aqua depths that he couldn't help but admire.

"Daddy had a stroke six years ago. He's been partially paralyzed on his left side and in a wheelchair ever since."

"I'm sorry to hear that, Cheyenne."

Nick knew how much she loved her father and how hard that had to have been for her. And no matter how much he despised the man, Nick didn't like to hear of anyone's suffering.

She glanced down at her hands. "When I dropped out of school to come home to care for him—"

"You had to quit school?" She'd always wanted to become a teacher and he hated that she'd had to give that up.

"I only had a couple of semesters left, but Daddy needed me more than I needed to finish school." She shrugged, but he could tell it still bothered her. "There wasn't any money for my last year at the university anyway."

Nick frowned. Bertram Holbrook had always been one of the wealthiest, most powerful men in the county. Or at least, that's what he'd always led everyone to believe.

"Surely—"

"No." Obviously embarrassed, she suddenly rose to her feet and walked over to the window between the floor-to-ceiling bookshelves. "Do I have to spell it out for you? We're broke. The only thing keeping us from being homeless is that contract."

He didn't know what to say. As far as the judge was concerned, Nick couldn't have cared less. But Cheyenne didn't deserve the burden of having to pay for the sins of her unscrupulous father or be forced to give up her dreams.

"What happened?" he asked, when he finally found his voice.

Her shoulders sagged as if the weight of the world rested on them a moment before she finally turned to face him. "Daddy had made some ill-advised investments and when the stock market took a nosedive, he was too incapacitated from the stroke to sell before he lost most of his portfolio."

"He had a lot of Web site stocks?" Nick guessed, remembering the crash of the Internet stocks several years back.

"What was left wouldn't even cover our utility bills for a month," she said, nodding. "Then, when the doctors told us he couldn't work any longer, things went from bad to worse."

"What about insurance and a pension? He should have had the same paid benefits that other county and state officials have."

Something didn't ring true about the whole situation. Either the judge had been an extremely poor planner or his thirst for money and power had finally backfired on him. Nick suspected it was the latter that had finally brought the man down.

She walked back over and sank into the chair. "After Daddy had the stroke and couldn't work, there wasn't enough money to keep up the premiums on the insurance and he'd withdrawn everything in his pension fund to invest in the stocks."

Nick would have thought the judge had more sense than to deplete every resource he had. But then, greed could do that. And if there was ever a more greedy, power-mad human being than Bertram Holbrook, Nick had never met him.

"You didn't know any of this?"

"No." She rubbed her forehead with a trembling hand. "Daddy never discussed finances with me. He always told me that I'd never have to worry about those things."

Nick would bet every dime he had that finances weren't the only things the man had kept her in the dark about. "I'm sure it all came as quite a shock when you found out."

She nodded. "I had no idea what we were going to do. Fortunately Emerald, Inc. contacted me about buying the Flying H right after I came to the conclusion there was no alternative but for us to file for bankruptcy." Her cheeks colored a deep rose. "Then, when it became clear there wasn't enough money from the sale of the ranch to pay off Daddy's medical and rehabilitation bills, Mr. Freemont told me the corporation would pay off the rest of our creditors, allow us to stay in our home and pay me a modest salary if I signed a ten-year contract to be the ranch foreman of the newly formed Sugar Creek Cattle Company. At the end of that time, our debts will be considered paid in full and I'll be free to renegotiate my contract or move on."

If Nick had thought things were strange before, they'd just taken a turn toward bizarre. But the more he thought about it, the more it sounded like Emerald had learned of the Holbrook's money problems and, in the bargain, seized the opportunity to mete out a bit of revenge for the judge's treatment of him and his mother all those years ago.

Unfortunately it wasn't Bertram Holbrook who was having to pay the price for Emerald's retaliatory actions. Cheyenne was the one who'd practically sold herself into servitude to bail the old man out of his financial woes. And it didn't sit well with Nick one damned bit that his indominable grandmother had obviously been taking advantage of Cheyenne.

"Do you mind if I keep this for a couple of days to look over?" he asked, picking up the contract. If there was a way to get them both out of this mess, he intended to find it. "I need to figure out if you owe me or Emerald, Inc."

She shrugged one slender shoulder as she rose to her feet. "You might as well, since it appears that I work for you now, instead of Emerald, Inc."

"Where are you going?"

From the look on her face, she couldn't wait to end their meeting. "Unless you have something more you want to discuss, I've got work to do."

He did, but first he wanted to talk to Emerald. "I'll go over this and see what the exact wording is, then we'll discuss it tomorrow afternoon while we inspect the herds."

"Can't you do that on your own?" She sounded close to going into a panic at the thought of spending time with him.

Nick smiled. "I could, but it's standard practice for the foreman to show the new owner around. Besides, I'm sure I'll have a few questions about the way you've been running the operation."

Clearly unhappy, she hesitated a moment before she nodded. "Fine." Walking to the door, she turned back. "I'll be here tomorrow after lunch. Be ready."

"I'll have the horses saddled."

"The truck would be faster."

"I'd rather ride."

She glared at him for several long seconds before she finally nodded. "All right...boss." Then, opening the door, she walked out into the hall and slammed it shut behind her.

Once he was alone, Nick inhaled deeply. He hadn't drawn a decent breath since Cheyenne had walked into the room. He wouldn't have believed it was possible, but she was even prettier today than she'd been yesterday. Her turquoise T-shirt had brought out the blue-green of her eyes and the sun shining through the window behind her when she'd turned to face him had accentuated the golden highlights in her long brown hair.

His temperature soared at the mental image and shaking his head at his own foolishness, he did his best to ignore the tightening in his groin. But then, it had always been that way with Cheyenne. From the first moment he saw her at the homecoming dance his senior year, he hadn't been able to think of anything but making her his wife and living out the rest of his days trying to prove himself worthy of her.

Thinking back on that summer after his high school graduation, he still couldn't get over how naive they'd been. He and Cheyenne had gone steady throughout his senior year, even though her father had forbidden her to have anything to do with Nick. Neither of them had understood the judge's intense dislike of Nick, but they'd managed to sneak around to see each other at school functions and met in town every Saturday afternoon to hug and kiss their way through a double-feature matinee at the movie theater. And despite Bertram Holbrook's concentrated efforts to keep them from seeing each other, by the end of the summer they'd fallen in love and were desperate to be together.

Nick couldn't remember which one of them had hatched up the plan to run away and get married. Truth to tell, it really didn't matter. It was what they'd both wanted and they'd heard that for a couple of hundred bucks the clerk over in the next county would issue a marriage license to anyone, whether they were of legal age or not. So he'd worked at the feed store on weekends and saved every dime he could until he had enough to make Cheyenne his bride.

Then, one hot night in late August, he'd picked her up at the house of one of her friends and they'd driven across the county line to get married. But just before they were pronounced husband and wife, the judge and his cohort, Sheriff Turner, had shown up to stop the ceremony.

Nick rubbed the tension gathering at the back of his neck. Until yesterday afternoon, his last remembrance of Cheyenne had been watching her sob uncontrollably as her father led her away from the little church to his car.

But things had a way of working out for the best. Marrying his high school sweetheart had been the lofty illusion of an eighteen-year-old boy with more hormones than good sense. He was a grown man now and no matter how alluring he found Cheyenne, there was no danger of falling under her spell a second time.

Besides, after discovering that his father was an irresponsible player who had thought nothing of walking out on not one, but three women he'd impregnated, who was to say that Nick hadn't inherited the same "love 'em and leave 'em" gene? After all, he was the one who'd lost interest in every relationship he'd had since leaving Wyoming.

Picking up the contract, he scanned the contents of the document a little closer. There had to be a clause concerning termination of the agreement—a way to free them from having to work together.

His frown turned to a deep scowl when he found it. In the event that Cheyenne quit or her position as foreman was terminated for any reason, the balance of the money immediately became due and payable to Emerald, Inc. No exceptions.

He should have known Emerald would cover all the bases. She hadn't gained the reputation of being an invincible force in the boardroom or become one of the richest, most successful businesswomen in America by accident.

As he dialed his grandmother's private number, he took a deep breath to control his anger. Although he no longer had feelings for Cheyenne, he didn't like the idea of Emerald taking advantage of her or circumstances that were beyond her control.

Instead of Emerald, Luther Freemont answered. "I'm sorry, Mr. Daniels. Your grandmother is unavailable at the moment. May I take a message?"

Nick could tell the man had him on the speakerphone and knew the old gal was probably sitting right there at the desk listening to every word he said while her assistant ran interference for her. "Maybe you can help me, Luther. I have a few questions about Cheyenne Holbrook's employment with the Sugar Creek Cattle Company."

There was a long pause before the man spoke. "What would that be, sir?"

"I'd like some more information on Ms. Holbrook's salary, the balance on what she owes Emerald, Inc. and if she's my employee or Emerald's."

Another long pause signaled that the man was most likely looking to Emerald for direction. "I'm not at liberty to say, sir. I'm afraid you'll have to discuss that with Mrs. Larson."

Irritated with the entire situation, Nick muttered a pithy curse. "Tell Emerald to give me a call as soon as possible."

"I'll be sure to do that. Is there anything else I can help you with, sir?"

Nick couldn't resist teasing Emerald's stiff and formal personal assistant. "As a matter of fact, there is, Luther."

"Yes, sir?"

"You sound like a robot. Loosen up and stop being such a tightass."

"I'll take that under advisement, sir," the man said with a hint of laughter in his voice.

Nick grinned when he heard the definitive sound of a woman laughing in the background a moment before the connection ended.

"Daddy, I have to go up to the summer pastures to check the herds this afternoon," Cheyenne said as she put their lunch plates in the dishwasher. "Will you be all right until I get back?"

Her father nodded as he backed his wheelchair away from the table. "I'll be fine, princess. Gordon called this morning to tell me he's going to stop by for a while." He chuckled. "I'm sure he's got some hot piece of gossip he'd like to share."

Cheyenne smiled wanly. She'd never cared for Sheriff Turner, but he and her father had been friends for over twenty years and her father always looked forward to his visits.

She kissed her father's cheek. "There's some lemonade in the refrigerator and peanut butter cookies in the cookie jar if you two get hungry."

Smiling, he patted her arm. "What would I do without you, princess?"

"I'm sure you'd do just fine, but that's something you won't ever have to worry about." Checking her watch, she gave him a quick hug, then grabbed her truck keys from the counter. "You and Sheriff Turner stay out of trouble."

Her father laughed. "Now what could a county sheriff and a crippled old judge possibly do to get themselves in hot water?"

"Let me think." Tapping her index finger on her chin, she acted as if she had to give it a lot of consideration. "I'm sure you'll turn down the extra cigar that Sheriff Turner just happens to bring with him?"

"Of course I'll turn it down. Just like I always do." Her father's eyes twinkled mischievously. "I wouldn't think to do anything else, princess."

They both knew he was telling a fib. The sheriff always tried to time his visits to coincide with her working on another part of the ranch in order for her father to smoke a cigar—something his doctors had advised him to cut out. But he had very few pleasures left in life and she decided the occasional cigar he enjoyed once or twice a month while he visited with his best friend wasn't going to do that much harm.

Smiling, she opened the door to leave. "Just remember, if the sheriff wants to have a cigar there's no smoking in the house. You'll both have to go out onto the back porch."

Her father waved for her to leave. "You just be careful out there in the pastures. You might run across a wolf, or worse."

Cheyenne's stomach twisted into a tight knot. She wouldn't encounter a wolf somewhere along the way, she'd be riding right along beside one.

Nodding, she ducked out the door before he had a chance to see the guilt she knew had to be written all over her face. It had been three days since she'd run across Nick repairing that section of fence and she still hadn't found the courage to tell her father about him being back in the area or that he owned the very house they lived in.

For one thing, she wasn't sure how her father would react. He'd already had one stroke. She certainly didn't want to run the risk of him having another when he learned that she was working for Nick. And for another, she didn't want or need to listen to him tell her how disreputable Nick was or that she'd do well to steer clear of him. She knew firsthand how unreliable Nick was.

Cheyenne sighed heavily as she climbed into her truck and drove the five miles to the Sugar Creek ranch house. She really didn't have a lot of choice in the matter. Even if they figured out who held the promissory note—Emerald, Inc. or Nick—heaven only knew she didn't have the money to repay it in order to get out of the work agreement.

Ten minutes later, when she pulled into the ranch yard and got out of the truck, the first thing she noticed was the bay and sorrel geldings standing saddled and tied to the corral fence. They were waiting for her to take Nick to see the cattle company herds— his herds. But he was nowhere in sight. And that suited her just fine. The less time she had to spend with him the better off she'd be.

Walking over to the horses, she patted the sorrel gelding's neck. She'd been more humiliated than she'd ever been in her life during their meeting yesterday when she'd had to tell him that she and her father were practically destitute. But that hadn't stopped her from noticing that the boy she'd once loved with all her heart had grown into a devastatingly handsome man or that whenever he turned his deep blue eyes her way, her chest tightened with an ache she'd thought she'd long ago gotten over.

"You're late."

Her stomach did a little flip at the sound of Nick's deep baritone and, turning around, she found him standing with one shoulder propped against the edge of the barn door, his arms crossed over his wide chest. She swallowed hard and tried not to notice how his chambray shirt emphasized the width of his shoulders or how his worn jeans hugged his muscular thighs and rode low on his narrow hips. As he pushed away from the barn and walked toward her, her pulse sped up and she felt as if she couldn't breathe.

"I had things to do," she said, hating the breathless tone of her own voice. "Besides, this shouldn't take long. Both herds are pastured within a few miles' ride of each other."

He nodded as he untied the two horses, then handed her the sorrel's reins. "I need to be back before supper."

"We'll be back well before then," she said, mounting the gelding.

"Good. I have plans."

Cheyenne couldn't believe the twinge of disap-

pointment coursing through her. She couldn't care
less if he had a date. She really couldn't. As long as
he left her alone, he could date and bed the county's
entire female population and it wouldn't bother her
one bit.

"If you'd like to postpone checking the herds, it
won't bother me. I have other things I need to be
doing anyway."

He effortlessly swung up onto the bay and rode up
beside her. "No, I want to see what we've got so that
when I go to the auction tomorrow night, I can compare what we have to what's being sold. Then I'll
have a fair idea of how much I can get when I sell
our cattle."

"You're selling out?"

Panic sent a cold chill snaking up her spine and
caused her stomach to twist into a painful knot. If he
sold everything, how was she supposed to pay off the
remainder of her debt?

"Don't worry, you'll still have a job," he said as
if he'd read her mind. "I'm starting a new breeding
program that will make the Sugar Creek a major
force to contend with in the beef industry. And I can't
do that with the cattle we have now."

"You're not going to start raising some obscure
breed that no one has ever heard of, are you?"

"Not hardly." Laughing, he shook his head as they

nudged the horses into a slow walk. "The Sugar Creek has always raised Black Angus and we always will. The same as the Flying H. But they're going to be free-range cattle. No more supplements, growth hormones or commercial cattle feed. We're starting an all-natural operation."

Relieved to hear that she wouldn't have to worry about finding a way to pay back money she didn't have—at least for now—she nodded. "Free-range stock of all kinds are becoming very popular."

"It's getting bigger by the day and we're missing out on a fast-growing market." When he turned his head to look at her, he adjusted the wide brim of his black Resistol so that their gazes met. "The way I figure it, between the two ranches there's a little over a hundred and fifty thousand acres of prime grazing land and plenty of good grass to cut for hay to feed the cattle in the winter months."

He definitely had her interest. It could take several years for an operation like that to reach its peak. Maybe if he was busy planning how many acres he'd use for graze, how many for hay and where and how to market the beef, she'd be free to do her job and get through the next four years of her contract without having a lot of contact with him.

"When are you going to start selling off the herds and bringing in the new stock?"

"Within the next couple of weeks. I'm going to talk to the auction house tomorrow night about selling off the cattle in lots of ten to fifteen. I think I'll get more out of them that way."

She frowned. With the cold Wyoming winter just around the corner, it seemed like a bad time to be bringing in a new herd. "When will the new stock arrive?"

"Next spring."

Glancing over at him as they rode across the pasture behind his house, she couldn't help but wonder where she fit into the equation. With no stock to feed or any need to chop ice for the cattle to get water from the ponds and streams this winter there really wasn't going to be any work for her to supervise.

When they reached a gate at the back of the pasture, she started to dismount, but Nick was quicker and jumped down from the bay to open it. "I'm betting you're wondering what you'll be doing with your time this winter."

She led the bay as she rode the sorrel through the opening into the next field. "Well, now that you mention it, it did cross my mind."

He chuckled. "Don't worry. There'll be more than enough work for both of us." Taking the bay's reins, he swung back up into the saddle. "After the herds are sold, we'll be busy planning how many acres per head of cattle we'll need, how we intend to rotate them and how many acres of hay we'll need to cut in the summer to get them through the winter."

Her heart skipped a beat. "We? Why can't you do that yourself?"

He stared off across the Sugar Creek Valley at the Laramie Mountains in the distance. "I'm changing your job description. From now on, you'll be working in the office and I'll be out supervising the men and managing the daily operation."

"Excuse me?" She reined in the gelding at the edge of the creek the ranch had been named for. "What office are you talking about?"

Stopping the bay, he shrugged. "My office at the Sugar Creek."

Cheyenne felt a chill travel from the top of her head to the soles of her feet. How on earth was she going to keep her distance from him if she had to work in his office? In his home?

"You mean until the new cattle arrive in the spring?"

He shook his head. "From now on. I've missed being out in the fresh air and feeling like I've actually accomplished something when I go to bed so tired that I'm asleep before my head hits the pillow."

She couldn't help it, she laughed out loud as she urged the sorrel across the slow moving, shallow water of Sugar Creek. "Give me a break. You can't tell me you'd rather be out in weather so cold your breath freezes on your lips or so hot that you feel like your brains are baking inside your hat."

"I'm serious, Cheyenne." He rode up the bank on the other side of the creek. "I've been stuck being a desk jockey for the past eight years and I'm tired of it."

It wasn't any of her business nor did she care what he'd been doing for the past thirteen years, but curiosity got the better of her. "What kind of job did you have?"

"I developed software for a bank's online customers to pay bills and transfer funds from one account to another."

"You graduated from college." She couldn't keep from sounding wistful.

"Yep. I have a degree in software development and computer applications."

"And you gave up all that to come back here to shovel manure and cut yourself to ribbons stringing barbed wire fence? Are you nuts?"

He grinned. "Put that way, it doesn't sound real smart, does it?"

Laughing, Cheyenne shook her head. "I'll bet your mother is very proud of you for earning your degree, but fit to be tied that you won't be using it. She always wanted you to go to college." It suddenly occurred to her that she hadn't asked about his mother. "By the way, how is she doing?"

His smile faded and stopping his horse at the top of a rise, he gazed out over the herd of sleek black cattle grazing in the shallow valley below. "Mom died about a year after we moved to St. Louis. She never knew that I went to college, let alone graduated."

"Oh, Nick, I'm so sorry. I didn't know." She'd always liked Linda Daniels and hated to hear of the woman's passing. "Had she been ill?"

Cheyenne knew from experience how hard his mother's death had to have been for Nick. She'd lost her own mother when she was very young and had it not been for the love of her father, she wasn't sure she would have survived. But Nick hadn't had anyone to lean on. His mother had never married and it had always been just the two of them.

"Mom knew she didn't have long to live when we left here," he said quietly.

"Was that why you went to St. Louis? I think I remember you mentioning that your mother had a cousin there."

Nick turned to stare at Cheyenne. The sincerity in her blue-green eyes convinced him that she didn't have a clue why he'd run away in the middle of the night like a coyote with a backside full of buckshot. And that had him wondering just what the good judge had told her about his disappearance the night they were to have been married.

"That's where we went to live," he said, turning his attention back to the herd of cattle in the valley below. "But that wasn't the reason we left here."

He could tell from her intense stare that she was baffled by his answer, but she didn't pursue the issue further. Instead she reined her horse toward the path leading down into the meadow. But the gelding balked, then gingerly held his front hoof off the ground as if it might be injured.

"I think we have a problem," Nick said as they both dismounted to examine the sorrel's left front leg. Bending down, he gently examined the inside center of the animal's hoof. "The sole looks swollen."

"It's probably a stone bruise."

Straightening, he nodded. "That would be my guess. Looks like we'll have to ride double."

She shook her head as she patted the gelding's neck. "It's only a few miles. You go ahead and I'll walk him back."

"I don't think so, sweetheart." He took the reins from her. "There's no way in hell I'm going to ride back to the house and leave you out here alone with a lame horse."

"You can go faster without me." She took a step back. "You said yourself that you have a date tonight and I certainly don't want to be the cause of you being late."

Nick stared at her for several long seconds. Had there been a bit of sarcasm in her voice?

He knew he should let it go, but some part of him had to know. "Does it bother you that I might be seeing someone, Cheyenne?"

"Not at all." Her laughter was as hollow as the old bee tree out behind his barn. "I don't know why you'd wonder something like that. I gave up caring what you do a long time ago."

He knew she was lying and for reasons beyond his comprehension, he wanted her to admit the truth. "You never could lie worth a damn, sweetheart."

"I'm not lying."

"Yes, you are." He stepped forward and putting his arm around her waist, drew her to him. Lowering his voice, he whispered close to her ear. "You don't like caring, but you do."

"D-don't flatter yourself, Nick Daniels. What you do or who you do it with is none of my concern."

"Is that so?"

"Absolutely."

The breathless tone of her voice and the tremor he felt pass through her slender body belied her words and, unable to stop himself, Nick pushed the brim of her ball cap up out of the way and lowered his head. "Let's just settle the issue here and now."

Three

When Nick covered her mouth with his, Cheyenne's heart began to pound like she'd run a marathon and every cell in her body tingled to life. She tried to remain unaffected, tried to fight the heat filling every fiber of her being. She didn't want to feel anything for him but contempt.

This was the man who had broken her young heart all those years ago, the man who had left her behind without a word or even a backward glance. He'd proven what her father had said about him to be right on the money—there wasn't anything more to Nick Daniels than a handful of empty promises and a boatload of heartaches. But try as she might, she couldn't stop the honeyed warmth flowing through her veins or the overwhelming need to kiss him back.

At eighteen, Nick the boy had kissed her with the soft, innocent reverence of youthful love. But as his lips moved over hers now, then urged her to open for him, she found that Nick the man kissed her with a thoroughness that caused her head to spin and made every bone in her body feel as if it had been turned to rubber.

When he tightened his hold and she felt the hard contours of his body pressed to her much softer curves, her pulse throbbed and she gave up all pretense of resisting. His breathtaking exploration of her tender inner recesses stole her breath and wiped out all thought of the past, present or future. At the moment, all she wanted to do was savor the delicious sensations flowing from the top of her head all the way to her curled toes inside her scuffed boots.

With her hands trapped between them, she had to grasp his shirt in order to keep her balance. But the flexing of his rock-hard pectoral muscles beneath the fabric sent her pulse racing and caused her knees to give way completely. Moving his hands from her back to cup her bottom, he positioned his leg between hers to help support her.

Cheyenne's heart stopped, then took off like a

runaway train at the feel of his strong thigh wedged against the most feminine part of her. A flash of unexpected need, so strong it sent shivers up her spine, streaked through her and caused her to moan from the sheer pleasure of it.

The uncharacteristic sound shocked her back to reality and pushing against him, she shook her head. "No. Stop."

He immediately set her away from him, then stepping back gave her a look that sent her temperature up at least ten degrees. "I guess we settled that, didn't we, sweetheart?"

His confident comment and knowing smile were as effective as a bucket of ice water and chased away all traces of desire. "I suppose we did." She took the sorrel's reins and, leading the injured animal, started walking back the way they'd come. "I'm sorry to disappoint you, Nick, but you're going to have to face facts. That spark we used to have between us is long gone."

Before she'd gone two steps, his hand on her arm stopped her. "Is that why you were clinging to me? Or why you brought up my going out on a date in the first place?"

Cheyenne stared at his large hand wrapped around her upper arm a moment before she pulled away from his grasp. "I merely pointed out that you'll be late if you insist that we ride back to the house together." She gave him a smile that she hoped with all her heart set his teeth on edge. "You're the one who seems to think it should matter. Not me."

"Whatever you say, Cheyenne." Grinning, he shook his head as he took the sorrel's reins from her and dallied them to the bay's saddle horn. "Come on. We're wasting time."

She wasn't looking forward to walking three miles in boots, but it was preferable to riding double with him. Especially after that kiss.

"You go on. I'll walk."

"This isn't negotiable."

Mounting the bay, Nick held his hand out to help Cheyenne up onto the horse. She didn't look any happier about the situation than he was, but, grasping his arm, she allowed him to pull her up to sit behind him on the gelding's broad back.

They rode in silence for some time and it wasn't lost on him that she held on to the back of the saddle instead of wrapping her arms around his waist. And that suited him just fine. The less physical contact they had, the better.

What the hell had he been thinking when he'd taken her in his arms, anyway? Why had it been so imperative that he make her admit it bothered her to think of him with another woman?

He'd acted like some kind of macho jerk out to

prove a point. And the only thing he'd succeeded in doing was proving to himself that he was more like his father than he wanted to admit.

From everything Nick had heard about Owen Larson, he'd been the kind of man who used the steamroller approach with women—overpowering them with his charm, seducing them in order to prove to himself that he could. And although Nick hadn't kissed Cheyenne with seduction in mind or because he wanted to prove his virility, he had wanted to overwhelm her and make her admit that she still cared for him.

As they crossed Sugar Creek and started up the bank on the other side, he felt as if he'd been struck by a bolt of lightning when Cheyenne had to put her arms around him for a more secure hold. The warmth of her body and the feel of her breasts pressed to his back did strange things to his insides and had him struggling to draw his next breath.

He'd gotten over her years ago and he had absolutely no interest in rekindling anything they'd once shared. But that didn't stop his body from responding to her in a way that made sitting astride a horse damned uncomfortable, if not dangerous.

Deciding he needed to put a little space between them or risk emasculating himself, he pulled his horse to a stop. "We'll let the sorrel rest a bit before we go on."

"I think that's a good idea," she said, sliding from the back of the bay.

After he let the horses get a drink, Nick ground-tied them to graze, then joined Cheyenne, sitting under the shade of a large cottonwood tree. Wanting to ease the tension between them, he searched for a neutral topic.

"Catch me up on all that's happened around here since I've been gone."

"There hasn't been much." She shrugged as she plucked a blade of grass to twirl it between her slender fingers. "Your friend, Tom Little Bear, is making a career in the Marines. He married a North Carolina girl while he was stationed at Camp Lejeune and the last I heard, they had four children and another one on the way."

Nick laughed. "That sounds like Bear. He always said he wanted a big family."

Cheyenne smiled. "His sister, Marleen, has eight children."

"What about your friends?" he asked casually. "Did Sally Hanley finally convince Doug Carson to take a trip down the aisle?"

"Yes, but they couldn't make it work. They divorced after three years and Sally ended up marrying Gerald Reynolds. They run the Bucket of Suds Bar and Grill in Elk Bluff."

They sat in silence for some time as Nick assimilated all the changes that had taken place in the thirteen years he'd been gone. But as he sat there pondering everything Cheyenne had told him about their friends, he couldn't help but wonder if she'd found someone special.

The thought caused a burning in his gut and had him wondering if he'd lost his mind. It was none of his business who she'd seen after he left. He'd forfeited that right a long time ago.

Standing up, he offered his hand to help her to her feet. "Are you ready to go?"

When she nodded and took his hand a charge of electricity streaked up his arm, then spread throughout his chest. She must have felt it too because once she stood up she dropped his hand so fast he was surprised she didn't end up hurting her wrist.

"You're not the only one who needs to get home," she said, checking her watch.

Grinning, he teased, "Got a hot date?"

She gave him a smile that sent his blood pressure sky high. "As a matter of fact, I do."

He instantly stopped grinning and the burning in his gut that he'd experienced earlier at the thought of her with another man returned with a vengeance. "Then we'd better get going." He caught the horses and mounting the bay, he pulled her up behind him.

"When you see loverboy tonight, tell him that you won't be available tomorrow evening."

"Why?"

"You'll be working."

Her glare could have melted metal. "And just what will I be doing?"

Traditionally, ranchers gave their hired help Saturday night off. But for reasons he wouldn't even allow himself to consider, he didn't want Cheyenne available to anyone but him.

"I've decided to take you to the stock auction with me."

As Nick watched the Cardinals shut out the Diamondbacks, he struggled with his insistance that Cheyenne accompany him to the stock auction tomorrow night. He hadn't originally intended to take her along. So what the hell had gotten into him?

He'd found it rather humorous when she'd mistakenly thought his plans for the evening included a woman. But her admission that she had a date tonight had tied him up in such a knot that it had damned near knocked him to his knees. And for the life of him, he couldn't figure out why.

What they'd once had together was past history and it would be completely unreasonable for him to expect her not to have moved on with her life. He had. And although he wasn't overly proud of the fact that he hadn't been able to sustain a relationship for longer than a few months without losing interest, it wasn't like he hadn't had his share of women in the years since they'd parted ways.

But whether it was rational or not, just the thought of Cheyenne in the arms of another man sent a searing pain straight to the pit of his belly and had him ready to punch something or somebody.

Taking a swig of beer from the longneck bottle in his hand, he shook his head as he blindly stared at the ball game. He had a feeling he knew exactly what his problem was. When he and Cheyenne had been kids sneaking around behind her father's back to be together, he'd never crossed the line with her, never taken her virginity and truly made her his. Not that he hadn't wanted to or that she wouldn't have been willing. But Nick had been determined not to be anything like the man who'd gotten his mother pregnant, then left her high and dry to face the consequences. And that meant not making love to Cheyenne until he'd done the right thing and made her his wife.

He took a deep breath. He didn't expect her to still be a virgin at the age of twenty-nine, but the thought that some other man had touched her and taken her innocence was enough to turn him wrong side out. That was supposed to have been his claim, his right as her husband. But that was no longer an issue after all this time.

Shaking his head, he closed his eyes and leaned his head back against the chair. Thirteen years ago, his obsession with her and her father's unexplained hatred of him damn near cost him a prison sentence and he wasn't about to jeopardize the chance Emerald had given him to reclaim what was rightfully his. But the truth of the matter was, he still wanted Cheyenne physically. He wasn't happy about wanting her. But he did. It was just that simple.

As he questioned his sanity, a thought suddenly occurred to him. He was no longer that green as grass kid he'd been back then and Cheyenne was no longer jailbait. And although he had no intention of becoming emotionally involved with her or any other woman, he couldn't think of one good reason why they couldn't enjoy a satisfying physical relationship.

He knew for certain she was as attracted to him as he was to her. And as long as they kept it all in perspective and their emotions in check, there shouldn't be a problem.

Now, the uppermost question on his mind was how to go about convincing Cheyenne that it was the best way for both of them to get each other out of their systems once and for all.

* * *

Cheyenne kept her head lowered as she preceded Nick through the crowded auction barn and up the bleachers to find a couple of empty seats. She wasn't the least bit happy about being seen out in public with him. Nearly all of the ranchers and ranch foremen attending the sale knew her and her father and she was positive that several of them remembered Nick. And although he'd changed a lot in thirteen years, she had no doubt that someone would recognize him.

Normally that wouldn't be a big deal. She was Nick's employee and there was absolutely nothing going on between them. But she'd yet to tell her father that Nick was back in the area, let alone that he was the new owner of the Sugar Creek. What if one of her father's acquaintances mentioned that they'd seen her at the auction with Nick before she found a way to break the news of his return?

Slumping into one of the chairs, she pulled the bill of her ball cap a little lower and prayed that the first lot of cattle would be herded into the arena soon. Once the auctioneer started the bidding, everyone's attention would be focused on the action in the ring and off the matter of who was in attendance.

"You're awfully quiet," Nick said as he settled into the seat beside her.

"I'm just waiting for the sale to start." She glanced

around to see if anyone noticed them. Breathing a little easier when she found that no one seemed interested, she asked, "Did you talk to the manager? Is he agreeable to auctioning off lots of ten to fifteen head of cattle at a time?"

Nick nodded as he looked over the sale bill. "I called earlier today and he said he'd be more than happy to accommodate my request."

She frowned. "If you've already made the arrangements, then why are we here?"

"Prices. I want to see what the going rate is so that I can calculate what I think we'll get for the herds."

"You could have done that yourself."

"I wanted company," he said, shrugging.

Glaring at him, she folded her arms beneath her breasts and without thinking, muttered, "You could have asked your date from last night to accompany you. I'm sure she would have been a lot happier to be here than I am."

Nick's slow smile made her warm all over, but just as he opened his mouth to comment on her ill-chosen words, the auctioneer welcomed everyone to the night's event and instructed the gate man to let the first animals up for bidding into the arena. It appeared that she'd been saved from having to explain herself, at least for the time being.

Over the next few hours, she began to relax a bit as she watched a procession of cattle, horses and sheep herded into the arena—some individually, some in lots. Surely by the end of the auction Nick would forget that she'd mentioned his date again.

What she couldn't understand was why she kept bringing it up. She didn't care that he was seeing another woman. She really didn't. And maybe if she kept telling herself enough times, she might even start to believe it.

But when the gavel came down for the final time and Nick took her hand to keep them from being separated in the crowd departing the auction barn, his smile told her that he not only hadn't forgotten her slip of the tongue, but he had every intention of commenting on it.

"Would you like to know what my plans were last night, Cheyenne?" he asked as they walked the short distance to his truck.

"No." She didn't particularly want to hear the details, even if she didn't care that he was seeing someone.

"Are you sure?"

"Yes." Why was he being so persistent?

"I'll tell you about my evening, if you'll tell me about yours."

His eyes lit with mischief and she could tell he

wasn't going to let the matter drop. "Oh, good heavens! Tell me and get it over with."

Opening the passenger door to his truck, he smiled. "Ladies first."

Thinking quickly, she smiled. "I took Sebastian MacDougal to bed with me and spent the entire evening with him."

Nick's expression turned dark. "Who the hell is this Sebastian character?"

"Just someone I know," she said, shrugging as she climbed into the truck.

"Is he from around here?"

"Not that it's any of your concern, but no. He's not from around here." Smiling, she buckled her shoulder harness. "He's from the United Kingdom."

She almost laughed out loud at the deep scowl on Nick's handsome face. If only her evening had been as exciting as what she'd just described. But she wasn't about to admit that the man in question was the hero in a suspense novel she'd been reading.

"What about your evening?" she asked when he walked around the front of the truck and slid in behind the steering wheel. "I've told you about mine. Now it's your turn."

"Mine wasn't anywhere near as wild as yours." He gave her a look that made her warm all over as he started the truck's engine. "I stayed home and watched the Cardinals kick the Diamondbacks' butts, then I went to bed. Alone."

"What happened?" she asked before she could stop herself. "Was your date canceled?"

"No. I did exactly what I intended to do. I watched the ball game."

"But you said—"

He shook his head as he put the truck in gear and steered it from the parking lot. "I told you I had plans and that I wanted to get back home before supper. You were the one who insisted that I had a date."

His evening hadn't included a woman? No wonder he'd been amused when he asked her if she was bothered by the thought of him seeing someone. Her reaction had confirmed that it did.

"Why didn't you correct me?" She wasn't about to take all the blame for the misunderstanding. After all, he hadn't made the slightest attempt to set the record straight.

He smiled. "I had my reasons."

Not wanting to listen to him tell her how transparent she'd been, she decided it would be in her best interest to change the subject. "Did you find out who I owe in the event I find myself without a job at the Sugar Creek?"

"I'm still waiting on a call from Emerald, Inc. for clarification, but the best I can decipher from your contract, you're in the clear as long as you continue to work for me." He shook his head. "If you're worried about being out of a job—don't. I have no plans to replace you or anyone else."

On the one hand, it was a relief to know she wouldn't have to come up with the thousands of dollars it would take to pay off the debt. But on the other hand, it appeared there was no way out of working for Nick for the next several years.

"It doesn't make sense to me how I can work for you and the Sugar Creek Cattle Company and still owe Emerald Inc. I would have thought that when you bought the cattle company, you'd have also gained control of my contract." She stared out the windshield at the brilliant display of stars dotting the midnight sky. "Is it just me, or is there something about this whole deal that doesn't add up?"

Unwilling to admit that the Sugar Creek had been given to him or that the mighty Emerald Larson was his newfound grandmother, Nick made no comment. Hell, he hadn't gotten used to the idea himself. Besides, he needed to talk to Emerald before he discussed things with Cheyenne.

On the surface, it did look like she and her father should owe him the balance of the loan. But Nick had a feeling that Emerald fully intended to retain control of Cheyenne's contract until it was completely paid off. What he couldn't figure out was why. And until he talked to his domineering grandmother, it would be best to keep quiet.

When he steered the truck into the yard and parked beside the house, he started to get out and open the passenger door, but Cheyenne beat him to it. She was already halfway to her truck when he managed to stop her.

"Would you like to come in for a while?"

"I don't think that would be a good idea," she said, shaking her head.

Without thinking, Nick reached out and loosely circled her waist with his arms. "What's the matter? Are you afraid Sebastian will find out?"

She placed her hands flat on his chest, but instead of shoving him away, her fingers seemed to caress his chest muscles through the fabric of his shirt. "M-maybe."

"How serious are you about this Sebastian character?" he asked, wondering how far she'd take the ruse.

"Why do you care?" She sounded slightly winded.

"I don't." Pushing the wide brim of his Resistol back, he lowered his head to nuzzle the satiny skin along the column of her neck. "When are you going to admit that Sebastian is the lead character in Baxter Armstrong's latest mystery novel?"

To his immense satisfaction, she shivered against

him. "Wh-what makes you think that Sebastian's fictional?"

He laughed. "I read the book a couple of weeks ago."

"Then why—"

Kissing the frown from her forehead, he smiled. "I wanted to see just how far you'd go with your little story."

She shook her head. "It wasn't a story. I told the truth. I took the book to bed with me and woke up this morning with it on the mattress beside me. I can't help that you assumed I was having a wildly erotic night with someone."

Nick knew that he should let well enough alone and drop the matter. Instead he found himself pulling her closer. For reasons he'd rather not dwell on, he wanted to wipe out the memory of the men in her past, to make her forget anyone but him.

"This is insane, Nick." He felt a slight tremor pass through her at the contact of her body pressed closely to his. "What we had between us is ancient history."

"You're right, sweetheart." Tightening his arms around her, he lowered his head to brush her mouth with his. "I'm not concerned with the past. It's the present that I want to explore."

As his mouth settled over hers, he could tell she was trying to remain impassive, trying to deny the myriad the sensations coursing between them. But when he coaxed her to open for him, she readily complied and melted against him.

Encouraged by her response, Nick savored the taste of her and the feel of her soft body pressed to his. Her breasts crushed to his chest, the nipples taut with longing scored his skin through the fabric of his shirt and caused a flash fire to race through every fiber of his being.

But when she wrapped her arms around his waist and shyly stroked his tongue with hers, the heat gathering in the pit of his belly tightened his groin with an intensity that robbed him of breath. He wanted her. And if the way she was clinging to him was any indication, she wanted him just as much.

Moving his hands from her back, then up along her sides, he slid them to the underside of her breasts. Her impatient whimper and the tightening of her arms around his waist when he paused assured him that she wanted his touch. Cupping the soft mounds through the layers of her clothing, he gently caressed and teased the tight tips until she moaned with pleasure.

The sound of her own passion seemed to startle her, and he knew from the sudden rigidity of her slender frame that the moment was over.

Nick eased away from the kiss, then stepping back, he smiled down at her. "Be here first thing

Monday morning. We need to start making decisions about dividing up the herds."

She blinked, then propping her fists on her shapely little hips, gave him a look that would have dropped a lesser man dead in his tracks. "I don't know what game you're playing here, Nick Daniels. But you can count me out."

If he'd ever seen a more beautiful woman, he couldn't remember when. Even with her ponytail threaded through the back of an old red ball cap and a frown marring her pretty features, she could easily win the top title in a beauty contest.

"I don't play games, sweetheart."

"Then what was that all about?" she demanded, sounding out of breath.

He smiled. "I was just telling an old friend good night."

She shook her head. "Good night is a handshake, a pat on the shoulder or a 'see you later.' It is not a kiss hot enough to blister paint."

Grinning, he rocked back on his heels. "So you thought my kiss was that hot, huh?"

"I didn't—" She stopped, then glaring at him, shook her head. "Stop trying to turn this back on me. You were the one who—"

Before she could get a good head of steam worked up, he took her back in his arms and kissed her until they both gasped for breath. When he raised his head, he was pleased to see her scowl had been replaced by a slightly dazed expression.

"Good night, Cheyenne. Drive carefully on your way home."

She stared at him for several seconds before she turned and without a word walked the distance to her truck.

As he watched the taillights of her truck disappear into the dark night, Nick took a deep breath and willed himself to relax. It appeared that convincing Cheyenne they could have a satisfying physical relationship was going to be easier than he'd first thought.

Turning toward the house, he climbed the steps and headed upstairs to a cold shower. He wasn't proud of the fact that he was consciously planning to seduce her. That really made him no better than his philandering father.

But his need for Cheyenne was a weakness that was too strong to resist. And as long as he made sure neither of them developed an emotional attachment, there was no chance of either of them getting in over their heads or being hurt.

Four

"**Y**ou were out pretty late last night, princess." Bertram Holbrook rolled his wheelchair up to his place at the head of the kitchen table. "Did the auction run longer than usual?"

Cheyenne nodded as she opened the refrigerator to take out a carton of eggs substitute and a package of bacon. "There was a lot of stock being sold." She wasn't about to tell him that she'd also been detained at the Sugar Creek Ranch after the auction, who had detained her or why.

"Is the company looking to buy some more cattle?" he asked conversationally.

Unable to meet her father's questioning gaze, she busied herself arranging strips of bacon in a skillet. "I've been told that we're going to sell off these herds and bring in all new stock."

Her father frowned. "What's wrong with the cattle we have? Aren't Black Angus good enough for those corporate bigwigs?"

"There's nothing wrong with our stock." She turned to put bread in the toaster. "We'll still be raising and marketing Black Angus beef. But our herds will be free-range cattle."

"That's going to cost a small fortune to replace all those cattle. Why in the name of Sam Hill does the company want to do something like that?" He shook his head. "It looks to me like it would make more sense to use the stock they've got and just stop feeding them store-bought feed."

"There's a lot more to it than that, Daddy." She finished making their breakfast, then, setting a plate at each of their places, she poured them both a cup of coffee and sat down at the table across from him. "Besides, it's not my place to question what's planned for the Sugar Creek. My job is to follow orders and put the plan into action."

"That's the problem with these corporations trying to play around at being cattle ranchers," he said disgustedly. "They jump on the bandwagon every time something new comes along. Then they wonder why they aren't making money."

She shrugged. "Actually I think it's a good move. The market for free range beef is really growing right now and it doesn't look to stop any time soon. More people than ever are wanting their food to be raised naturally and that includes beef free of growth hormones and supplements."

He smiled. "You do make a pretty good argument, princess. If you think it's a good idea, then I'm sure it is."

They fell into silence as they ate and Cheyenne tried to think of a way to break the news to him that Nick Daniels was not only back in the area, he was the new owner of the Sugar Creek Cattle Company and the one responsible for changing the status quo. She knew that the longer she put off telling her father, the harder it would be.

For one thing, he wasn't going to be the least bit happy that Nick had returned. And for another, he was going to resent that she hadn't told him about it immediately. But his blood pressure and the possibility of another stroke had to be considered, too. If her father got upset, it could very well cause him more problems.

Lost in thought, it took a moment for her to realize that he'd asked a question. "I'm sorry. What was that, Daddy?"

"I asked if you saw anybody you knew at the sale barn last night."

Feeling more guilty by the second, she rose to her feet to clear the dishes from the table. "I wasn't all that happy about having to be there, so I really didn't pay that much attention. But I suppose the usual crowd was there."

Her father was silent for a moment before he quietly said, "I'm sorry, princess."

She turned to face him. "What for?"

"You shouldn't have to work so hard or be going places you don't want to go." The sadness etched in his once handsome face and the regret in his faded blue eyes broke her heart. "If I hadn't had the stroke, you'd be a schoolteacher instead of working off a debt that isn't yours."

Tears burned her eyes as she walked over and knelt down beside his wheelchair. "Oh, Daddy, please don't blame yourself. You couldn't help that you got sick. And I really don't mind ranch work." She smiled through her tears. "Remember what you told me when I was younger? You always said that I was the best cowboy you ever saw."

He put his arms around her shoulders and hugged her as close as the wheelchair would allow. "You're the best of everything in my life, princess. I don't know what I'd do without you."

She hugged him back. "I don't want you worrying about that because it isn't an issue. I'm taking care of everything."

Later that evening, as Cheyenne went about the task of feeding her gelding and Mr. Nibbles, the pony she'd had since she was five, then checked on a couple of calves she'd isolated because they'd shown signs of pink eye, she thought about what she had and hadn't told her father. She'd tried to be as honest as possible without telling him a lie. But dancing around the truth was getting more difficult with each passing day. And if that wasn't enough to have to contend with, the guilt of not telling him about Nick was weighing on her like a ton of bricks.

Sitting on a bale of hay outside her horse's stall, she weighed her options. Her father's health was frail at best and she didn't want to cause him any more problems. But she had four years left to work for Nick or Emerald, Inc. or whoever held her contract. And there was no way she could avoid telling him about Nick for that long.

She took a deep breath and started walking toward the house. Her father was having a fairly good day and the news might not affect him as badly as she feared, as long as she stressed there was no danger of her falling for Nick again. The only problem was, she wasn't sure who she'd be trying to convince of that fact—her father or herself.

But when she entered the kitchen, her heart plummeted. She could tell from the accusing expression on his face that he knew.

"I can't tell you how disappointed I am in you, princess. Why didn't you tell me that Daniels bastard is back?"

Instead of the remorse she expected, a huge sense of relief washed over her. "I'm sorry, Daddy. I didn't want to upset you and I wasn't sure how to tell you without doing that."

Her father sadly shook his head. "I would've rather heard it from you than learn about it from J. W. Schaefer."

"Was he at the auction last night?" she asked, not at all surprised that one of her father's acquaintances had seen her and Nick. Being a judge in a small county, Bertram Holbrook was well-known by nearly everyone, and so was his daughter.

"He was sitting a couple of seats away from you," her father said, nodding. "But that's not important. What I want to know is why Daniels is back here. And why were you with him? After the way he left here like a thief in the night thirteen years ago, I can't understand why you'd want to have anything to do with him."

Cheyenne hated having to tell him the rest of the

news. He was upset enough and she certainly didn't like the idea of upsetting him even more. But there was no way around it. He had to know everything.

"Nick is the new owner of the Sugar Creek Cattle Company, Daddy. He's my boss now. I don't have a choice."

He stared at her for several long seconds, then to her dismay, her father suddenly seemed to be much more calm. "Really? I wonder how he came up with the money for that?" He shook his head. "Did he give you any explanation about why he high-tailed it out of here all those years ago?"

Before she could answer that she had no idea, the phone rang. Answering on the second ring, she wondered how much worse her day could get when she discovered Nick on the other end of the line.

"Cheyenne, I know this is your day off and I'm really sorry about asking you this. But I need you to get over here right away." The urgency in his voice alarmed her.

"What's wrong?"

"I've got a mare in labor and she's showing signs of distress."

"Of course I'll help. Have you called Doc Connors? He's the veterinarian we've been using since Doc Haywood retired."

"Yes, but he's tied up at the McIntire ranch with

a possible outbreak of bovine tuberculosis and he's not sure when he'll be able to get here."

There was no hesitation in her answer. An animal was in trouble and it was her job as ranch foreman to see that it got the help it needed. "I'll be there in fifteen minutes or less."

When she hung up the phone, Cheyenne turned to her father. "I have to go help Nick with a pregnant mare having trouble giving birth."

Looking a bit distracted, he nodded. "Go ahead and do what you have to do, princess. I've been thinking about giving Gordon and a couple of my other cronies a call to see if they wanted to play cards this evening anyway."

As she gathered the first-aid kit she kept for animal emergencies around the ranch, her father proceeded to call Sheriff Turner and set up a game of poker. She thought it was a bit odd that her father had so readily dismissed the subject of Nick's return, considering how much he'd always disliked Nick. But Cheyenne didn't have time to speculate on her father's abrupt turnaround. The lives of a mare and her unborn foal were dependent on her doing her job. And that's exactly what she intended to do.

While Nick waited for Cheyenne to arrive, he got the agitated mare up and walking around the large birthing stall. He'd seen this type of problem before in other horses and although it had been a long time, he still remembered what to do when a foal's head failed to appear with both forelegs.

Sometime during the stage two phase of labor the foal had failed to position itself properly for the delivery. By getting the mare to walk, it would hopefully stop her from pushing and reduce the pressure on the foal. With any luck, the fetus would fall back into the womb enough to reposition itself for a normal birth.

"What seems to be the problem?" Cheyenne asked in a soft, low tone as she slowly approached the stall.

"We have a retention of the head," Nick answered just as quietly. Keeping the mare calm was crucial and any loud noise or sudden moves could increase her anxiety and cause more problems.

Easing into the stall, Cheyenne asked, "How long have you had her up and walking?"

"About forty-five minutes." He stopped the mare to check her hindquarters. "If the foal repositions, I think we'll be okay and have a normal birth. But if it doesn't present properly, I may have to reach inside and help."

Cheyenne stepped up to take hold of the mare's halter. "I'll keep her walking while you wash your arms with disinfectant."

As he walked down the wide center aisle of the

barn, Nick was thankful for Cheyenne's tranquil presence. She'd always had a way with animals and he was going to have to depend on her to help keep the mare calm in the event something intrusive had to be done.

When he stepped into the stall a few minutes later, Cheyenne was patting the horse's sweat-soaked neck and crooning to her softly. "She's tried to lie down several times, but I wanted to wait until you returned, in case she needs our help."

He nodded. "Let's get her down and see how it goes."

Without any encouragement from the two humans, the mare immediately lay down on her side on the thick bed of straw and began pushing to bring her colt into the world. Within minutes, first one tiny hoof, then the other emerged.

Nick found himself holding his breath, waiting to see if the foal's head presented as it should. When it did, he had to force himself not to let out a loud whoop of joy.

But his jubilation was short-lived when the mare suddenly relaxed as if her job was complete. Kneeling down beside her, he laid his hand on her belly. The contractions had stopped after the emergence of the foal's shoulders.

"Damn! I was afraid something like this would happen."

"She's too tired. I think you're going to have to help her." Worry was written all over Cheyenne's pretty face as she continued to pat the animal's sweat-soaked neck and he could tell she feared they'd lose both the foal and the mare. The same as he did.

He hadn't wanted to intervene if he didn't have to. But it appeared that the matter had been taken out of his hands. Nature wasn't going to take its course and he didn't have a choice.

Sitting behind the exhausted mare, Nick braced his boots flat on the floor of the stall for traction and, grasping the foal's fetlocks, slowly began to pull. He hoped the steady pressure of his efforts would restart the mare's abdominal contractions. But when it became apparent that it wasn't working, Cheyenne moved into position beside him without having to be told what to do and took hold of one of the foal's front legs.

"Ready?" he asked through gritted teeth.

When she nodded, they worked together and, careful not to injure the animal, they slowly began the arduous task of pulling the foal from the mare. Working for what seemed like hours, but in fact was only a matter of minutes, they finally succeeded and the new baby slid out onto the soft bed of straw.

While Cheyenne caught her breath from the physical exertion, Nick quickly cleared the bluish-white amniotic sac away from the foal's nose and muzzle. To his relief, the colt immediately moved its head and started breathing without further assistance, then rolled to its sternum to make the job a little easier. Turning his attention to the mare, Nick was further relieved to discover that, although exhausted from her ordeal, she appeared to be fine.

"We did it," Cheyenne said, throwing her arms around him.

They were still on their knees in the straw and her exuberant reaction damned near knocked him over, but he didn't care. He felt the same as she did. They'd seen the mare through the crisis and had good reason to celebrate.

"We sure did." Wrapping her in a bear hug, he pulled her close. "We make a hell of a team, sweetheart. If I hadn't had your help, I'd have probably lost both of them."

As he drew back to stare down at her, the feel of her soft body against his and the emotional bond they shared from having weathered the crisis together was too strong a connection to resist. Without thinking twice, Nick lowered his head to capture Cheyenne's lips with his.

Tunneling his hands through her glossy hair, the golden-brown strands flowed over his tanned skin like silk threads and the instant his mouth touched hers, an electric current traveled all the way from the top of his head to the soles of his feet. A need stronger than anything he'd ever experienced overtook him. He wanted her, wanted to lose himself in her sweetness and forget that they'd spent thirteen years apart or that they'd never have a future together. All that mattered was here. Now.

He leisurely savored her lips as he reacquainted himself with their softness. When Cheyenne splayed her hands across his back and pressed herself closer, the feel of her lush breasts crushed to his chest sent a shock wave straight to the most sensitive part of his anatomy.

She sighed at the contact and he instinctively knew she was experiencing the same intense need he was. Her acceptance of his kiss encouraged him and he slipped inside to taste the sweetness that was uniquely Cheyenne. Stroking her tongue with his, he teased and coaxed her into exploring him, but when she returned the favor, his heart thumped his ribs like a bass drum and the blood flowing through his veins felt as if it had been turned to liquid fire.

As she tentatively acquainted herself with him, it took everything Nick had in him not to take charge of the caress. But he sensed that she needed to feel in control, needed to come to terms with what he'd already accepted. They were going to make love. And, if their inability to keep their hands off of each other was any indication, it was going to be soon. The thought sent his hormones into overdrive and not only was his arousal immediate, the intensity of it left him feeling light-headed.

Unable to remain passive any longer, he tugged the tail of her T-shirt from the waistband of her jeans, then ran his hands along her sides to cup the underside of her breasts. When they were kids, he'd never taken the liberty of exploring her body, never touched her in any way that could have been considered inappropriate. But they were no longer teenagers and as far as he was concerned, there was nothing out of line between two consenting adults.

When he used his thumbs to tease her taut nipples through her lacy bra, her moan of pleasure vibrated against his lips and sent heat streaking to every cell of his being. "Does that feel good, Cheyenne?" he whispered.

She nodded. "We shouldn't be doing this."

"Do you want me to stop?"

"No."

He chuckled. "I shouldn't be touching you. But you don't want me to stop?"

"Yes...no..." She shivered against him. "I...can't think."

"It's okay, sweetheart." He rose to his feet, then pulled her up to stand in front of him. Staring at her upturned face, he smiled at the rosy blush of passion painting her porcelain cheeks. "I'm not going to lie to you. I want you, Cheyenne. I want to kiss every inch of your body, then sink myself deep inside you and watch you come apart in my arms when you find your release." He touched her satiny skin as he shook his head. "But I can't promise you anything beyond the pleasure. I'm not looking to start a relationship with you, nor do I want a commitment from you."

His lower body tightened further when her little pink tongue darted out to moisten her perfect lips. "In other words, you want sex with no strings attached?"

Put in such basic terms it sounded cold and calculating and he'd like nothing better than to deny it. But his conscience was stronger than his desire to finally claim her body.

"I didn't want to phrase it that way, but yes. That's exactly what I want."

Five

Even though she'd gotten over Nick years ago and the very last thing she wanted to do was become involved with him again, Cheyenne couldn't believe the level of desire that filled her at his admission that he wanted her. "I think I'll be going now. You should be able to handle things from here with the mare and colt."

He stared at her for several long moments before he nodded and stepped back. "Thanks for coming over to help. I really appreciate it."

Thankful that he wasn't going to pressure her, she shrugged as she knelt to repack the first-aid kit. "No need to thank me. Taking care of the Sugar Creek livestock is part of my job description." When she stood up and walked to the stall door, he started to follow her, but she shook her head. "There's no need for you to show me out. I know the way."

Needing to put distance between them, but unwilling to let him see how tempted she'd been by his confession, she forced herself to walk slowly from the barn and over to where she'd parked her truck. She felt Nick's gaze following her as she put the first-aid kit in the back, then opened the driver's door and climbed in behind the steering wheel.

As she started the engine and drove from the ranch yard, she had mixed emotions about what Nick was proposing. On the one hand, she didn't want a relationship with him any more than he wanted one with her. She'd suffered the sting of his rejection once. She certainly didn't want to spend years trying to get over him again. But on the other hand, whether she liked it or not her body craved his touch and she wanted him as badly as he wanted her.

She slowed the truck to a stop and, taking a deep breath in an effort to settle her frayed nerves, stared out the windshield at the quiet, starless night. She couldn't believe she was even considering his outrageous suggestion. But the truth of the matter was, she was tired of always doing the right thing, of always being the person someone told her she should be. Just once she'd like to throw caution to the wind and do something completely out of character, simply because it was what she wanted to do, instead of what everyone expected of her.

But could she have an affair with Nick without endangering her heart in the bargain? Was it possible for a woman to share her body with a man and not become emotionally attached? Did she even have the courage to try?

Cheyenne wasn't sure how long she sat there waging her internal debate or when she came to a decision. But before she had the chance to change her mind, she steered the truck back onto the road and drove back to the Sugar Creek ranch.

What she was about to do was the most impulsive, insane thing she'd ever done in her entire life. But it was too late to back out now. When she pulled her truck to a stop, Nick was still standing in the open doorway of the barn and from his seductive expression she could tell he knew exactly why she'd returned.

Suddenly unable to find the courage to get out of the truck, she was aware that he had started walking toward her. The closer he got, the faster her pulse raced and when he opened the door and took her hand in his to help her down from the seat, her heart skipped several beats.

Neither spoke as they walked the short distance to

the house and climbed the porch steps. But when they entered the foyer, Cheyenne stopped.

"Your housekeeper and her husband—"

"Live in the foreman's cottage down the road." He gently cupped her cheek with his callused palm and gave her an encouraging smile. "I promise we're alone, Cheyenne."

A tiny shiver coursed through her at the sultry look in his hooded blue gaze as he once again took her hand in his and led her upstairs to his bedroom. But instead of stopping beside the bed, he led her into the master bathroom.

"We're going to take a shower together," he said, removing her ball cap, then the elastic band holding her ponytail. He threaded his fingers through her hair as he lowered his head to hers. "Then I'm going to give you more pleasure than you've ever imagined."

Tender and soft, his kiss warmed her to the depths of her soul and as his mouth moved over hers, she refused to think of the possible consequences of her actions or that she was playing a fool's game with a man she couldn't trust. At the moment, all she wanted to do was feel his hard body pressed to hers and taste the passion on his firm male lips.

When he coaxed her to open for him, she readily complied and the feel of his tongue stroking hers sent a flash fire racing to the pit of her belly and caused every cell in her being to tingle to life. Wanting to get closer to him, she wrapped her arms around his waist and splayed her hands over the firm muscles of his broad back.

It didn't matter that Nick was the last man she should be kissing or that her decision could very well be the biggest mistake of her life. She was too caught up in the feel of his strength surrounding her, his hands molding her to him and his strong arousal pressed to her lower abdomen.

Her heart pounded against her ribs and her mind began to spin when he broke the kiss and, holding her gaze with his, slid his hands from her back to her sides, then up under the tail of her T-shirt to pull it over her head. He tossed it to the floor, then made quick work of unfastening her bra.

His gaze never wavered as he drew the straps from her shoulders and she shivered in anticipation of his touch. Heaven help her, but she wanted to feel his hands on her, wanted him to explore her in ways that she'd never experienced before.

But just when she thought he was going to caress her heated body, he took a deep breath and knelt to remove their boots and socks. When they were both barefoot, he reached to unbuckle her belt. He seemed to be devoting his total concentration on each task and not once did he look at her body.

Once he had the leather strap unfastened, he pushed the button through the buttonhole, then slowly eased the zipper down. Her heart pounded so hard, she was surprised it didn't leap out of her chest when he hooked his thumbs in the elastic at the top of her panties and eased them and her jeans down her legs.

When he straightened, his blue gaze seemed to touch her everywhere and instead of feeling the self-consciousness she'd expected, she felt more feminine than she'd ever felt in her life. "You're even more beautiful than I imagined, Cheyenne." Smiling, he guided her hands to the snaps on the front of his chambray shirt. "Your turn, sweetheart."

Her fingers trembled as she slowly opened each one of the metal closures and when she finally parted the garment to push it from his wide shoulders, her breath caught. When they'd been teenagers, she'd seen him without a shirt and thought he had a nice physique. But the lanky body of the eighteen-year-old boy she'd known had grown into the impressively muscular body of a man. And he was absolutely gorgeous.

As she unbuckled his belt and reached for the snap at the top of his jeans, the sight of his bulging fly had her hastily amending her assessment of him. Not only did Nick have an impressive body, but he was the perfect specimen of a thoroughly aroused man in his prime. The room suddenly felt several degrees warmer and she couldn't seem to get her fingers to work.

"I think you'd better do this," she finally said, surprised that her voice sounded a lot more steady than she felt.

The sexy sound of his low chuckle sent a wave of longing straight to the pit of her belly and made her knees feel as if they had been turned to rubber. "You're probably right. Metal zippers can be damned dangerous to a man in my condition."

Watching Nick carefully pull the zipper down, then push his jeans and white cotton briefs down his muscular thighs caused tiny sparks of electric current to skip over every nerve in her body. When he kicked his clothes aside and she caught a glimpse of his magnificent body, her heart stalled. His chest wasn't the only impressive part of his superb physique.

"You're perfect," she said aloud.

He shook his head and pulled her into his arms. "Not as perfect as you."

The contact of feminine skin with hard male flesh and the feel of his strong arousal pressed to her soft lower belly sent the tingling sensation racing to her very core.

"You feel so damned good, sweetheart." His deep voice was rough with desire and caused an answering shiver of compelling need to slide over every inch of her.

When she finally managed to draw a breath, she nodded. "So...do you."

Caught up in the delicious sensations swirling throughout her body, she wasn't sure when Nick turned on the water and moved them under the warm spray. But the feel of water sliding over her sensitized skin helped restore some of her sanity.

She'd never in her life showered with anyone and until that moment, she'd never considered how intimate it could be. If he'd given her the opportunity, she might have even been a little embarrassed by how truly exposed she was. But Nick didn't give her the chance.

Turning her away from him, he poured a dollop of shampoo into his hands and began to work it into her long hair. His fingers felt wonderful massaging her scalp and any traces of apprehension she might have had disappeared immediately.

When he rinsed her hair, he gave her a quick kiss before washing and rinsing his own. Then, taking a bar of soap, he worked it into a lather and began to slide it over her shoulders and collarbone. Placing it in the built-in soap dish, he slowly ran his soapy hands up along her ribs to cover her breasts. The friction of his palms caressing her, the calluses chafing her pebbled nipples sent ribbons of desire threading their way throughout her body.

As he leisurely smoothed his hands over her upper torso, Cheyenne closed her eyes and reveled in the delicious sensations coursing through her. Massaging her everywhere he touched, Nick created a need within her like nothing she'd ever known before. And by the time he reached her lower belly, she was certain she'd go completely mad from the intense longing building deep inside of her.

"You're making me crazy," she said, turning and bracing her hands on his wide chest.

"Trust me, sweetheart. It's only going to get better."

His mouth came down on hers with an urgency that stole her breath and she eagerly returned his kiss with a boldness that might have shocked her if she'd been able to think about what she was doing. But with the tantalizing fog of passion clouding her mind and his hands slowly skimming the insides of her thighs, all she could do was feel.

At the same time as he slipped his tongue inside to stroke her tender inner recesses, he placed one arm around her back to steady her, then used his other hand to part the delicate folds of her femininity. Sparkles of light danced behind her closed eyes and her knees threatened to give way at the exquisite tightening in her womb.

Just when she thought she'd go into total melt-down, he gently broke the kiss and, putting a bit of space between them, handed her the soap. "I scrubbed your back, now it's your turn to scrub mine."

Cheyenne realized that in slowing down his sensual exploration, he was actually heightening her anticipation of things to come. Taking a deep breath, she smiled as she ran the bar of soap over his heavily muscled chest and rippling stomach.

"I don't know how to tell you this, cowboy. But you need a lesson in female anatomy if you think that was my back."

His sexy grin caused her stomach to flutter. "I'll tell you what. I'll teach you about the male body, if you'll teach me about a woman's."

Her heart skipped several beats when he took the soap from her. She'd bet her next paycheck that he knew a lot more about the female form than she knew about a man.

"Lesson number one," he continued, guiding her hand to him. "This is what you do to me, how much you make me want you."

At the same time as her fingers encircled his engorged flesh, Cheyenne watched his jaw tighten and his eyes close a moment before he shuddered against her. An overwhelming sense of feminine power overtook her as she explored his body. Testing the strength and weight of him, she had no doubt about the depth of his desire for her.

He suddenly opened his eyes and caught her hands in his to hold them to his chest. "I think we'd better dry off and take this to bed while I still have the strength to walk."

Turning off the shower, he dried them both with fluffy towels, then giving her a kiss so tender it brought tears to her eyes, he picked her up and carried her into the bedroom. When he set her on her feet beside the bed, she pulled the comforter back and lay down while he turned on the bedside lamp and removed a foil packet from the nightstand.

She caught her lower lip between her teeth to keep it from trembling as she watched him place the condom under his pillow. She was nervous, but her anxiety had nothing to do with having second thoughts and everything to do with her inexperience. But when Nick stretched out beside her, then gathered her to him, her apprehension was quickly forgotten as the feel of his strength overwhelmed her.

His mouth touched hers in a feathery kiss. "I wanted to take this slow, but I'm so damned hot for you, I'm not sure that's going to be an option."

Before she could respond, his lips claimed hers and his need, the taste of his passion sent pleasure racing to every cell of her being. As his tongue swept over her mouth, then darted inside to stroke her, she savored his hunger and reveled in the excitement building deep within her.

When he slid his callused palm along her side, then caressed her breast, a heavy coil of need settled in the pit of her stomach and she couldn't stop a frustrated moan from escaping on her ragged sigh. Wanting to touch him, to explore his incredible body the way he was exploring hers, Cheyenne placed her hands on the thick pads of his pectoral muscles. His flat male nipples puckered in response and his groan of pleasure rumbled up from deep in his chest.

He nibbled kisses along the column of her throat to her collarbone, then down the slope of her breast, causing her breath to come out in tiny little puffs. But as his mouth closed over the hardened peak, the sensation of his warm, wet tongue on her sensitized skin had her wondering if she would ever breathe again.

"You're so soft...so sweet," he murmured as he slowly moved his hand down her abdomen to the juncture of her thighs.

She gasped when he parted her, then teased her with a gossamer touch. The tightening deep inside her lower belly increased tenfold and she couldn't seem to lie still.

"Nick, please!"

"Easy, sweetheart," he whispered as he continued

to tease the tiny nub of intense sensation. "I'll take care of you."

A tremor passed through her and she caught her breath at the empty ache forming in her lower body. "I need...please—"

His kiss was so tender, so poignant she felt as if she would melt. "Do you want me, Cheyenne?"

"Yes."

"Now?"

"Yes."

"Where?"

She was quickly losing her mind and all he could do was ask questions?

"Please...I need you...inside."

He raised his head and gave her a smile filled with the promise of things to come before he reached beneath the pillow for the foil packet. Her heart raced and her breathing became shallow as she watched him arrange their protection.

But when he nudged her knees apart, then settled himself over her, she closed her eyes and braced herself for whatever happened next.

"Look at me, Cheyenne."

When she did as he commanded, he held her gaze with his as he guided himself to her, then slowly, carefully pushed his hips forward. The exquisite pressure she felt as her body stretched to accommodate him was indescribable and instead of the pain she expected, her entire being hummed with a longing to be completely filled by him.

Nick could have never in his wildest dreams imagined the incredible degree of hunger that Cheyenne instilled in him. It was as if he'd finally found the other half of himself when he fitted his body to hers to make them one.

But as he savored the feeling, his heart suddenly stalled and he went completely still at the barrier he met within her. "What the hell—"

The unusual tightness surrounding him, the unexpected resistance and the flash of pain clouding her aqua eyes could only mean one thing. Until that moment Cheyenne had never been with a man.

"You're a virgin," he said, careful to hold his lower body perfectly still.

"Not…anymore." She gave him a tremulous smile. "I'm pretty sure…you just took care…of that…issue," she said breathlessly.

"But you're twenty-nine."

"And you're thirty-one." She grinned. "But I don't think either of us is ready for social security just yet."

"You've never done this before." He knew he wasn't making a hell of a lot of sense. But he was having the devil of a time believing that in the past thirteen years she hadn't found someone she wanted to be with. At least once.

"Does that make a difference?" she asked, suddenly sounding defensive.

Gathering her to him, he smiled as he kissed her stubborn little chin. "No, sweetheart. It doesn't make a damn bit of difference. I just wish that you had told me, that's all."

"Why?"

"Because if I hadn't been trying to take things slowly and make this last, I could have hurt you more than I did."

His body demanded that he complete the act of making her his, but he gritted his teeth and did his best to ignore it. Cheyenne needed time to adjust to the changes caused by his invasion.

She reached up to touch his cheek with her delicate hand. "I'm fine. Really."

"Are you sure?" Her eyes had softened and her body had relaxed some, but he needed to make sure.

When she nodded, he slowly pulled back, then moved forward, ever watchful for any sign of her discomfort. Detecting none, he set a slow pace and all too soon he felt himself climbing the peak of fulfillment.

Unwilling to complete the journey without her, Nick reached between them to lightly caress her feminine secrets. Her immediate tightening around him indicated that she was reaching for the summit and, deepening his strokes, he held himself in check as she found her pleasure and came apart in his arms.

Only then did he unleash the tight control he'd struggled to maintain and give in to his own release. He hoarsely whispered her name as he thrust into her one final time and felt the triumphant of completion as he emptied himself deep inside her tight body.

Several moments later, when he found the strength to lever himself away from her, he rolled to the side and gathered her into his arms. "Are you all right?"

"I can't believe how incredible that was." The awe in her soft voice reassured him that she hadn't found the experience as unpleasant as he'd feared it might be after learning it was her first time.

"I promise that next time will be even better," he said, kissing the top of her head.

She snuggled closer. "I don't see how that's possible."

Chuckling, he leisurely ran his hands over her satiny skin. "Just give me a minute or two to recover and I'll show you."

They lay in companionable silence for several long moments before she raised up to glance at the clock on the nightstand. "Oh, dear heavens! I didn't realize it was so late."

She started to pull from his arms, but Nick held her close. "What's your hurry, sweetheart?"

"I need to get home."

He brushed his lips over hers. "Spend the night with me, Cheyenne."

"I can't. I have to get home to see about my father. He'll be worried." When she tried to get up a second time, Nick let her go.

As he watched, she scurried into the bathroom and when she emerged a couple of minutes later she was fully dressed.

Rising from the bed, he removed a fresh pair of jeans from his closet and pulled them on. "I'll walk you out to your truck."

"There's no need." Her expression was unconcerned as she shrugged one slender shoulder. "That's the beauty of a 'no-strings' arrangement. You don't have to observe the conventions of a relationship."

"Maybe so, but that doesn't mean a man shouldn't be a gentleman about things," he growled. It was completely ridiculous, but her words irritated the hell out of him. "Besides, I want to kiss you goodnight."

Her smile sent his blood pressure soaring. "A simple kiss was what got all this started in the first place."

Placing his arm around her shoulders, he walked her down the stairs and out onto the front porch. "If

I kiss you again, will you reconsider spending the night with me?"

"No."

He kissed her until they both gasped for breath. "You're sure?"

She looked a little dazed as she started down the porch steps. "Right now, I'm not even sure of my own name."

"Good night, *Cheyenne*," he said, laughing.

As he watched her truck disappear down the lane, Nick leaned his shoulder against the newel post and stared up at the night sky. Nothing would have pleased him more than to spend the night with her, then wake up tomorrow morning with her in his arms.

When his body tightened at the pleasant thought, he shook his head to clear it. "That doesn't sound like a no-strings affair," he muttered, suddenly disgusted with himself.

Walking back into the house, he headed straight for the bathroom and a cold shower. How the hell could he still burn for her after the most incredible sex of his life?

But some time later, as he lay shivering in his empty bed, Nick was still having a problem wrapping his mind around the idea that up until a couple of hours ago, Cheyenne had still been a virgin. Surely she'd had other boyfriends after he left Wyoming— if not in high school, at least in college.

Why had she waited until now to lose her virginity? Hadn't she found a guy in the past thirteen years that she'd had special feelings for?

When they'd been teenagers, she'd certainly given every indication that she'd thought he was that special. But out of respect for her and not wanting to be anything like the man who'd spawned him, Nick had been determined to make Cheyenne his wife first.

With his heart racing, his body jackknifed and he sat straight up in bed. Had she waited all this time because she hadn't felt as close with any other man as she had with him? Did she still feel that way?

His mind reeled from the implications. Earlier, in the barn when he'd laid his cards on the table and told her up-front that he didn't want a relationship with her, but that he did want them to have sex, she hadn't been able to get away from him fast enough. But not fifteen minutes later, she'd come back and accepted his terms. Then, after honoring him with the gift of being the first man to touch her, of making the most amazing love with him, she'd reminded him theirs was a no-strings affair.

Collapsing back against his pillow, Nick shook his head. How the hell was a man supposed to understand what was going on when he was getting such mixed signals? And why was he letting it get to him?

He hadn't come back to Wyoming to take up

where he left off with Cheyenne Holbrook, nor did he want to. Unbeknown to him, his mother had requested that after her death Emerald hold his land in order for him to reclaim it when she decided he was ready. That's why he'd returned and that's exactly what he intended to do.

Besides, he and Cheyenne were two different people now and it was best the way things had turned out. The likelihood of them sharing anything more than a few laughs over old times and some really amazing sex was slim at best.

After all, he was Owen Larson's son and he'd proven time and again that relationships weren't his strong suit. It was probably just a matter of time before he lost interest in Cheyenne and the last thing he wanted to do was hurt her.

He frowned as he stared up at the ceiling. But she seemed to be doing all right with their arrangement—maybe even better than he was. He couldn't believe the level of irritation that ran through him when she'd told him that he didn't have to walk her out to her truck. But that was probably due to her inexperience with the dynamics of a no-strings affair. She didn't realize that whether emotions were involved or not, after a woman shared her body with a man, she deserved to be treated like a lady.

Satisfied that he had it all figured out and once

again had his priorities straight, he turned to his stomach and concentrated on getting a good night's sleep. But instead of ways to improve the ranch or the new free-range program he intended to start, his last thoughts before he went to sleep were of making love to a beautiful girl with long golden-brown hair and aqua eyes named Cheyenne.

Six

"**D**addy, did you hear anything unusual after I got home last night?" Cheyenne asked her father as she came in from outside.

When her father looked up from the crossword puzzle he'd been working, he shook his head. "No, why, princess?"

"Because I have four flat tires on my pickup truck." Walking straight to the phone, she punched in the number for the county sheriff's office. "And it looks like someone used an ice pick to puncture holes in the side walls."

His expression indignant, he slapped his puzzle

book down on the table. "Who in tarnation would have the nerve to come onto my property and do such a despicable thing?"

Cheyenne held up her index finger to silence his outburst when the county dispatcher picked up on the other end of the line. "Wilma, this is Cheyenne Holbrook. Could you please send a patrol car out to the Flying H Ranch? I'm afraid we've had some trouble with vandals."

"Cheyenne, honey, are you and your dad all right?" the woman asked anxiously.

"We're fine. But I can't say the same for my truck." Cheyenne sighed. "I have four tires that resemble Swiss cheese."

"I'll send Gordon out right away to take your statement and fill out a report."

Cheyenne cringed at the sound of the sheriff's name. She'd never liked Gordon Turner and the less she had to do with him the better. "That's not necessary, Wilma. Just send one of the deputies."

"Good heavens, Cheyenne. Are you looking to get me fired? Gordon is going to insist on taking care of this himself since it happened out there at the judge's ranch."

The woman immediately turned away to radio the sheriff. When she came back on the line, Wilma announced, "He says he'll be there in about twenty minutes."

Sighing, Cheyenne thanked the woman, then hung up the phone. For the sake of her father's pride very few people knew that they were no longer the owners of the Flying H. She supposed having to deal with Sheriff Turner was a small price to pay to keep her father's dignity intact.

"Is Gordon on his way?" her father asked, backing his wheelchair away from the table.

She nodded. "Wilma said he should be here in a few minutes."

Her father waved his hand toward the door. "Push me out onto the back porch. I want to make sure he knows who to question about this trouble."

She pushed his wheelchair out onto the covered porch, then locked the wheels. "We've never had this kind of problem before. Why would you think you know who punctured my tires when I can't think of a soul who would do something like this?"

"Think about it, princess. We've never had trouble like this before." He pointed to the west. "But Nick Daniels moves back into the area and in sight of a week you have four flat tires. Didn't I always tell you he was nothing but bad news?"

Shocked by his vehemence, she shook her head.

"No, Daddy. I don't think so. What would Nick gain by vandalizing my truck?"

"He could be trying to get you to quit your job." Her father sounded a little less passionate, but no less convinced that Nick was guilty of the crime.

"If he didn't want me working for him, I'm certain Nick would tell me so and terminate my contract with the Sugar Creek Cattle Company."

"I'm not so sure about that," her father said stubbornly. "That boy was up to no good thirteen years ago and you can bet he's up to no good now. Once a troublemaker, always a troublemaker."

Cheyenne patted his shoulder in an effort to calm him down as they waited for the sheriff to arrive. She wasn't about to tell him that unless it was some kind of bizarre mating ritual no one ever heard of, she seriously doubted that Nick would flatten all four of her tires after making love to her so tenderly only a few hours before.

"Whatever you say, Daddy."

"I mean it, Cheyenne." He took hold of her hand. "There are things about that Daniels boy you don't know anything about."

His insistence and the earnest expression on his face unsettled her. "What are you talking about, Daddy? I don't remember—"

"You know I'm not at liberty to talk about the aspects of past cases, princess," he interrupted. "But believe me when I tell you, that boy is no good and never will be."

"Nick?"

Looking up from the ranch records, he smiled. "What can I do for you, Greta?"

"Cheyenne's here."

"It's about damn time. She's over three hours late."

At first, he'd wondered if she'd overslept. But the later it got, he'd started to worry that he might have hurt her more last night than she'd let on.

Standing up, Nick walked around the desk, but something about his housekeeper's frown stopped him dead in his tracks. "What's up?"

"Sheriff Turner is with her. They're in the great room." Greta lowered her voice. "Do you want me to call Carl?"

Nick had no idea why he was being paid a visit by Gordon Turner, but he was no longer an inexperienced teenage boy. He could fight his own battles and he damned well wasn't going to let the man run roughshod over him again.

"There's no need to call Carl, Greta. I can take care of whatever the sheriff wants."

He waited until the woman started back toward the kitchen before he crossed the hall into the great room.

"Sheriff Turner. Cheyenne." He nodded a greeting. "I'm guessing this isn't a social call."

Turner grunted. "Not hardly. Just where were you last night, Daniels? And what were you up to?" The sheriff's sanctimonious expression was meant to intimidate, but only served to make him look like a puffed-up bullfrog.

"I've already told you that Nick and I had to help a mare with a difficult birth," Cheyenne said, turning on the man.

Sheriff Turner shook his head. "I want to hear where he was after you left here to go home. And I want to hear it from him, not you, Ms. Holbrook." Turning back to Nick, he narrowed his eyes. "I'm waiting, Daniels."

Nick met the man's accusing glare head on. "I was right here all night."

"Is there someone who can verify that?"

"No. After Cheyenne left, I was alone the rest of the evening." Nick didn't like the sheriff's condescending attitude or the direction his questioning was headed. "Why do you ask?"

A vein began to throb at the man's temple. "I'm the one asking the questions here. All I want from you is answers."

"Oh, for heaven's sake. It's not like it's a state secret, Sheriff." Cheyenne looked angry enough to bite nails in two. "Someone punctured all four of my truck tires last night," she said, turning to Nick. "I tried to tell him that you had nothing to do with it, but he won't listen."

Sheriff Turner stubbornly folded his arms over his barrel chest. "The judge said to question Daniels here, and that's what I'm doing."

Anger, swift and hot welled up inside of Nick at the mention of the judge. It appeared that disabled or not, His Honor, Bertram Holbrook, still had Gordon Turner dancing to his tune.

"Are you accusing me of having something to do with the vandalism, Sheriff?"

"I didn't say that." Some of the sheriff's arrogance seemed to slip and he couldn't quite meet Nick's steady gaze. "I'm just trying to investigate what happened."

"I was here. Alone." Nick hardened his voice so there was no mistaking his meaning. "And unless you have evidence that says otherwise, I suggest you look elsewhere for whoever caused the trouble, because it wasn't me."

A dull flush colored Sheriff Turner's puffy cheeks. "I'll be watching you, Daniels. Don't think I won't." When he turned to leave, he motioned for Cheyenne to follow him. "Come on, Ms. Holbrook. I'll give you a ride back home."

Cheyenne shook her head. "I'll have Nick drive me home later."

"Your father—"

"Knows that I'll be home later," she said, glaring at the man.

The sheriff looked as if he wanted to argue the point, but when it was clear that Cheyenne was going to stand her ground, Turner wisely chose to leave without her.

"I'm so sorry about this, Nick," she said when they heard the front door close. "I tried to tell my father and the sheriff that I didn't think you had anything to do with the incident, but they wouldn't listen. They insisted that you needed to be questioned about it since you'd been in trouble before."

He frowned. Unless she was talking about the night they tried to elope, he'd never in his entire life done anything to land his ass in trouble with the law. And it didn't set well that after he'd moved to St. Louis he'd been falsely accused of doing things without the benefit of being there to defend himself.

"Would you like to refresh my memory? I don't seem to recall doing anything illegal. Just what was it that I was supposed to have done?"

She looked confused. "I'm not sure. Daddy said he couldn't talk about past cases. But I told him that I was sure if you had done something it couldn't have been anything more than a boyish prank."

Although he'd never been able to figure out why, Nick had always known the judge had no use for him. But he'd never dreamed the man would stoop so low as to make up a pack of lies about him.

More furious than he could ever remember, he chose his words very carefully. "Out of respect for you, I'm not going to call your father a liar, Cheyenne. But rest assured, I have never in my entire life broken the law. Not at eighteen. Not now."

"I don't...understand."

He could tell that his impassioned statement and the intensity in his voice startled her. He regretted that. But it couldn't be helped. It was past time for her to face facts. Everything she'd been led to believe about him had been colored by her father's hatred toward Nick's family.

But as much as he wanted to set the record straight, he needed time for his anger to cool. When he explained why he and his mother had left Wyoming in the dead of night, he fully intended to keep his head about him and his temper in check. None of it was Cheyenne's fault and he didn't want to leave her with the impression that he blamed her.

"Don't worry about it, sweetheart. We'll discuss it later." Taking her in his arms, he pressed a kiss to her forehead. "Do you have any idea how amazing you were last night?"

"Not really." He felt some of her tension ease away as he held her close. "I'm not sure…"

When he nibbled at the delicate hollow behind her ear, her voice trailed off. "Were you sore this morning?"

Her porcelain cheeks colored a pretty pink. "A little."

"I'm sorry, sweetheart." He hated that he'd caused her even the slightest discomfort. But he could damn sure see that it didn't happen again. "We'll have to wait a few days before we make love again."

"Don't you mean *have sex?*"

Leaning back, he frowned. "Same thing."

She shook her head. "Making love carries the connotation of an emotional attachment. Having sex is the coming together of two individuals for the purpose of mutual satisfaction." She pulled from his arms and started walking toward his office. "But I'm not here to argue semantics with you. I'm here to get some work done."

It made absolutely no sense, but Nick had the urge to punch something. What Cheyenne said was true. Theirs was an affair with no emotional involvement. That's what he wanted and that's what she was giving him.

But every time she reminded him of that fact it pissed him off. And for the life of him, he had no idea why.

By Friday afternoon, Cheyenne found it extremely hard to concentrate as she sat in Nick's office staring at the preliminary list of cattle to be taken to auction on Saturday night. She'd spent most of the week thinking about the tire incident and Nick's assurance that he'd had no part in it.

Her father and the sheriff continued to suspect he'd been responsible for the vandalism, but it really made no sense. For one thing, puncturing tires was more of a juvenile act than something a grown man would do. And for another, she couldn't think of a single thing that Nick would gain from it.

Her father insisted that Nick had been in trouble with the law when he was younger, and he'd never lied to her. But Nick had been very convincing when he'd sworn that he hadn't. And unless she counted him telling her when they were teenagers that he'd love her until his dying day, to her knowledge he'd always been truthful with her, too.

So who was she supposed to believe? A father who had always had her best interest at heart? Or the man who had captured her heart when she was sixteen and really never let it go?

Her breath caught and she had to swallow around

the sudden tightening in her throat. Did she still love
him? Was that the reason she'd made the uncharacteristic decision to have an affair with him?

Glancing up, she looked at Nick sitting across the
desk from her. In some ways he hadn't changed since
they were teenagers and in others he seemed to be a
entirely different person than he had all those years
ago. There was an edge to him now, a strength that
she hadn't noticed when they were kids.

When he'd talked to the sheriff, she'd been left
with the distinct impression that Nick wasn't the type
of man to start a fight, but he definitely wouldn't back
down from one. And she'd bet every last thing she
owned that whether it was a physical or verbal battle, he'd be the last man standing once the final punch
had been thrown.

Coupled with the gentle way he'd always treated
her, his commanding presence and take-charge attitude only added to his sex appeal. And it was no
wonder she found him completely irresistible.

Suddenly feeling as if the walls were closing in on
her, she stood up. "I'm going to take a break and get
a breath of fresh air." When he looked up from the
ranch's cattle registries, she added, "I'll be back in a
few minutes."

"I could use a break, too." He rose to his feet and
started around the desk, but to Cheyenne's relief the

phone rang. When he checked the caller ID, he smiled apologetically. "I need to take this call."

"That's fine." Actually, it was more than fine with her. Her sole reason for taking a break had been to spend a few minutes alone to try to sort through her feelings. "I'll be on the porch when you're finished with your phone call."

As she walked out onto the front porch and sat down on the suspended wooden swing, she stared out at the mountains in the distance. What in heaven's name was she going to do?

She was caught in an impossible situation with no way out. She loved Nick—had always loved him. For years, she'd tried to tell herself that she'd gotten over him, that she'd only had a foolish schoolgirl crush she'd mistaken for love.

But now she knew that hadn't been the case. All he'd had to do was kiss her and she was right back where she'd been thirteen years ago. She'd given her heart to him then, and as much as she would like to take it back now, she couldn't. Unfortunately for her, he'd made it clear that he didn't want it now any more than he had back then.

Her breath caught at the futility of it all. If she had the money to pay the balance on the promissory note she'd signed with Emerald, Inc., she'd resign as foreman of the Sugar Creek Cattle Company and move her and her father as far away as possible. But she didn't have enough in her meager savings account to even pay the interest on the loan.

Biting her lower lip to keep it from trembling, she didn't see any way out of the situation. She was trapped for the next four years, listening to her father's constant reminder that the man she loved was no good and couldn't be trusted, and knowing there was no chance of Nick ever loving her in return.

She took a deep shuddering breath. He was, and always had been, her biggest weakness and she'd made a huge mistake in thinking she could settle for anything less than his love.

But was she strong enough to call a halt to their "no-strings" affair, then work with him day in and day out until she'd fulfilled her contract? Would she be able to walk away at the end of the four years without making a fool of herself? More importantly, could she hide her feelings for that long without him finding out the way she felt about him?

Deciding she didn't have a choice, she stood up. If she had any chance of surviving, she knew what she had to do. She had to end their physical relationship now or risk losing what little sanity she had left. And as long as he didn't kiss her, she should be able to carry through on her decision.

* * *

"I'm glad to hear you've finally gotten over passing out every time you see a needle, Hunter." Nick laughed as he listened to his older brother tell about the E.M.T. courses he'd been taking. Until a few weeks ago, he hadn't even known that he had two brothers. But after discovering that his mother wasn't the only woman his father had loved and left to face single motherhood alone, the bond forming between him and his brothers meant more to Nick than anything had in a very long time. "How much longer before you get certified?"

"If I can pass this damned course without having to deal with too many needles, I'll get my certificate in about two weeks. Then I have to get checked out to fly choppers again." Hunter sighed heavily. "I'm still not a hundred percent sure that I want to do this. I just don't trust Emerald not to have something up her sleeve with this medical evacuation service that she's not telling me."

"Yeah, the old gal has a way of omitting details and twisting facts to get us to dance to her tune," Nick said, thinking about the things she'd conveniently failed to tell him concerning the expansion of the Sugar Creek ranch.

"Caleb told me about the mess she's gotten you into. Do you have that straightened out yet?"

"No." Nick released a frustrated breath. "Emerald

hasn't returned my phone calls and old Luther is as noncommittal as ever."

Hunter chuckled. "I'm still wondering where she found that guy. He's definitely not normal."

"Not by a long shot," Nick agreed, laughing.

"I guess I'd better get back to studying about compound fractures," Hunter said, sounding less than enthusiastic. "Good luck getting things straightened out with your foreman's contract."

"Thanks. I have a feeling I'm going to need it." As an afterthought, Nick added, "I can't wait to see what Emerald has in store for you."

Hunter groaned. "If it's anything like what she's gotten you into, I think I'd just as soon quit now and save myself the hassle."

Nick couldn't help but laugh. "And miss all the fun?"

After finalizing plans with Hunter to fly down to Albuquerque in a couple of weeks to surprise their brother, Caleb, on his birthday, Nick hung up the phone and stood to go in search of Cheyenne. She'd probably have to find someone to take care of her father for a few days, but that could be worked out. He had every intention of taking her with him and he wasn't taking no for an answer.

He had no idea why it was suddenly important to him that she meet his brothers. The fact of the matter was, he really didn't want to know. He had a feeling he wouldn't be overly thrilled with what he discovered if he tried to analyze his reasoning.

"Some things are better left alone and this is one of them," he muttered as he opened his office door and walked right into Cheyenne. Catching her by the shoulders to keep her from stumbling backward, he laughed as he pulled her to him. "Whoa, sweetheart. Where were you headed in such a hurry?"

"I…need to talk to you about—"

"We'll talk later," he said, lowering his mouth to hers.

The feel of her petite frame pressed to his chest was more temptation than he could resist. It had been the better part of a week since they'd made love and with each passing day, his need for her had grown into an unbearable ache.

As he moved his lips over hers, blood surged through his veins and a spark ignited in his gut. Her soft, feminine body pressed to his sent heat coursing straight through him and a shockwave of desire directly to the region south of his belt buckle.

Caught up in the feel of her perfect lips beneath his and the rapidly building hunger overtaking every fiber of his being, it took a moment for him to realize that she was pushing against him. "Hey, where do you think you're going?"

"Greta—"

He tightened his arms around her. "Greta left right after lunch. She and Carl are going down to Denver to spend the weekend with their daughter and her family."

"W-we're...alone?" If he didn't know better he'd swear there was a hint of panic in her voice.

Deciding he'd imagined it, he kissed his way from her cheek down the slender column of her neck. When he raised his head to meet her wide-eyed gaze, he smiled. "All alone, sweetheart."

Seven

A momentary wave of panic swept through Cheyenne when Nick's mouth covered hers. But she quickly ceased thinking of why it was so important that she call a halt to their affair or the risk she was taking of losing what was left of her sanity. Nothing mattered but the fact that she was in his arms once again.

When he eased his lips from hers to capture her gaze with his, the heat in his deep blue eyes caused her insides to hum with an anticipation that robbed her of breath. "I want you, Cheyenne." Low and slightly rough, his voice wrapped around her like a warm velvet cape and sent a wave of goose bumps shimmering over her skin. "I want to sink myself deep inside you and make our bodies one."

She knew she was playing a dangerous game and there was a very real possibility of losing what was left of herself. But if all she could allow herself to have with him was this one final moment, she'd cherish the memory of what they shared, no matter how much heartache she suffered later. Right now, she needed to taste the desire in his kiss and feel the strength of his passion as he claimed her one last time.

"Make love to me, Nick."

Without a moment's hesitation, he swept her into his arms and carried her up the stairs to his bedroom. When he set her on her feet at the side of his bed, his sexy smile chased away the last shadow of her doubts and she knew in her heart she'd lost her internal battle the moment he'd touched her.

After bending to quickly remove their boots and socks, he straightened, giving her a look that threatened to melt every bone in her body. "As much as I want to make love to you, I need to know. Are you still sore, sweetheart?"

Her cheeks heated at his intimate question. "The soreness went away after a day or two."

"Do you have any idea how pretty you are when

you blush?" he asked as he removed the elastic band holding her ponytail.

"I've never associated embarrassment...with feeling attractive." Her pulse sped up and her breathing became shallow when he trailed his fingers down her throat to her collarbone.

"I think you're pretty when you're happy, sad, angry—" he lightly ran his fingers over her shoulders, then down her arms to catch her hands in his "—and I even think you're pretty when you're embarrassed." Smiling he brought her hands to his lips to kiss each one. "When we were young, I thought you were the prettiest girl I'd ever seen. Now that we're grown, I *know* you're the prettiest woman I've ever seen."

Before she could get her vocal cords to work, he placed her hands on his shoulders, then reached down to tug the bottom of her tank top from the waistband of her jeans. Slipping his hands beneath the hem, the calluses on his palms sent waves of delight straight to the core of her as he caressed her ribs and the underside of her breasts.

"Raise your arms for me," he whispered close to her ear.

When she did as he commanded, he swept the lavender garment over her head and tossed it to the floor. Then, cupping her cheek with one hand, he kissed her with a tenderness that brought tears to her eyes as he reached behind her with the other hand to make quick work of unfastening her bra.

"How do men...do that?" she asked, feeling more than a little breathless.

"Do what?"

"Unfasten a bra one-handed faster than most people can snap their fingers."

A frown marred his handsome face as he leaned back to look at her. "How do you know—"

"Girl talk with some of my friends."

His rich laughter made her warm all over as he tossed the scrap of lace on top of her tank top, then nibbled kisses from her ear around to her throat. "Never underestimate the talents of a man on a mission, sweetheart."

At the feel of his lips on her sensitized skin, Cheyenne closed her eyes and let her head fall back to give him better access. A tingling excitement began to course through her veins, heating every inch of her as it made its way to pool in the pit of her belly. When he used his tongue to soothe the fluttering at the top of her collarbone, then kissed his way down her chest to the slope of her breast, she felt as if she'd melt into a puddle at his feet.

Caught up in the delicious sensations Nick was creating deep within her soul, her heart skipped several beats when he took her nipple into his mouth to draw on it deeply. Certain she'd burn to a cinder at any moment, she gripped his shoulders as the pooling of need in her lower body intensified.

"Do you like that?" His moist breath against her breast felt absolutely wonderful.

"Mmm."

"I'll take that as a yes." Turning his attention to her other breast, he treated the hardened peak to the same delightful torture.

Wave after wave of desire washed over her and it came as no small surprise when she realized that Nick had unsnapped her jeans and lowered the zipper without her knowledge. Sliding her jeans and panties down her thighs, he quickly added them to the growing pile of her clothes on the floor.

"This isn't fair. I'm completely naked and you still have all of your clothes on," she said, reaching out to unfasten the metal snaps on his Western-style shirt.

Knowing it would be their last time together, she forced herself to go slowly, to savor and enjoy the exploration of his magnificent body. She wanted to memorize every moment, commit every detail of their lovemaking to memory.

As she unsnapped first one gripper, then another, she kissed every inch of newly exposed skin and by the time she parted his shirt, Nick looked like a man in pain. "I think you're killing me."

"Do you want me to stop?" She grazed his flat male nipples with the tips of her fingers and was rewarded by his low groan of pleasure.

"Hell no, I don't want you to stop."

The hungry look in his dark blue eyes encouraged her and pushing his shirt off of his broad shoulders, she tossed it aside, then placed her hands flat on his bare chest. His warm male flesh felt absolutely wonderful beneath her palms and as she mapped the ridges and planes of his muscular physique, he took several deep, shuddering breaths.

Smiling, she trailed her index finger down the shallow valley dividing his rippling stomach muscles. "Your body is so beautiful, so perfect."

"It can't hold a candle to the perfection of yours, sweetheart," he said, shaking his head as he cupped her breasts with his hands.

The feel of his thumbs lightly chafing her tight nipples as he gently caressed her fullness sent her temperature soaring. He continued teasing her and by the time she unbuckled his belt and reached for the stud at his waistband, her fingers trembled from a need deeper than anything she'd ever experienced. Working the metal button free, she paused as she toyed with the tab at the top of his fly.

"It appears that you might have a bit of a problem."

"You caused me to be like this, sweetheart." The smoldering heat in his cobalt gaze caused the butterflies in her stomach to go absolutely wild and sent a shiver of anticipation up her spine.

Slowly brushing her hand across the faded denim, she smiled when he sucked in a sharp breath. "I'm responsible for this?"

"Yeah." He leaned forward to nibble kisses from her shoulder, up her neck to just below her ear. "Now, what are you going to do about it?"

Carefully lowering the zipper, the sight of his arousal straining against his cotton briefs filled her with an irresistible urge to touch him. Running her index finger along the hard ridge, she felt a moment of panic when he jerked as if he'd been shocked with a jolt of electricity.

"Is that uncomfortable?"

"Sweetheart, if you don't get the rest of my clothes off…it's going to be damned near unbearable. Real quick."

Cheyenne couldn't get over how empowering it felt to know that she'd brought him to such a heightened state of need. "That wouldn't be good."

"No, it wouldn't."

The hunger in his steady gaze encouraged her and, sliding her hands beneath the elastic at the top of his briefs, she slid them and his jeans over his narrow hips and down his powerful thighs. When he stepped out of them, then kicked them aside, the sight of his fully aroused body caused her heart to stall.

Crooking his index finger, he gave her a sexy smile. "Come here."

When she stepped into the circle of his arms, the feel of woman against man, skin against skin from shoulders to knees caused a delicious shiver of anticipation to slide through every part of her. But when he cupped her bottom in his large hands and lifted her to him, a sizzling awareness swirled from the top of her head to the soles of her feet, leaving her slightly dizzy from its intensity.

The honeyed heat deep in the most feminine part of her quickly changed to the empty ache of unfulfilled desire and she couldn't have stopped a moan of frustration from escaping if her life depended on. "I need you. Now."

"Easy, sweetheart." His kiss was filled with pure male passion and awakened a yearning in her deeper than she'd ever dreamed possible.

By the time he broke the kiss, she felt as if she would go up in a blaze of glory at any moment. Nick must have experienced the same sense of urgency because he reached into the bedside table to remove a foil packet and quickly arranged their protection. Then, settling himself on the side of the bed, he guided her to straddle his lap.

"Put your legs around me," he whispered hoarsely as he lifted her to him.

When she did, she reveled in the exquisite stretching of her body as he slowly eased her down onto his aroused flesh. Closing her eyes, Cheyenne felt a completeness that she knew in her heart she could never feel with any other man as he joined their bodies and made them one.

"You feel...wonderful," she said, wrapping her arms around his wide shoulders.

"I was about to say the same thing about you." His voice sounded strained and she could tell he was holding himself in check, making sure she was ready before he continued.

Opening her eyes, she raised one hand to thread her fingers in his thick, dark blond hair. Her heart ached with the need to tell him how special he was to her, how much she loved him. But knowing he didn't feel the same, she swallowed back the words and chose to show him how she felt about him.

"P-please...make love to me, Nick."

His gaze held hers as without a word he guided her in a leisurely rocking motion against him. When he slowly increased the pace, her head fell back as wave upon wave of exquisite pleasure radiated over every cell in her body. His lips caressing the sensitive skin of her throat and collarbone escalated the building tension deep inside her and all too quickly, she felt her body begin to tighten as the coil of need prepared to set her free.

He must have sensed her readiness because he tightened his arms around her. "I've got you, Cheyenne. Let go, sweetheart."

If she'd been able to find her voice, she could have told him that she didn't have a choice, that her body demanded she turn loose and reach for the completion they both sought. But her release from the captivating spell overtook her and she was cast into a vortex of incredible sensation.

Quivering from the waves of satisfaction flowing to every corner of her being, Cheyenne felt Nick's body move within her one final time, then stiffen as he found his own shuddering liberation from the passionate storm. As she clung to him, they both made the journey to a place where they basked in the perfect union of two bodies becoming one heart, one mind, one soul.

Tears filled her eyes and she tightened her arms around him in an effort to make the moment last. But as she slowly drifted back to reality, she knew the time had come to end the madness. She only hoped she had the strength to carry through with her decision and tell him their affair was over.

Nick couldn't believe the myriad of emotions tightening his chest. The possessiveness he'd been battling since seeing Cheyenne the first day of his return to the Sugar Creek ranch had grown into a force he could no longer fight. And it scared the living hell out of him.

He'd been a damned fool to think he could engage in any kind of physical relationship with her and not form some sort of bond. But to his relief, she'd apparently been just as affected by their affair. It hadn't been lost on him that she'd stopped referring to their coming together as having sex and started calling it what it was—lovemaking.

His chest tightened further and he suddenly found it hard to breathe. Had he done the unthinkable? Had he fallen in love with her again? Had he ever really stopped loving her?

Thirteen years ago, he'd been an infatuated teenage boy with a case of raging hormones and an inherent sense of honor. And in his attempt to avoid being anything like his irresponsible father, he'd confused lust for love and decided they had to be married before he made love to Cheyenne.

That explained his feelings for her in the past. But what about the way he was feeling now? Was he once again mistaking lust for something deeper, something far more meaningful?

His heart pounded hard against his rib cage and he had to force himself to breathe. The last thing he needed right now was to complicate his life by falling for Cheyenne again.

Deciding it would be better to sort everything out later when he was alone and could think more clearly, he kissed her satiny cheek and concentrated on the present. "Any discomfort this time?"

She shook her head. "No."

"Good."

They sat holding each other for some time before she started to pull away from him. "What's your hurry?" he asked, tightening his arms around her.

"I need to…get home." The tone of her voice warned him that something had upset her.

He lifted her from his lap to sit beside him on the bed. But instead of snuggling against him, she quickly stood up and started gathering her clothes from the pile on the floor.

"What's wrong, sweetheart?"

Instead of answering, she hurried into the bathroom. When she came out a few minutes later, he was waiting for her. There was no way in hell she was leaving until she explained what the problem was.

Placing his hands on her shoulders, he shook his

head. "You're not going anywhere until you tell me what's going on."

"Nothing...everything."

She looked about two seconds away from crying and it twisted his gut into a painful knot to think he might have caused her distress. "Slow down and tell me what's bothering you."

"I can't do this again." Her voice was so soft and tremulous, he almost hadn't heard her.

His heart stalled. She'd said there was no discomfort, but had he unknowingly hurt her in some way?

"Are you all right?"

"Don't worry about me. I'll be fine." Her sad smile caused his gut to twist.

"Then what's wrong?"

A lone tear slid down her pale cheek. "You can't change what happened any more than I can." She wouldn't look him in the eye when she motioned toward his clothes on the floor. "Will you please put something on? It's very distracting to try holding a conversation with a naked person."

"What do you mean we can't change what happened?" Frowning, he turned her loose to reach for his jeans and briefs. "If I did something that's upset you, I'm sorry."

As he started pulling on his jeans, she walked out

into the hall. Turning back, the sadness in her aqua eyes just about tore him apart.

"It's not what you did, Nick. It's what you can't do."

"Dammit, Cheyenne, wait a minute. You're talking in riddles."

In a hurry to follow her, he struggled to get his fly zipped, then started after her. But the sound of the front door closing behind her stopped him halfway down the stairs.

He had no idea what had just happened or why, but he had every intention of finding out. Turning, he went back to his bedroom for his shirt, then sitting on the side of the bed to pull on his boots, he thought about what she'd said.

For the life of him, he couldn't figure out what she'd been talking about. What didn't she think they could change? And what was it that she thought he couldn't do?

If she'd been referring to what happened thirteen years ago, she was right. He couldn't change the past. But he could damn sure explain what happened that night and why he and his mother had left Wyoming under the cover of darkness.

But as much as he wanted to set the record straight once and for all, he decided to wait until they drove back from the auction tomorrow evening to tell Cheyenne the truth about that night. She was too upset right now to listen to what he had to say and he wanted her full attention when he told her the role her father and the sheriff had played in one of the darkest days of his life.

By the time Cheyenne parked her truck in front of her house, she had her emotions under control. But only just barely. She knew she'd handled the situation with Nick badly. But that couldn't be helped. She'd done the best she could under the circumstances and if he didn't realize that she was ending their affair, he'd figure it out soon enough.

He'd probably wonder why she'd changed her mind. He might even question her about it. But after a time, he'd accept that it was over and move on to find a woman who could keep her emotions in check. Considering that he didn't love her, that shouldn't take too long.

"You look tired, princess," her father said as she let herself into the house through the back door. He was sitting in his wheelchair at the kitchen table with several of his old case files spread out in front of him. Slipping several of the papers into a folder, he stacked them on his lap. "Aren't you feeling well?"

No. She wasn't sure she'd ever feel good again.

"I do have a bit of a headache, but it's nothing. I'll be fine."

His eyes narrowed. "You had to work close to that blackhearted excuse for a human being again today, didn't you?"

"Daddy, please." She rubbed her throbbing temples. "I'm really not up to another lecture on how reprehensible you think Nick is."

His expression hard, he shook his head. "I just hate that you have to work for that illegitimate son of a—"

"Daddy!"

His features softened a bit. "I'm sorry, princess. But you're too good to be anywhere near Daniels, let alone have to work for him."

She knew her father only wanted the best for her and found the entire situation extremely frustrating. But neither one of them could change the fact that she had four more years on her contract with the Sugar Creek Cattle Company and there was no sense in belaboring the issue.

"Please, let's not talk about it now." She moved to take the files from him. "Do you want me to put these in your office?"

To her surprise, he held on to the files and shook his head. "Sit down and put your feet up. I'll put these back in the file cabinet, then we can talk about driving down to the Bucket of Suds Bar and Grill for supper. My treat."

"But I'd planned on making a meat loaf," she said

halfheartedly. She really didn't feel like cooking, but she hated for her father to use what little spending money she gave him each month on her.

"We can have meat loaf another time." He turned his wheelchair around and started rolling it toward his office. "You deserve a night off."

Two hours later, as she and her father sat at a chipped Formica table at the back of the Bucket of Suds, enjoying plates piled high with spaghetti and meatballs, Cheyenne felt as if the world had come to a grinding halt when Nick walked through the entrance. Hadn't she suffered enough turmoil in her life for one day? What on earth was he doing here? And what would her father do if he saw Nick?

As she stared at him, her chest tightened. She loved him so much she ached with it. And seeing him day in and day out without being held by him, loved by him was going to make the next four years drag out like a life sentence.

"Princess, did you hear what I said?"

Turning her attention to her father, she shook her head. "I must have been daydreaming."

"I said we should eat out like this more often." He smiled. "It feels good to get out of the house for a while."

She was glad to see that her father was enjoying his night out. Because of the demands of her job, she didn't have a lot of time to take him places and she knew he had to get bored staying at home all the time. She just hoped that he continued to enjoy himself and didn't recognize Nick. Fortunately the restaurant was packed with the usual Friday night crowd and the chances of that happening were fairly good.

Keeping an eye on Nick sitting at the bar, she did her best not to let on that anything was out of the ordinary. "I don't think our budget will allow us to eat out every week, but I think we can afford to do this once a month," she said, smiling.

Her father nodded. "It's something we can look forward to."

Aware of every move Nick made, Cheyenne knew the second he rose from the bar stool and headed toward their table. She tried to dissuade him with a surreptitious shake of her head, but she could tell by the determined look in his eye her effort was futile.

He nodded a greeting as he passed their table on his way to the jukebox. "Good evening, Judge Holbrook. Cheyenne."

"Who is that young man?" her father asked. "He looks familiar."

Cheyenne took a deep breath. "That was Nick Daniels, Daddy."

Her father's congenial expression quickly changed to a glare. "What's he doing here?"

"Probably for the same reason we are. His house-keeper went to Denver for the weekend and I assume he's here to eat dinner."

She swallowed hard when she recognized the beginning notes of the song she and Nick had always called theirs in high school. Why had he chosen that particular song out of all the ones on the jukebox?

"Housekeeper?" her father interrupted her thoughts. "Where's his mother? Didn't she come back to Wyoming with that whelp of hers?"

"Linda Daniels passed away about twelve years ago, Daddy."

"Linda's gone?" She could have sworn she saw a hint of sadness cross his face. But just as quickly as it appeared, it was gone.

Deciding she'd only imagined the change in his demeanor, Cheyenne nodded. "Nick said she knew she didn't have long to live when they left here to go to St. Louis."

As he walked back toward the bar, Nick stopped at their table. "When you left this afternoon, I forgot to tell you that we'll start loading the cattle we're taking to auction after lunch tomorrow."

Before she could respond, her father slammed his fork down on the table. "It's a damn fool idea to be selling off good stock the way you're doing. Of course, you never did have a lick of sense."

"Daddy," Cheyenne warned. Creating a scene in a public place would make the day go from difficult to unbearable.

"It's all right, Cheyenne." Nick smiled, but it was anything but friendly. "Your father has a right to his opinion." Although he'd spoken to her, his gaze never wavered from her father's.

"If you've said your piece move on, Daniels. You're ruining my appetite." As an afterthought, her father added, "And from now on, unless my daughter is on the clock, I don't want you anywhere near Cheyenne. Is that understood?"

Nick shook his head. "In case you hadn't noticed, she's an adult now, Judge. Who she does or doesn't see is her call. Not yours."

The level of hostility between Nick and her father shocked her. "I think you'd both better calm down. This isn't the time or place to be having a conversation like this."

"I was leaving anyway." When Nick finally turned his attention her way, the heat in his sensual gaze robbed her of breath and sent a shiver of awareness all the way to her soul. "I'll see you tomorrow afternoon, Cheyenne."

As he walked away, her father continued his diatribe, but Cheyenne had no idea what he was ranting about. There had been a wealth of meaning in the look Nick had given her and there was no mistaking his intention.

He had questions and he wasn't going to rest until he had the answers.

Eight

By the time the auction was over the next evening and Cheyenne waited for Nick to collect the money from the sale of the cattle, she felt ready to jump out of her own skin. Her nerves were completely shot, and for good reason.

She and Nick had worked together the entire afternoon to get the cattle loaded in trailers and moved to holding pens at the sale barn, then sat together while the animals were auctioned off to the highest bidders. Neither of them had mentioned the run-in he'd had with her father the night before, nor had he asked her why she'd had a sudden change of heart about their affair. But that was about to change.

They had a little over an hour before they got back to the Sugar Creek ranch and the complete privacy of his truck for their conversation. There wasn't a doubt in her mind what they would be discussing or that it was going to be one of the longest drives of her life.

"Ready to go?"

Lost in thought, she jumped at the unexpected sound of Nick's voice only inches away. "As ready as I'll ever be."

He smiled as he tucked the check he'd received from the auction officials in his shirt pocket, then put his arm around her shoulders to walk her to his truck. "Would you like to stop somewhere for a bite to eat before we head back?"

The feel of his body pressed to her side sent a deep longing straight to her soul. "N-no. I need to get home."

The last thing she wanted was to prolong the time they spent together. The more she was with him, the stronger the temptation became to rethink her decision.

"You've worked hard today." Opening the passenger door for her, he lightly ran his index finger from her ear along her cheek to her lips. "I'm sure you're tired."

Her skin tingled where he touched her and it took every ounce of willpower she had not to lean toward him. "I'm used to it." She forced herself to ignore the longing that streaked through her and got into the truck. "It's my job."

He shook his head. "Not anymore. Remember? You'll be in the office and I'll be out doing the ranch work."

If he thought she was going to argue with him, he was mistaken. She'd worked for six long years out in all kinds of weather and an easier job in the comforts of a heated office in the winter and air-conditioned in the summer didn't sound at all bad. And as long as she was alone in that office, she might even manage to retain a scrap of what little sanity she had left.

When he walked around the front of the truck and got in behind the steering wheel the look in his eye warned her that the conversation she'd dreaded was about to begin. "Your father looked fairly healthy last night, considering that he's had a stroke."

She nodded. "I can't get him to see a doctor as often as he should, but he's recovered everything but the ability to walk."

They rode in silence for some time before Nick asked, "What did your father tell you about the night I left Wyoming?"

His question wasn't what she expected. She'd thought he'd want to know why she'd ended their affair.

"Daddy didn't tell me anything until he received

the news that you and your mother were no longer at the Sugar Creek. Why?"

"I figured as much."

Confused, she turned to look at him as he gunned the truck's powerful engine. "What is that supposed to mean?"

He took a deep breath and she could tell he was doing his best to hold his temper. "Before I tell you what really went down that night, why don't you tell me what happened after your father led you away from the church?"

Cheyenne had expected them to be discussing her father's behavior the night before and her decision to end their no-strings arrangement. She couldn't imagine why Nick wanted to talk about the events of thirteen years ago.

"I don't see the need to drag up the past," she said, shaking her head. "My father broke up our wedding and you left without even telling me goodbye. End of story."

The lights from the dashboard illuminated his face just enough for her to watch a muscle work along Nick's lean jaw. "That's not exactly the way it all unfolded that night, Cheyenne."

She shook her head. "It doesn't matter now."

"Yes, it does."

Sighing heavily, she thought back on the night

she was to have become Nick's wife. "After my father and the sheriff stopped our wedding, Daddy took me home and that was it. We didn't talk about it, until a couple of days later when he told me that you and your mother had left the area."

"What did he say?"

There was no sense mincing words. He was well aware of how her father felt about him. "Daddy pointed out that if you had really cared anything about me, you would have told me where you were going or at the least, told me goodbye."

Nick's particularly nasty oath startled her. "I'll bet he didn't bother telling you why we left, did he?"

"How could he? My father didn't know any more about your leaving than anyone else."

His hollow laughter caused a chill to slither straight up her spine. "That's where you're wrong, sweetheart. Your father and the sheriff had firsthand knowledge of why I left Wyoming."

She was becoming more than a little irritated by his intimations that her father had something to do with it. "Well, since everyone seems to know all about it but me, why don't you fill me in on the big secret?"

Nick stared out the windshield for several long seconds before he finally spoke. "After your father and the sheriff put you in the patrol car and left me standing there on the church steps, I drove home and told my mother what happened. She wasn't any happier about our trying to elope than your father, but for different reasons. She told me if she knew anything about Bertram Holbrook that we hadn't heard the last of the incident." He cast her a meaningful glance. "And she was right."

A cold dread began to settle in Cheyenne's stomach. She could tell by the look on his face that the accusations Nick was about to make against her father were going to be ugly and hurtful.

Swallowing around the lump in her throat, she asked, "Just what was it that my father was supposed to have done?"

She watched Nick's hand tighten on the steering wheel. "Around midnight that evening, my mother received an anonymous phone call, telling her that your father was filing charges and that the sheriff would be out the next morning to arrest me for statutory rape."

Gasping, she shook her head. "I don't believe you. My father would never do something like that."

Nick steered the truck to the side of the road and turned off the engine. When he turned to face her, his anger was evident in the tight lines around his mouth and the sparkle in his deep blue eyes.

"Don't fool yourself, Cheyenne. Your father was a powerful judge, who, for whatever reason, despised me and my mother. And I had taken his underage daughter—his only daughter—across the county line to marry her."

"But—"

"He had the motive, the resources and the hatred to pursue the issue." His gaze caught and held hers. "Face it, Cheyenne. Your father had every intention of seeing that I rotted away in a jail cell for the better part of my life."

Her stomach churned and she felt as if she might be physically ill. "I-if what you say is true, then why didn't you stay and fight the charges?"

"Think about it, sweetheart. Your father knew the law inside and out. And he had plenty of people to see that his goal was accomplished." He smiled sardonically. "What chance do you think I would have had at getting a fair trial with one of your father's colleagues sitting on the bench?"

Her mind reeled from the implications of it all. If what Nick told her had actually happened, it would have ruined his life. But she couldn't believe her father would do something so vile, so vindictive.

Taking her hand in his, Nick shook his head. "You have to believe me. The last thing I wanted to do was leave you behind that night. But as my mother pointed out, I didn't have any other options. I either got the hell out of Wyoming while I could or stay and face a guaranteed prison sentence."

Tears filled her eyes as she struggled with what he'd told her. "Why didn't you call...or write to let me know what had happened?"

"I tried to get in touch with you, but your father made sure that didn't happen." He reached down to release her safety harness, then pulled her to his wide chest. "I called every day for a month, sweetheart. But your father always answered the phone and wouldn't let me talk to you, or the answering machine picked up. I left messages, but it's my guess that he erased them before you heard them. I also sent a few letters, but I doubt you ever saw them, either."

She numbly shook her head. "No."

His arms holding her so securely to him were a comfort, but she felt completely overwhelmed and needed to be alone to sort out everything. "I..." Her voice caught. "P-please take me home."

Apparently sensing her need to come to terms with what he'd told her, Nick kissed the top of her head, then releasing her, started the truck.

As they drove in silence through the quiet night, Cheyenne thought about everything Nick had said. What was she supposed to believe?

The man he had described was nothing like the kind, loving father she'd always known. And until that very moment, there had never been a time in her life that she doubted her father having anything but her best interest at heart.

But as much as she hated to admit it, what Nick said made sense. At the time of the incident, her father did have the power and connections to pursue charges against him. And after seeing her father's hostility toward Nick last night, she couldn't deny that it was a possibility.

Why had her father always had such a low opinion of the Daniels family?

She'd never known anyone nicer than Linda Daniels, and even though the woman had had Nick at a time when it wasn't as socially acceptable to be an unwed mother, no one in the area had seemed to care. No one, that is, but her father.

Could that be the reason her father had such contempt for Nick? Had he viewed Nick as less of a person because his mother hadn't married his father?

But that made no sense. Why should her father be bothered by Nick's illegitimacy when no one else was?

Deciding there were no easy answers, Cheyenne rested her head against the back of the seat and tiredly closed her eyes. She had no idea who or what to believe anymore.

One of the two men she loved with all her heart had deceived her. And it didn't matter whether it was her father or Nick, when she discovered the truth, she knew without a doubt that it was going to break her heart.

Nick cursed his carelessness as he parked his truck beside the house and got out to climb the porch steps. He should have known better than to try to stretch a section of barbed wire fence without both work gloves. But like a damned fool, when he'd driven up to the north pasture that morning and discovered that he'd lost one, he'd gone ahead and tried to do the work without the protection of the thick leather covering his hands. Now he had a deep gash in his left hand and the fence still needed to be repaired.

"Greta, you'd better get the first-aid kit," he called when he entered the house.

"What's wrong?" Cheyenne asked, walking out of his office. She stopped short and her face went deathly pale. "Oh, dear Lord! What happened?"

Glancing down at the bloodstains on the front of his shirt, he held up his hand. "I tangled with some barbed wire."

"Let me see." She gently took his hand in hers and carefully unwrapped the blood-soaked handkerchief he'd wrapped around the wound. Looking up at him, she shook her head. "This is more than a scratch, Nick. Why weren't you wearing your gloves?"

Her soft hands holding his almost made him forget how much the gash hurt. "I could only find one of them and didn't want to drive all the way back here to get another pair."

Rolling her eyes, she shook her head. "You're going to need several stitches to close this."

He tried to pull his hand from hers. "I'll just wash it out with some peroxide and wrap it in gauze."

"No, you're not. You're going to the doctor."

"Am not."

"Yes, you are."

When their gazes locked, he couldn't believe how good she looked to him or how much he'd missed seeing her. For the past week, he'd given her the space he knew she needed and managed to be out of the house each morning before she arrived to work in his office. He'd even postponed taking the rest of the herds to auction in order to give her the coming weekend off.

But standing here staring at her now, he decided that space be damned. He wanted nothing more than to take her in his arms and kiss her until they both needed oxygen.

"Here's the first-aid kit," Greta said as she hurried down the hall. She stopped beside Cheyenne, took one look at his hand, then shook her head. "That's going to need more than anything we can do for you."

"He needs to see a doctor," Cheyenne said stubbornly.

"I couldn't agree more." Greta frowned. "Have you had a tetanus shot lately?"

Nick nodded. "About fifteen years ago."

"You're definitely going to the clinic," Cheyenne said, glaring at him.

Nick cringed when he thought about the injection they'd have to give him to numb his hand in order to stitch the wound shut, as well as the inoculation. Apparently an aversion to needles ran in the family because he suddenly understood why Hunter had had problems passing out every time he saw one.

"I don't like doctors."

"That's tough. You're going." Cheyenne held out her hand. "Give me your truck keys."

"If I go—and I'm not saying that I am—I can drive myself," he said stubbornly. He liked having her fuss over him. But this seeing-a-doctor business was getting out of hand.

"Nick." The tone of her voice warned him that she meant business.

Reluctantly placing the key ring in her outstretched hand, he shook his head. "This is ridiculous."

"Come on, cowboy." She tugged him along by his shirtsleeve. "The ordeal will be over with before you know it."

* * *

Two hours later, as Cheyenne drove them back from the clinic in Elk Bluff, Nick finally began to relax. His encounter with the barbed wire hadn't damaged any of the tendons in his hand and he hadn't humiliated himself by passing out when the doctor brought out the biggest hypodermic needle he'd ever seen to numb his hand.

"Are you in pain?" Cheyenne asked, steering his truck onto the highway leading out of Elk Bluff.

The concern in her voice caused a warm feeling to fill his chest. "Nope. In fact, I can't even feel my hand."

She smiled. "Just wait until the anesthetic wears off. I'm betting you'll feel plenty."

"Well, aren't you just a bright little ray of sunshine?" he said, tempering his sarcasm with a wide grin.

She laughed. "Seriously, you should probably take a couple of days off from working around the ranch to keep from tearing the stitches loose."

"I was thinking I might go down to Colorado this weekend to check out a free-range operation, then drive on to Albuquerque and spend some time there, so that won't be a problem."

"Oh." Pausing, she added, "I…hope you have a good time."

"I'm sure I will." Nick could tell Cheyenne was

curious about where he was going and who he'd be with, but she wasn't going to ask. "I'm going to help a relative celebrate *his* birthday."

"I didn't know that you had family down that way." Was that relief he heard in her voice?

He smiled. "Until just recently, I didn't know about it, either."

"It must be nice to have an extended family," she said, sounding wistful.

"Didn't your mother have a sister down in Laramie?" he asked, thinking back on what she'd told him about her mother.

She nodded as they drove up the lane leading to his house. "Yes, but we lost touch after a while and I haven't heard from her in years."

When she parked his truck and they went into the house, he motioned for her to follow him into the office. Picking up the envelope he'd received the day before from the Emerald, Inc. offices in Wichita, he pulled out a bank draft.

"I guess this answers our question about who you work for." Handing her the paycheck, he added, "But since I won't be here and there isn't any stock to tend, I'm giving you the weekend off."

Her fingers brushed his when she reached for the check and a charge of electric current streaked up his arm, then spread throughout his chest. Without thinking twice, he stepped forward and loosely wrapped his arms around her waist.

"Nick, I—"

"Shh. I'm not pressuring you to do something you can't or don't want to do." He lightly touched his lips to hers. "I just want to give you something to think about while I'm gone."

To his satisfaction as he settled his mouth over hers, Cheyenne melted against him and returned his kiss with a hunger that matched his own. Her sweet taste and the feel of her delicate frame pressed to him from shoulders to knees had the blood rushing through his veins and his body aching to claim her, to make her his once and for all. But he'd made her a promise and even if it killed him, he was going to prove to her that she could trust him.

After the confrontation with her father, then their talk on the way back from the auction, he'd decided she wasn't the only one who needed the space to think over a few things. In the past week, he'd done quite a bit of soul-searching on his own and reached several conclusions. Whatever genes he'd inherited from his irresponsible playboy father, the "love 'em and leave 'em" gene wasn't one of them. And although he'd fought with everything he had in him not to fall for Cheyenne again, he knew now that he'd never really had a choice in the matter.

She was his obsession—an addiction for him from which there was no cure. He'd pledged his love to her thirteen years ago and he knew now that was why he'd been unsuccessful at sustaining a relationship with anyone else. His heart had belonged and always would belong to Cheyenne. And whether she realized it or not, she felt the same way about him.

Breaking the kiss, he smiled as he stared into her beautiful aqua-green eyes. "While I'm gone, I want you to do something for me."

"Wh-what?"

He touched her satiny cheek with his finger. "I want you to think about us. I want you to think about me and how I make you feel. When I get back, we'll talk, sweetheart."

As the gray light of dawn began to chase away the dark shadows in her bedroom, Cheyenne lay in bed staring at the ceiling. She'd spent the entire night thinking about what Nick had said yesterday afternoon when he'd kissed her.

Didn't he realize he'd been all she could think about since finding him making repairs to that fence three weeks ago? Wasn't he aware that when he kissed her, nothing else seemed to matter but that she was in his arms? Or that when he made love to her she lost all sense of herself?

She scrunched her eyes shut to stop the wave of tears threatening to overtake her. She loved him— had never stopped loving him. But he'd made it clear that he didn't want her love and had no intention of returning it. And even if Nick did love her, she wasn't sure she could trust him.

He'd told her so many things about her father that she still had a hard time believing were true. Unfortunately, as much as she'd like to dismiss his accusations, she couldn't.

At the time, her father had been a powerful county judge with an intense dislike for Nick's family. And even though her father had always shown her nothing but love and kindness, she knew that he wasn't the same with others. His reputation of being very rigid and intolerant was legendary. But surely he wouldn't have misused his power to try ruining Nick's life, simply because Nick had tried to marry her.

She'd thought about confronting her father with Nick's accusations, but his blood pressure had been running a little high ever since they'd met up with Nick at the bar and grill. The last thing she wanted to do was run the risk of exacerbating her father's health problems with her questions.

"Cheyenne!"

The sound of her father's voice coming over the intercom system she'd had installed after his stroke caused her to sit straight up in bed. It wasn't unusual for him to rise around dawn each morning, but from the panic in his voice, she could tell something was terribly wrong.

She depressed the talk button on the unit beside her bed. "I'll be right there, Daddy."

"Hurry! The barn is on fire."

Cheyenne's heart pounded and her mind raced as she ran down the stairs. How many animals were in the barn?

The calves she'd isolated a few weeks ago had already been turned back into the herd after she'd successfully treated them for pink eye. But her gelding and Mr. Nibbles were still in the barn.

"Call the county fire department," she ordered as she ran past her father for the back door.

Sprinting down the wheelchair ramp and across the backyard, she ignored the pain of pebbles bruising the bottom of her bare feet as she crossed the gravel driveway. A chill snaked up her spine at the eerie glow she saw illuminating the otherwise dark interior of the barn and she was thankful that in deference to the August heat she'd worn a pair of gym shorts and a tank top to bed the night before. She had to get her gelding and the pony out of there and she didn't need the added encumbrance of her nightgown tangling around her legs.

"I called Gordon," he shouted as he wheeled his chair out into the yard after her. "He's contacting the county's volunteer firefighters."

"They'll never get here in time," she said, running toward the barn entrance.

"Cheyenne, no!"

Her father's panicked voice caused her to pause momentarily, but she continued on. Two animals were depending on her to lead them out safely and she wasn't going to let them down.

Nine

As the sky began to lighten, Nick steered his truck onto the road leading back to the Sugar Creek ranch. He'd left way before daylight to make the drive down to the free-range cattle ranch he'd heard about in Colorado. But the more miles he put between him and Cheyenne, the more he realized that leaving her behind was the last thing he wanted to do. They'd already spent thirteen years apart and as far as he was concerned, one more minute away from her was too damned long.

He had every intention of driving over to the Flying H later in the day, telling her father to get over whatever it was the man had against him and ask

Cheyenne to take a trip with him back to that little church across the county line. Only this time the outcome would be different. Come hell or high water, he was going to make her his wife.

Nick glanced toward the Holbrook place as he drove past and uttered a phrase he reserved for dire circumstances and smashed thumbs. Smoke billowed from the barn's hayloft and flames were visible along the outside wall.

Turning the truck around, he sped up the driveway to come to a sliding halt in the loose gravel. As he jumped from the truck, the sight of Cheyenne running into the burning barn caused fear to grip his insides and his heart to stall.

Bertram Holbrook jumped from his wheelchair surprisingly well for a man who was supposed to be partially paralyzed and began waving frantically toward the barn. "Get her out of there!"

Without thinking twice, Nick ran into the barn after Cheyenne. Catching her around the waist from behind, he spun her around and started pulling her toward the door. "What the hell do you think you're doing?"

She squirmed free of his grasp. "I have to get my horse and the pony."

"You get out of here. I'll get them," he shouted above the crackle of the rapidly spreading flames. "Which stalls are they in?"

She shook her head. "I'll get one while you get the other." Before he could stop her, she ran down the center aisle toward the fire.

Following her, Nick threw open a half door on one of the stalls and took hold of the halter on a fat, little chestnut pony. As he tugged the frightened animal along, he stopped at the stall where Cheyenne tried to catch a large buckskin gelding.

"Take the pony and go out the side door," he yelled, pushing her aside to keep the terrified horse from trampling her as it moved nervously around the stall.

When he grabbed the gelding's halter, Nick felt a sharp pain shoot up his arm as the stitches in his hand broke free, but he did his best to ignore it. Then, leading the panicked animal out into the center aisle, he fought to breathe as the choking smoke swirled around him and the terrified horse.

A loud cracking sound from somewhere overhead caused the gelding to shy away from him and Nick had to use every ounce of strength he possessed to bring the animal under control. Praying that Cheyenne and the pony had already made it to safety, he hurried to get himself and the buckskin out of the burning structure before the loft came crashing down on top of them.

He immediately released his hold on the gelding and let the horse run free when they reached the side door of the barn and the safety of the outside. Looking around for Cheyenne, relief washed over him when he spotted her several yards away. He started toward her, but he'd only gone a few feet when the sudden throbbing pain in his hand threatened to buckle his knees. He stumbled and might have fallen had she not rushed over to help steady him, and together they moved away from the burning building.

"Are you...all right?" he asked between fits of coughing.

She nodded, tears streaming down her face as she wrapped her arms around his waist and pressed herself to him. "I was so frightened that I might lose you."

His chest tightened with emotion and forgetting all about his hand, he held her close. "Why were you frightened, sweetheart?" He had a feeling he knew the answer, but he wanted to hear her say the words.

"Because I—"

Her answer was cut short when a heavy hand came down on Nick's shoulder. "There's no way you're getting out of this one, Daniels. I've got the evidence to prove your guilt this time."

Releasing her, Nick turned to face his assailant. "What the hell are you talking about, Sheriff?"

The potbellied lawman waved a leather glove in front of him. "This is yours, isn't it?"

Nick nodded as he stared at his missing work

glove. It would take a blind man or a fool not to see that he was being set up. Again.

"I thought as much," Sheriff Turner said, looking smug.

"Where did you find it?" Nick asked calmly. The sheriff had to have taken it from his truck the day he'd questioned Nick about the vandalism to Cheyenne's tires.

"It doesn't matter. It was found on the judge's property and you've already admitted it's yours." The man shook his head. "You should've stuck to misdemeanors. Arson is a felony and mark my words, you'll do time over this."

"Nick didn't set the fire," Cheyenne said, shaking her head.

Sheriff Turner shrugged. "I have proof that says otherwise. Besides, Daniels here left his ranch over an hour ago, then conveniently showed up here to help with the fire."

Nick gritted his teeth as he stared at the sorriest excuse for an officer of the law he'd ever seen. "How would you know that, unless you were watching my place, Sheriff?"

"I was out on patrol," the sheriff said, sounding a little less sure of himself.

"Before daylight?" Cheyenne shook her head. "You have deputies for that."

A dull flush began to spread over the man's face. "Now listen here, little girl—"

"Give it up, Gordon. It's over."

"Bertram, I've got Daniels right where we want him," Sheriff Turner said, reaching for the handcuffs clipped to the back of his belt.

Cheyenne turned to see her father coming toward them. He walked with a limp, but it was nothing that would keep him confined to a wheelchair. Nor were his movements and balance those of a man who was unpracticed at walking.

She felt the blood drain from her face as reality slammed into her like a physical blow. If her father had deceived her about his disability, he was certainly capable of everything Nick had alleged happened all the years ago.

As if sensing that she needed his strength, Nick put his arm around her shoulders. His silent support caused emotion to clog her throat.

"Why...Daddy?" Cheyenne asked brokenly. "How could you...be part of something...like this?"

For the first time in her life, she watched her father's shoulders sag and a look of utter shame to cross his face. "I—"

"Watch what you say, Bertram," the sheriff warned.

"What's the matter, Turner?" Nick's arm tightened around her. "Are you afraid the judge will name you as his accomplice?"

"Keep it up, Daniels, and I'll add resisting arrest to the arson and trespassing charges."

"You're not going to do a damn thing." Releasing Cheyenne, Nick turned on the sheriff. "Before you and the judge hatched up your plan, you should have made sure whose property you were torching. I own the Flying H Ranch."

"You're talking crazy," Turner blustered. "This place has always belonged to the Holbrooks."

"That's where you're wrong, Sheriff." Cheyenne glanced at her father. "Would you like to tell him, or should I?"

Her father suddenly looked ten years older. "I lost the ranch right after I had the stroke. Daniels is the owner of the Flying H now."

"And if there are any charges made, I'll be the one making them," Nick said, his tone leaving no doubt in Cheyenne's mind that he meant business.

She felt as if her heart broke all over again at the thought of her father being arrested. But what he and the sheriff had tried to do to Nick was incorrigible and she couldn't blame him for wanting to make them pay for what they'd done.

Despite a cool morning breeze, sweat popped out

on the sheriff's florid face as he glanced at her father. "If I go down, I'm taking you with me, Bertram."

She watched Nick step to within inches of the man's face. "Because I know how much it would hurt Cheyenne to see her father arrested, I'm going to shoot you a deal, Sheriff. And if you're smart, you'll take it because it's the only way you're going to keep yours and the judge's asses out of jail."

Sheriff Turner nodded. "I'm listening."

Nick pointed toward the remnants of the blazing barn. "This is your last official investigation. You're going to go back to Elk Bluff and file a report that this fire was an accident. Then you're going to turn in your resignation as County Sheriff, effective immediately."

"Now, see here—"

"You'd better think about it, Turner," Nick interrupted. "I've heard that lawmen and judges don't fare too well behind prison walls."

Cheyenne swallowed around the huge lump in her throat. She'd never loved Nick more. Even after all that her father and the sheriff had done to discredit him and set him up to face criminal charges—not once, but twice—he was willing to drop the matter in order to keep from hurting her.

"I think you'd better go, Mr. Turner," she advised the suddenly subdued sheriff. The sound of a distant siren grew closer. "That should be the county's volunteer fire department. I think they can take care of what's left of the barn, while you fill out that accident report and draft your resignation."

As the portly sheriff slunk back to his patrol car, Cheyenne turned to her father. "Let's go into the house for privacy. You owe Nick and me an explanation."

As Nick sat across the table from the judge in the Holbrook's kitchen, his hand throbbed unmercifully. But he wasn't going to drive down to the clinic in Elk Bluff to have the wound repaired until he had answers to the questions that had haunted him his entire adult life.

Before he could ask what the man had against him, Cheyenne must have noticed the fresh blood soaking through the bandage on his hand. "Oh, Nick, you've torn the stitches loose. You need to see the doctor."

He shook his head. "Not until I hear what your father has to say."

She stared at him for several moments, then, taking a deep breath, turned her attention to the silent man sitting on the opposite side of the table. "Why, Daddy? What could Nick have possibly done to you to deserve the way you've treated him?"

The tremor in her voice and the disillusionment in her eyes caused Nick's gut to twist into a painful knot. He felt her emotional pain all the way to his soul and he vowed right then and there that even if it killed him, he would never allow anything to hurt her again.

"I never meant for it to go this far," the judge said, sounding tired. Nick noticed that he kept his head lowered and couldn't quite meet their questioning gazes. "I only wanted to make you look bad. I never wanted anyone to get hurt."

"You're lucky no one did." Nick shook his head. "I think I lost ten years off my life when I saw Cheyenne run into that burning barn."

For the first time since Nick arrived, Bertram Holbrook looked him square in the eye, and for once there was no trace of animosity in the man's steady gaze. "I can't thank you enough for getting her out of there, Daniels. I don't know what I would've done if you hadn't shown up."

"Who set the fire—you or the sheriff?" Cheyenne asked.

"Gordon. But it wasn't supposed to get out of hand." The judge stared at his loosely clasped hands on top of the table. "It was supposed to be minor like the tire incident."

"That still doesn't answer my question. What do you have against Nick, Daddy? Why have you always despised him and his mother?"

The judge was silent for several long moments before he raised his head to look at Nick. "There was a time in my life that I wanted nothing more than to marry your mother. She was my high school sweetheart and I had it all planned out. After I finished college and law school, I was going to marry Linda, practice law and raise a family."

Shocked, Nick searched his memory, but he could never remember his mother mentioning that she and Bertram Holbrook had ever been anything but acquaintances. But before he could find his voice to ask the judge what happened between them, the man went on with his story.

"It all might have worked out, too, if she hadn't made that week-long shopping trip to Denver." The old man tiredly shook his head. "That's when I lost her. Once she met your daddy, she didn't want anyone else. I even offered to marry her and raise you as my own child after that philandering bastard left her alone and pregnant. But she wouldn't hear of it. She never would tell me the name of the man who stole her heart, but I hated him just the same. And I'm ashamed to say that hatred carried over to you."

"But what about Mama?" There was a tremor in Cheyenne's voice that tightened the knot in Nick's gut. "Didn't you love her?"

A lone tear spilled from Holbrook's eye. "Yes, princess. I loved your mother very much."

Tears streamed down Cheyenne's face and Nick moved his chair closer to hers and put his arm around her shoulders. "Then why did you—"

"Looking back over the way I've acted all these years...I'm not proud of it," the man said haltingly. "But I carried a grudge toward you and your mother, boy. And I couldn't stand the thought of you being with my precious daughter."

Nick wasn't sure what to say. For one thing, he was astounded that what little Bertram Holbrook had known about Nick's father was more than he'd known himself. There had been a time when he was young that he'd questioned his mother about who his father was and how she'd met him. But she'd only smile and tell him that the time would come when he'd learn about the man and why she didn't want to talk about him. After a while, he'd accepted her silence and stopped asking. He knew now that his mother's reluctance to talk about his father was due to the affidavit that Emerald had had her sign, requiring his mother's silence and ensuring that he would be an heir to the Larson fortune.

"That explains why you've treated Nick so poorly," Cheyenne sobbed. "But why have you deceived me all these years about your ability to walk? Didn't you know how heartbreaking it was for me to see my once strong father in a wheelchair?"

As Nick watched, Bertram Holbrook seemed to shrink before his eyes. "After I had the stroke I was afraid of losing you, princess. I know I've made a lot of enemies and I don't have many friends in this county." Nick almost felt sorry for the man when he reached for Cheyenne's hand and she moved it away from him. "You've always been the light of my life, princess. Since your mother died, you've been the only one to love me unconditionally and I was afraid of losing that." Tears ran unchecked down the judge's face. "But in my desperation to keep from dying a lonely old man, I only succeeded in driving you away."

"But you're my father. Didn't you realize that I would always love you? That I had enough room in my heart for you as well as Nick?"

Sensing that Cheyenne and her father needed time alone to sort through what was left of their father-daughter relationship, Nick kissed her temple, then rose to his feet. "I think the two of you need some privacy to work this out. I'm going to drive down to the clinic and have the stitches replaced in my hand."

Cheyenne looked torn between going with him and staying to work out things with her father.

Giving her a smile he hoped was encouraging, Nick walked to the door. "Come over to my place this afternoon and bring the copy of your contract. We need to settle a few things of our own, as well as discuss how all this is going to affect your employment with the Sugar Creek Cattle Company."

By the time Cheyenne drove over to Nick's that afternoon, she felt emotionally drained. After a long, tearful discussion with her father, they'd come to an understanding. He'd agreed to enter counseling to help him deal with his propensity to manipulate and control people and situations, as well as work through his fears of being alone. And she was going to make her own choices without his interference.

Parking her truck at the side of the Sugar Creek ranch house, she took a deep breath and reached for the file containing her contract on the seat beside her as she readied herself for her meeting with Nick. She knew he cared for her, but he'd made it clear there was no chance of them having a relationship. And they both knew that made it impossible for her to continue working as the Sugar Creek foreman.

Before he fired her, she was going to do the only thing she could do. She was going to turn in her resignation, move away from the area and find another job to pay back the balance of her debt to Emerald, Inc.

When she got out of the truck and climbed the porch steps, Nick opened the door before she had a chance to knock. "You're late," he said as he took her in his arms, then kissed her until she gasped for breath.

"I...didn't realize you'd set a time for this meeting."

"I didn't."

His hand at the small of her back as he guided her toward his office burned through her clothing and sent a shaft of longing straight to her soul. "Then why did you—"

"Because we've wasted enough time getting things settled between us." He reached for the folder in her hand, then tore it in half. "As of right now, you're no longer my employee or Emerald, Inc.'s."

She opened her mouth to tell him that he couldn't fire her because she was quitting, but he didn't give her the chance.

"And if you're worried about paying back the debt—don't. I've already made arrangements with Emerald Larson."

She shook her head. "I don't want you paying my debts."

"We'll talk about that later." His sexy smile caused her heart to skip several beats. "Right now, we have more important things to discuss."

Backing away when he reached for her, she shook her head. "Nick, I can't do this. I can't continue a 'no-strings' affair with you."

To her surprise instead of being disappointed, he grinned. "That's not what I want from you, sweetheart."

Hope began to blossom deep inside of her, but she

ignored it. She couldn't allow herself to believe that he'd changed his mind.

"What do you want?"

He quickly stepped forward and taking her by the hand, led her over to his desk. Activating the speaker phone, he pushed the speed dial. "I want you to listen in on a phone call I'm about to make. But you have to promise not to say anything until I hang up. Would you do that for me?"

"Okay," she said slowly. She wasn't sure what she expected him to say, but listening in on his phone conversation wasn't it.

When she heard her father's voice on the other end of the line, she started to protest, but Nick held up his index finger to silence her. "Judge Holbrook, Nick Daniels here. I have something I need to ask you."

From the long pause, Cheyenne thought her father was going to hang up. "Go ahead," he finally said.

Nick gave her a smile that she thought would surely melt her bones. "Sir, we both know that you haven't changed your mind about me nor will you ever think that I'm good enough for your daughter. But there's one thing you and I have in common. We both love Cheyenne more than life itself. And if she'll have me, I'd like to make her my wife."

A happiness that she'd never dreamed would be hers again filled her body and soul. Nick didn't want them to continue their affair. He loved her and wanted to marry her.

"Are you asking for my permission?" Instead of the animosity she expected to hear in her father's voice, there was only quiet resignation.

"No, sir." Nick cupped her face with his hand as he stared into her eyes. "I don't need your permission to marry your daughter. Whether or not she agrees to be my wife is going to be her decision. What I want from you is your blessing. We both know how much that would mean to Cheyenne and I want whatever makes her happy."

Leaning forward, Cheyenne kissed his firm male lips. "I love you," she mouthed as they awaited her father's answer.

"You'd better be good to her," her father warned.

Nick's expression turned serious. "Judge Holbrook, you have my word that I'll spend every minute of every day for the rest of my life doing everything I can to make her happy."

There was a long pause, then her father said the words that filled her with such joy she could no longer hold back her tears. "If you're what Cheyenne wants, then I have no objections and I'll accept the marriage with no further protest."

"Thank you, sir. I swear, I'll never let either of you down." Ending the call, Nick brushed his lips over hers. "Cheyenne Holbrook, I love you. Will you do me the honor of becoming my wife?"

"Oh, Nick, I love you, too. So very much." She threw her arms around her shoulders and kissed him. "Yes, I'll marry you."

His kiss was filled with such passion, such love there was no doubt in her mind that he meant every word he'd said about making her happy for the rest of their lives.

When he raised his head, the smile on his handsome face held the promise of a lifetime of love and happiness. "I'd like to get married as soon as possible if that's all right with you, sweetheart. I think we've waited more than long enough to start our life together, don't you?"

She returned his smile. "I couldn't agree more."

"What are you doing next weekend?"

"I'm not sure, but aren't you supposed to go down to Albuquerque—" She stopped short. "Weren't you going to go down to Colorado today, then drive on to New Mexico for your relative's birthday?"

He shrugged. "I got as far as the Elk Bluff city limits before I turned around and headed back." The tenderness in his deep blue eyes stole her breath. "I was on my way back for you."

"You wanted me to meet your relatives?" she teased.

"Well, I do want you to meet both of my brothers, as well as get to know my grandmother better, but the reason I came back was to see if I could settle things with your father and ask you to marry me."

Surprised by his statement, she shook her head. "Whoa, cowboy. Brothers and a grandmother?"

Nodding, he explained, "It turns out my mother wasn't the only woman my father impregnated. My brother Hunter is a year older than I am and my brother Caleb is a year younger."

"How long have you known about them?" she asked, feeling envious. She'd always wanted siblings.

"About two months. I found out about them at the same time I learned Emerald Larson is my paternal grandmother."

"*The* Emerald Larson is your grandmother?" No wonder there was such confusion over who her employer was.

As he explained about Emerald's stipulations that the women tell no one who'd fathered their babies because she'd wanted them to grow up without the temptations that had corrupted their father, Cheyenne nodded. "I can understand that she was only trying to protect you and your brothers, but it would have been so nice for you to have all known each other sooner."

"We're getting acquainted now and finding that

we have a lot in common." He laughed. "We all wonder what our all-knowing grandmother is going to spring on us next. When she gave each of us a company to run, she told us we'd get no interference from her. But we're finding that the old gal still has a few surprises up her sleeve. And I have a feeling that in our case, she was doing a little matchmaking in the bargain."

"I'm glad she did," Cheyenne said honestly. She reached out and cupped his lean cheek with her palm. "It's taken thirteen years, but I'm finally going to marry the love of my life."

"I love you, sweetheart."

"And I love you, Nick Daniels. More than you'll ever know."

He kissed her until they both gasped for breath. "How big of a wedding do you want?"

"I think just family would be nice."

"That might be a problem." He gave her a sheepish grin. "Once Emerald gets wind of our getting married, she's going to jump right in and help. And believe me, sweetheart. She doesn't do anything on a small scale."

"Do you think she'd be content with a small wedding and a big reception?" Cheyenne asked hopefully.

Nick nodded. "As long as you put her in charge of planning it, I think she'll be fine."

Her mind reeled from everything that had happened in the past few hours. "I still can't believe this is finally going to happen."

"Believe it, sweetheart. Nothing is going to keep me from making you my wife."

Happier than she'd ever been, Cheyenne kissed the man she'd given her heart to so long ago. "I can't wait to start our life together."

Taking her by the hand, he led her toward the door. "I can't, either."

"Where are we going?"

His grin caused her entire body to tingle as he hurried her up the stairs and into his bedroom. "To start our life."

Epilogue

"**H**ave Cheyenne and the judge arrived yet?" Nick asked as he checked his watch.

"They just drove up." Hunter laughed. "I didn't think I'd ever see any man more impatient to get married than Caleb. But I swear, I think you have him beat, Nick."

"I've waited a long time to make Cheyenne my wife." Nick checked the pocket of his Western-cut suit. "Do you or Caleb have the ring?"

"And I thought I was nervous when Alyssa and I got married." Caleb laughed as he walked into the room. "If you'll remember, you gave me Cheyenne's wedding band when we got here."

A knock on the door signaled that the wedding was about to begin and, taking a deep breath, Nick smiled at his two best men. "I'll feel a lot better when that ring is on her finger and this is a done deal."

As he walked out of the room they'd used to wait for the ceremony to begin, Nick looked around at the interior of the church. Other than a fresh coat of paint on the walls and a different-colored carpet down the center aisle, it looked much the same as he remembered.

Once he and Cheyenne had gotten around to talking about where to get married, they'd both agreed that the obvious choice for the wedding was the little church where they'd tried to become husband and wife thirteen years ago. But this time things were different. This time, instead of leading her away in tears, her father was going to walk her down the aisle and place her hand in Nick's.

When Nick took his place beside the minister and looked at the handful of people sitting in the pews, his grandmother caught his eye. At first, Emerald had been disappointed that the wedding was going to be limited to family. But when she heard they were turning the reception over to her, she was like a little kid at Christmas. And Nick had no doubt that she'd made poor old Luther Freemont's life a living hell when she made him the liaison between her and the people she'd hired to pull it all together on such short notice.

As the organist began playing "Here Comes the Bride," he turned his attention to the back of the church and watched as the double doors opened and Judge Holbrook escorted Cheyenne down the aisle. When they reached the altar where he stood with his brothers and the minister, Nick stepped forward and her father placed her hand in his.

The judge's eyes were suspiciously moist when he kissed Cheyenne's cheek, then turned to Nick. "Take good care of my princess, son."

As the judge limped over to sit on the front pew, Nick stared into the eyes of the most beautiful woman he'd ever seen. "I love you, Cheyenne. Are you ready for this?"

Her smile was filled with such love it robbed him of breath. "I love you, too, Nick, and I've been ready to become your wife for thirteen years."

"Then let's not wait a minute longer," he said as they turned to face the minister.

"And true love prevails," Emerald whispered as the handsome groom kissed his beautiful bride.

"Inevitably," Luther Freemont agreed.

Theirs hadn't been an easy journey, but in the end Nick and Cheyenne's love had won out and they were finally going to realize their dreams. Nick's idea to turn the Sugar Creek Cattle Company into a free-range cattle operation had been brilliant and Emerald had no doubt that it would be a huge success in the beef industry.

She turned her attention to Cheyenne. If her sources were correct, and Emerald had every reason to believe they were, she would be celebrating the birth of her first great-grandchild early next summer, right after Cheyenne graduated from college with a degree in elementary education.

More than happy with the results of her second matchmaking attempt, her gaze settled on her eldest grandson. Hunter was going to be her biggest challenge of all. His was a deeply wounded soul in need of healing. But she had every confidence that what she had planned for him would be just what he needed to come to terms with the past and move forward with his life.

As the minister introduced Nick and Cheyenne as Mr. and Mrs. Nick Daniels, Emerald leaned over to Luther. "Two down and one to go."

* * * * *

Don't miss the final instalment of
THE ILLEGITIMATE HEIRS *mini-series.*
Betrothed for the Baby *is available in June 2007.*

0407/51

MILLS & BOON®

Desire™ 2-in-1

STRICTLY LONERGAN'S BUSINESS by Maureen Child

Kara Sloan was his ever-dependable, quiet assistant…until in a month of sharing close quarters Cooper Lonergan surprised her with a night of seduction.

PREGNANT WITH THE FIRST HEIR by Sara Orwig

Matt Ransome will stop at nothing to claim his family's one heir, even if it means a name-only marriage to a pregnant stranger. But perhaps it wouldn't be in name only for long.

❦

DYNASTIES: THE ELLIOTTS

MR AND MISTRESS by Heidi Betts

Scandal threatens to rock the Elliott family when business mogul Cullen Elliott wants to make his pregnant mistress his wife! Misty's past was scandalous…

HEIRESS BEWARE by Charlene Sands

Wealthy Bridget Elliott lost her memory and fell for a sexy stranger. All Mac Riggs knew about Bridget was that she came from money, but he wanted to uncover her secrets…

❦

FORCED TO THE ALTAR by Susan Crosby

Her handsome millionaire protector, Zach Keller, was insisting that for her safety they must marry. She had to find a way to deny him or have an unforgettable wedding night!

SEDUCTION BY THE BOOK by Linda Conrad

For two years he had isolated himself on his Caribbean island – could stormy passion with Annie Riley help him to overcome the past?

On sale from 20th April 2007

Available at WHSmith, Tesco, ASDA, and all good bookshops

www.millsandboon.co.uk

0107/SH/LC157

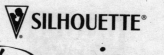

SILHOUETTE®

Desire™

Dynasties:

THE ELLIOTTS

Mixing business with pleasure

January 2007
BILLIONAIRE PROPOSITION *Leanne Banks*
TAKING CARE OF BUSINESS *Brenda Jackson*

March 2007
CAUSE FOR SCANDAL *Anna DePalo*
THE FORBIDDEN TWIN *Susan Crosby*

May 2007
MR AND MISTRESS *Heidi Betts*
HEIRESS BEWARE *Charlene Sands*

July 2007
UNDER DEEPEST COVER *Kara Lennox*
MARRIAGE TERMS *Barbara Dunlop*

September 2007
THE INTERN AFFAIR *Roxanne St Claire*
FORBIDDEN MERGER *Emilie Rose*

November 2007
THE EXPECTANT EXECUTIVE *Kathie DeNosky*
BEYOND THE BOARDROOM *Maureen Child*

**prima
new
beginnings**

There's the life you planned and there's what comes next...

DRAGONFLIES AND DINOSAURS
by Kate Austin

Randy Roman is taking a leave of absence from her life, and hitting the road. With each passing mile of farmland and prairie, she feels the thrill of freedom. But fate has a surprise for her, which will give Randy the courage to take a risk that will change her life...

OUT WITH THE OLD, IN WITH THE NEW
by Nancy Robards Thompson

Kate Hennessey is turning forty and has to confront the fact she no longer trusts her husband. Her world is ripped apart, but Kate might just find that putting the pieces together in a whole new way can bring unexpected rewards...

Because every life has more than one chapter...

On sale 20th April 2007

Available at WHSmith, Tesco, ASDA, and all good bookshops
www.millsandboon.co.uk

MILLS & BOON®

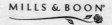

MILLS & BOON®

0407/23b

SPECIAL EDITION™

THE BABY TRAIL
by Karen Rose Smith

Baby Bonds

When someone abandoned a baby girl on Gwen Langworthy's doorstep, she couldn't just hand little Amy over to social services and forget her; so she hired tough, ex-FBI agent Garrett Maxwell to discover what had happened to the baby's parents.

A FATHER'S SACRIFICE
by Karen Sandler

Jameson O'Connell returned home to discover that a night of frenzied passion with Nina Russo had resulted in a baby boy. He insisted on claiming Nina as his bride. With their insatiable hunger for each other, would this ready-made family have a happy ever after?

THE WAY TO A WOMAN'S HEART
by Carol Voss

When widow Nan Kramer was forced to confront her son Justin's troubles, she didn't know where to turn. But then an old friend arrived on her doorstep, offering a shoulder to cry on and much, much more...

Don't miss out!
On sale from 20th April 2007

Available at WHSmith, Tesco, ASDA, and all good bookshops
www.millsandboon.co.uk

MILLS & BOON

INTRIGUE™

RILEY'S RETRIBUTION
by Rebecca York
Big Sky Bounty Hunters

A master of disguise, Riley Watson infiltrated Courtney Rogers' Golden Saddle ranch to capture a sinister fugitive. Riley was caught off guard by the pregnant ranch owner and he vowed to protect Courtney from a deadly showdown…

MORE THAN A MISSION
by Caridad Piñeiro
Capturing the Crown

She'd murdered the heir to the throne, and now the assassin was firmly in undercover agent Aidan Spaulding's sights. But Elizabeth Moore looked more like a princess than a prince-killer…and she faced the greatest threat of all: one to her heart.

BEAUTIFUL BEAST
by Dani Sinclair

When an explosion ended Gabriel Lowe's military career and left him scarred, his life became a shadow of what it once was. But the beautiful Cassy Richards was determined to warm his heart before an old enemy cut short both of their futures.

CAVANAUGH WATCH
by Marie Ferrarella
Cavanaugh Justice

When Janelle Cavanaugh's assignment took a deadly turn, she was given a ruggedly handsome, but infuriating, bodyguard. Risking his life was part of Sawyer Boone's job. Risking his heart was quite another matter.

On sale from 20th April 2007

Available at WHSmith, Tesco, ASDA, and all good bookshops

www.millsandboon.co.uk

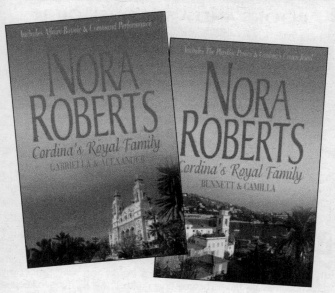

2 FREE

BOOKS AND A SURPRISE GIFT!

We would like to take this opportunity to thank you for reading this Mills & Boon® book by offering you the chance to take TWO more specially selected titles from the Desire™ series absolutely FREE! We're also making this offer to introduce you to the benefits of the Mills & Boon® Reader Service™—

- ★ **FREE home delivery**
- ★ **FREE gifts and competitions**
- ★ **FREE monthly Newsletter**
- ★ **Exclusive Reader Service offers**
- ★ **Books available before they're in the shops**

Accepting these FREE books and gift places you under no obligation to buy. you may cancel at any time. even after receiving your free shipment. Simply complete your details below and return the entire page to the address below. You don't even need a stamp!

YES! Please send me 2 free Desire volumes and a surprise gift. I understand that unless you hear from me. I will receive 3 superb new titles every month for just £4.99 each. postage and packing free. I am under no obligation to purchase any books and may cancel my subscription at any time. The free books and gift will be mine to keep in any case.

D7ZED

Ms/Mrs/Miss/Mr ....Initials ....

BLOCK CAPITALS PLEASE

Surname ....

Address ....

....

....Postcode..................................

Send this whole page to:
UK: FREEPOST CN8I, Croydon, CR9 3WZ